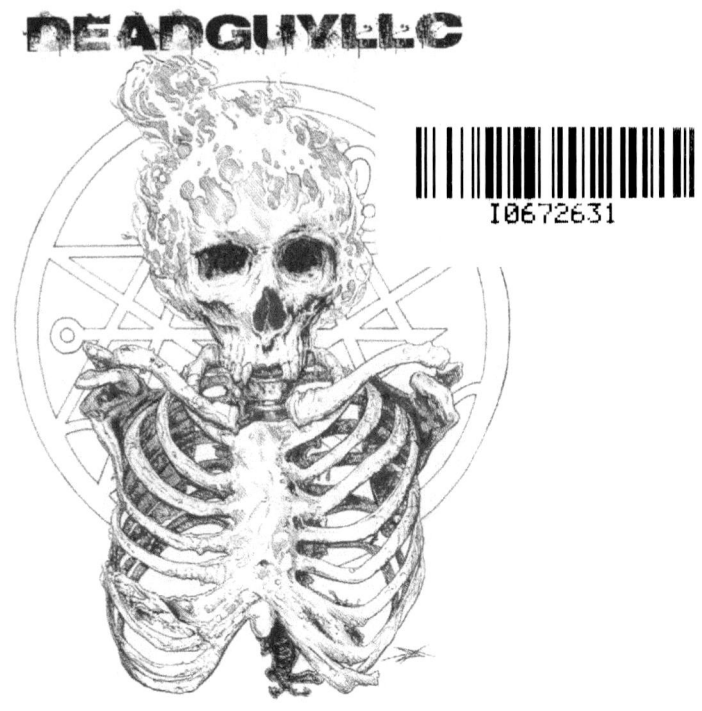

DEADGUYLLC

I0672631

Published by DeadGuyLLC.

Deadguyllc

The Joke is on Mankind

First Edition: May, 2025

Layout Dan Henk
All Art-Dan Henk

Copyright @Dan Henk

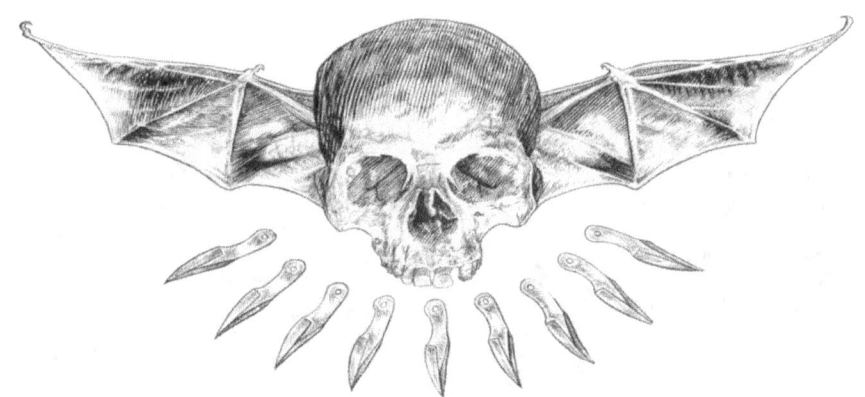

TALL TALES

"THE COSMIC MOUTH THAT WANTED TO EAT THE WORLD"

Jeff Strand

"Now do you want the *good* news?" Dr. Milker asked, after informing the public that humankind was doomed.

"Ummm...sure?" the stunned press secretary replied.

"The way things are going, we'll have driven humankind to extinction by then."

Everybody at the press conference just stared at him.

"I'm trying to add a bit of levity to the worst news that has ever been delivered," Dr. Milker said. "If you all want to wallow in doom and gloom, that's your prerogative. I, on the other hand, will be embracing a life of pure hedonism, indulging my darkest and most depraved fantasies. If you have any further questions, please direct them to my ass."

Dr. Milker flipped the audience the double bird, and then skipped away from the podium.

The press secretary took his place. "Okay, then. That was disturbing on all levels. Obviously, we'd like your takeaway to be that scientists are almost always wrong, and there's no need to panic."

A reporter up front raised his hand. The press secretary reluctantly pointed to him. "Yes?"

"It's inevitable that with only six weeks to live, many citizens of Earth will, for lack of a better phrase, make the most of it. Will our laws remain in place, considering the circumstances?"

"Are you asking if we're going to legalize rape?"

"Well, you didn't have to go straight to *rape*," the reporter said. "I was thinking more along the lines of looting. And, yes, perhaps some rape."

"The laws of the United States of America will remain intact. If you want to go feral, move to Canada."

Another reporter raised her hand. "I know we're supposed to wait until you call on us, but I thought I'd get started on the anarchy early. What did Dr. Milker mean by us being extinct by then?"

"It was a climate change reference."

"Ahh, okay. Frickin' scientists always have to get in a depressing zinger, don't they?"

"Yes. Anyway, this press conference is adjourned."

"Hold on, hold on," a third reporter said. "I'd like a little more detail about the form of our demise."

"He already told you. It's a giant mouth flying through space that's most likely going to eat our planet in a couple of bites."

"Right. What kind of mouth, exactly? A vampire mouth?"

"Who cares? It's a cosmic mouth three times the size of Earth."

"Does it have lips?"

"I don't know. Why is that relevant?"

"I can't decide if it's scarier or less scary if it has lips."

A fourth reporter raised his hand. "What about puppies and kittens?"

"What about them?" the press secretary asked.

"Will they be okay?"

"Are you asking me if puppies and kittens will be okay after the giant cosmic mouth devours the planet?"

"Yes. And I'm surprised it took this long for somebody to ask the question."

"Sure," the press secretary said. "They'll all be fine."

"Oh, good."

"We're done here. Go home to your families. And may God have mercy upon our souls."

* * *

I was that reporter. Not the rapey one. The one who asked if the mouth had lips.

Knowing that a cosmic mouth is rocketing toward your home planet, ready to bite it in half, changes you. Sometimes in a bad way. Like, maybe you've always fantasized about breaking into a nursing home and beating up all of the elderly residents, but you don't because there would be negative consequences, yet now you're all like, "To hell with criminal penalties! I'll be dead long before this case goes to trial, beeyotches!" and so you break into the nursing home and you start beating the absolute living shit out of geriatrics, cackling with laughter the entire time.

That's a change for the worse.

But sometimes the upcoming extinction of all life on earth, including fake life like plants, changes you for the better. That's what it did to me. I decided that no longer would I be an alcoholic reporter who cheated on his domestic partner and asked dumb-ass questions during press conferences. I would be…a hero.

I would devote the rest of my life to finding a way to defeat the cosmic mouth. Or die trying.

Well, no, I most likely wouldn't die *trying*, but I'd die after my efforts failed, like everybody else. I could have phrased that better. What I'm saying is that I wasn't a very good journalist.

I drove home. My domestic partner Suszie (her mother wanted to spell it "Susie," and her father wanted to spell it "Suzie," so they compromised) was in our driveway, holding a television set. She carried it into the house as I parked.

When I walked into the living room, there were a dozen television sets on the floor.

"Oh, hi," she said. "You heard the apocalyptic news, right?"

"Yes. I was at the press conference, so I actually reported the news. Why is our living room filled with TVs?"

"Thought I'd do some looting before the mouth got here."

"Okay. Why televisions?"

"If we're all going to die in a few weeks, I'll never be able to binge-watch all of the shows I want to see with just a single TV. *Grey's Anatomy* alone has 435 episodes. I worked it out, and if I have thirty-two TVs running 24/7, I can get caught up before the cosmic mouth eats us."

"*Grey's Anatomy* has 435 episodes?"

"Yeah."

"How do they keep coming up with new things for the characters to do?"

"I don't know. I haven't watched it. That's the problem."

"Okay," I said. "Not to be judgmental, but that seems like a strange way to spend the time you have left."

"I have an ulterior motive," Suszie admitted. "All of this visual and aural stimulation all at once will quickly drive me mad. If I can get myself all nice and insane, I can face my doom without worry."

I wanted to make an "oral stimulation" joke, but I knew what she meant, and I didn't want to squander my limited remaining time with a blowjob joke.

"I'm going to save the world," I informed her.

"Huh?"

"The world. I'm going to save it."

"You?"

"Yes."

"How?"

"I haven't figured that out yet."

"Oh. Well, okay. Good luck."

I knew I should break up with her. It was clear she didn't believe in me. I didn't expect her to grab a sword and vow to fight by my side, but *some* support would've been appreciated.

"We're finished," I told her.

"All right," Suszie said. "So you're moving out?"

Dammit! I hadn't thought this through. This was Suszie's home, and if I left her, I'd have to pack up all of my belongings and move them into a storage unit. That didn't seem like a very good use of my time.

"Can I take it back?" I asked.

"Sure."

"Thanks."

I helped her carry in the rest of the televisions. Then we spent a couple of hours getting them all connected to streaming services. After that, I left her to her self-induced insanity and went out in search of a solution to the apocalypse.

* * *

"Another beer?" the bartender asked me.

I nodded. Before you get all judgy, you should know that I do my best thinking when I'm a little buzzed.

Admittedly, I was drunk.

I got a little belligerent at last call, and the bouncers threw me out on my ass. I hadn't come up with a solution to the "giant mouth coming to eat our planet" during my binge-drinking, but to be fair, I hadn't made the problem worse.

* * *

I guess I should acknowledge that you already know the world was not devoured by a giant cosmic mouth. I mean, there could be a twist ending where we're all ghosts floating around space, or it could suddenly shift to the present tense where everybody is screaming as the mouth prepares to dine, but what actually happened is extremely well documented, and I'm not fooling anybody.

* * *

I wandered the streets, trying to figure out how I could defeat the mouth.

The best solution seemed to be to launch a nuclear missile at it. But, of course, I had no access to a nuclear missile, and certainly did not have the means to manufacture one.

Still, I could save the world by saying, "Hey, you should launch a nuclear missile at it!" I added that to my mental list.

Could the power of love defeat it?

Most likely not.

The power of friendship...?

No. These were terrible ideas. Well, not the nuclear missile one, that one was actually quite good, but the others sucked. Perhaps I should postpone brainstorming world-saving ideas for when I wasn't staggering around in a drunken stupor.

Could we reason with it?

Who was our planet's most charming human? Tom Hanks? Didn't Tom Hanks get nominated for an Academy Award for playing Mr. Rogers? Could Tom Hanks, in character as Mr. Rogers, convince the cosmic mouth that it was doing the wrong thing?

No! The government should bring in Samuel L. Jackson. If Samuel L. Jackson told the cosmic mouth to get the fuck away from Earth, motherfucker, it would most likely find another planet to eat.

That idea was brilliant. Get NASA to build the world's largest megaphone, and have Samuel L. Jackson ready to intimidate the mouth, with Tom Hanks waiting as backup.

I needed to remember this.

* * *

When I woke up the next morning, I scraped the dried vomit off my face, got up out of the gutter, and tried to remember my plan to defeat the mouth.

Yell at it? Be kind to it?

It was something along those lines, but I couldn't remember any of the other details.

Though my phone had been stolen during the night, it was light out, and so I should probably go into work. The vomit was also all over my shirt, but most of my fellow journalists had taken to alcoholism, so I wouldn't be the only one wearing that fashion statement.

I burst into my boss's office, where he was busy having sex with his secretary. Everybody knew he was banging his secretary, but previously he'd done it with the door closed.

"Should I come back later?" I asked.

"Nah, my mouth is free. What do you need?"

"I've figured out how to defeat the mouth."

"How?"

"Nuclear missile."

"Well, duh. There's already one pointed at it. They're waiting for it to come into range."

"Oh. I thought I was thinking outside the box."

"Nope. Totally in the box."

"Shit."

"Would you mind shutting the door on your way out? Darlene and I are about to break some taboos."

I left the office, feeling glum. I was starting to believe that I might not be the savior of our planet. But I still had a few weeks to figure something out...

* * *

"Here's my idea," I told my boss a few weeks later. He'd eaten Darlene, and was now having sex with his new secretary, who he'd forced to get plastic surgery to make her look like Darlene. She didn't look anything like her, but my boss had succumbed to madness, so it didn't matter.

My boss grunted at me, which I took as an invitation to share my idea.

"Two nuclear missiles!"

He grunted at me and pointed, which I took as a demand to get the fuck out of his office.

I had failed.

* * *

The mouth was now visible to the naked eye. Humans spent most of their day running around shrieking.

We shot nuclear missile after nuclear missile at that thing. The cosmic mouth kept eating them. Did it have a stomach? Did the missiles go into another dimension? Was its digestive system simply an empty void? Nobody knew. All we knew was that the mouth was still coming toward us.

"I love you," I told Suszie.

"Yagga gloop wooble," she said.

* * *

Finally, the mouth was here.

It extended its massive cosmic tongue.

Touched it to the earth's surface.

The mouth twisted into a grimace.

15

Then it reversed course, floating away from a planet whose flavor was not to its liking.

* * *

There was a great deal of relief. Maybe not from the millions of people who were crushed by the mouth's tongue, but everybody else was happy.

"Things are going to be incredibly awkward for a while," the press secretary announced. "We've all done things we're not proud of. If it's difficult for you to look your friends and family in the eye, just know that we're all in the same boat."

It would take a long time for things to get back to normal. How could you pretend you hadn't seen all of your professional colleagues masturbate in public? Would I ever forget about the underprivileged people I'd hunted for sport? How long would I be haunted by the memory of coming home one evening, after the world had been spared, to find that Suszie had cut off most of her own face?

Eventually, we could almost pretend the whole cosmic mouth thing never happened. There would be permanent changes to our way of life, such as the legalization of rape, but there were days when I could gaze into the sky and believe that the danger had never existed.

And then I'd suddenly remember, and freak the hell out

CAVITY CREEPS

Cody Goodfellow

S torage space #369 was four feet deep and eight feet wide, with a narrow, two-by-six appendix of useless "bonus space" they couldn't subdivide into another unit. It was just enough room to fit a modest human life and the body that had lived it. Filled to the ceiling with all of his records, books, sheet music and old instruments, the bonus space allowed Oscar Gurewich to sit in his favorite chair and listen to his phonograph.

This is your home, now. Don't cry, for God's sake. At least you have one... and all your precious, heavy possessions.

He was taking an awful chance. The old hi-fi was plugged into an extension cord that ran out under his rolldown door and along the corridor to the service closet, which he'd propped open with a strip of duct tape. But he had paid for this space with the money he'd earned. He didn't accept charity, but he'd be damned if he'd suffer in silence. And yet so long as no one tripped over his cable, he was outwardly as silent as the dead. He almost felt as if he was stealing something.

Oscar detested the headphones, but he couldn't risk being discovered. He had never knowingly broken a law or even a rule, and he really had no other choice, nowhere else to go. The world had taken everything else from him, and if he sold his things, who would want them? He would still be penniless, homeless and too old to start over, and without his music and memories, he would be less than an animal.

To dwell upon his circumstances, to honestly examine his fortunes and scheme upon any reversal, was pointless self-flagellation. The balm of Brahms' 4th Symphony soothed his nerves like no empty words ever could. In its elegiac opening tones, he found serenity, the sense that it was all part of someone's greater plan, but the flow soon turned stormy and defiant, making his heart race and his jaw clench.

He was in an unhealthy romantic jag tonight, having worn a hole in the Moldau and his whole Mahler catalog. Berlioz, Grieg, Saint-Saens and Tchaikovsky lay out of their yellowed onionskin sleeves, the brittle, heavy disks more like pressed anthracite than flimsy postwar vinyl. His dithering fingers fumbled the Moonlight Sonata out of the milk crate at his knee but replaced it. He was not strong enough for that one tonight.

When had the world lost its taste for such beauty? One could plot the "progress" in all human endeavors over the last century against the decline of music, from insipid jazz standards to the fecal sturm and drang of modern pop music, and observe an unmistakable correlation... but which was the symptom, and which the cause?

Perhaps, he reflected morosely, the end had begun with the recording of music itself. When playing music ceased to be a magical skill to conjure fleeting melodies out of tyrannical silence, and instead became a lot of common heat and noise that came out of a can, it lost its magic, its potent ability to speak to the soul; or perhaps men had sold or lost their souls first...

When Brahms himself submitted to record one of his Hungarian dances for Thomas Edison in 1889, perhaps he had seen the terrible changes the invention would wreak. Almost buried beneath the surface noise like a swarm of vicious rats, the master's muted piano work had the resigned air of a formal surrender.

As the 4th tossed and turned like a dreamer lost in troubled sleep, Oscar laid down the photo album he'd been leafing through and patted himself down for a tissue. The desiccated clippings swelled with the droplets of his tears. Discolored memories of his years with the San Diego Symphony and as a DJ at several short-lived classical FM stations, and his vacations in Vienna, with Elaine. They didn't come to life with the infusion of fluid. They only got wet.

Suddenly, he jerked upright and snatched the headphones off his head. Though his hearing was not what it once was and the music was very loud, he'd heard a rough pounding that spoiled the perfect counterpoint of the music. The sound didn't repeat itself, but he felt somehow guilty for retiring into the embrace of his headphones.

He knew he was not alone in trying to live in the storage spaces. He'd seen others who hopped the fence just before the office locked up, who snuck into their spaces and bolted themselves in with cut padlocks, and some vulgar idiots who left soda- and beer bottles refilled with urine in the outside lot. Such shameful circumstances did not make men eager to bond, but in the still of the night, you could hear men weeping, raging or ranting into imaginary telephones. The steel ducts that connected the four hundred spaces with the indifferent air conditioner distilled the chorus of raw emotions into a bland, murky tone poem of despair: Ligeti's *Lux Aeterna* for condemned choir. The monotonous clicking of some loose vent or faulty thermostat regulator often sounded for hours on end when the heaters blew their rank breath of combusted dust throughout the storage complex, providing a sort of robotic rhythm section. Sometimes, he thought he heard babies crying. It was enough to drive a man to opera.

Oscar was grateful for the headphones, then. When he looked at the stacks of heavy, antiquated LPs in their crumbling folios alongside Elaine's corny old rhumba records and Les Baxter and Dave Brubeck 45's and the battered instrument cases, he felt like much more than a broken music teacher. He felt as he supposed those young people in their Brobdingnagian monster trucks and paramilitary SUV's must feel, breezing along in implacable bubbles of creature comfort and blathering into cell phones with one half-lidded, heavily medicated eye on the ebb and flow of likewise disengaged traffic. More and more of them were marked with a bumper sticker from a local megachurch on the tinted rear window. *NOTW*, they defiantly proclaimed, with the T as a cross that looked more like a sword. *Not Of This World*. Back when someone had explained it to him, it'd seemed like the infantile height of modern stupidity, but now he wholeheartedly empathized. However high or low, hard or soft, the things of this world were an unbearable burden, and the longing to be free of them was not such a bad thing to feel.

He still had his possessions, his passions and his illusions. He had an air mattress, a gallon of fresh water to drink and clean himself, and a serviceable chamber pot. Eat your heart out, Sardanopolus. You *can* take it with you.

This was only temporary, to be sure. He still taught private lessons at Benoit Music on Ventura, though they paid barely enough to cover the storage space. He could try out again for the Los Angeles Symphony. Maybe this time, they'd deign to let him be an usher.

It had nearly killed him, lugging all this old junk into this tiny box of sheet metal, cinderblock and naked concrete, when the bank threw him out of the house on Vesper Street that he'd bought with Elaine eighteen years ago. He'd had to make his final trip with a stolen shopping cart, because they'd repossessed his camper.

When he walked from the storage space on Sepulveda to the library on Moorpark every morning, he passed the old green GMC with the Roll-Along shell sitting in the repo yard, that they'd bought when she was laid off from teaching middle school. That was all she'd wanted, to be footloose and fancy-free for the rest of their days, but her heart wasn't up to it and took her away before they could hit the road. Soon, the camper would be auctioned off, and someday, all this crap would fall to some scavenger who would no doubt groan at the dismal prospect of selling it on eBay. More and more spaces were turned out, of late, once the checks stopped coming. It was a wonder they hadn't found more renters packed away with the junk they couldn't pawn or part with, the best parts of them divided up long ago by the bank and the rats.

Enough. He didn't come here to wallow in self-pity. When he closed his eyes, he could almost dissolve into the music and rise above it all in a way that made him think death wouldn't be so bad, if it was like this. If Elaine was there, and music...

The last bombastic stabs of the 4th subsided into the fireside crackle of needle on looping groove. Saint-Saens next. *Carnival Of the Animals* was a juvenile parade of frivolity, but one of her favorites.

He dropped the record when he heard the sound again, damn it. Fists rapping on sheet metal.

His heart turned a backflip in his chest. He'd been found out. Too late to make any difference, he switched off his battery-powered camp lantern and tamped out the ember in his meerschaum pipe. What the hell was he thinking, smoking in here? Maybe if he just played dead, they'd move on. He was hardly worth the trouble, and they had to know he had nowhere else to go.

A warbling tremolo of wordless fear came through the wall, and someone banged again with their open hand. The sound wasn't coming from outside his door, but from the wall at his back.

Someone in the next space.

He'd resided in the storage facility for almost two months, and he'd never seen his next-door neighbor, nor had he any reason to seek him out. Tugging the headphones off, Oscar struggled to sound courteous. "Yes, what can I do for you?"

"Help me, please... can you help me?" Through the wall, he couldn't tell the man's age or background. The voice sounded bleary from sleep or drink or both, but there was a sour chord of hysteria in his tone that shivered the corrugated tin between them. "My light's gone out, it's dark and they're—I think they're... eating me..."

Oh dear, this didn't sound promising. Maybe the poor fellow was having night terrors or had committed the mortal sin of the modern age and gone off his meds. But no man is an island, Oscar reminded himself, not even here.

Scooting his chair away from the wall, he knocked over a stack of records in the dark. They skidded and cracked under his stocking feet. He cursed under his breath, an old habit from the days of Elaine's swear jar. He switched on the camp lamp and winced to survey the damage. The Mahler was a loss. Still, he tried to be civil. "Are you in distress? I don't have a phone."

"I need light! My batteries are dead, or... gone, I don't know, but they come when it's dark. I blocked my vent... you know about that, right? I can hear them, I think they're already in here with me, please—"

Was he talking about rats? Oscar had never seen one on the premises, though there were poison bait stations everywhere. "I don't have any extra batteries, and just the one lamp. Why don't you open your door?"

The lights in the corridors were on motion triggers and would switch on in fifty-yard stretches of the arterial corridor outside. A security guard was on duty in the front office and occasionally watched the video monitors, but he was studying for the LAPD exam—probably not for the first time—when he was awake at all. Surely a harsh blast of fluorescent light would wake him out of his nightmare, and Oscar Gurewich could mind his own business again.

The man on the other side snapped, "What the fuck do you think I am, new? I can't do that, I tried, but it's locked! Creeps locked me in! Fucking creeps..."

Well, that tore it. Oscar turned away from the wall, gingerly replaced his chair and picked up his headphones. Big, clunky old full enclosure Technics studio cans; he wouldn't have heard artillery or a Roman orgy in the next space, during his previous selections, *Marche Slave* and Holst's *The*

23

Planets. He wondered how long his neighbor had been making a drunken spectacle of himself. For surely that was all it was...

What would Elaine tell him, right now? He didn't need to ask his memory to replay her catalog of lectures. He didn't owe this stranger anything, but he owed it to himself not to have to look at a coward in the mirror every morning.

He grabbed the nylon rope leash and tugged his door open. It rolled jerkily up into its housing but refused to budge beyond waist-height. Oscar ducked under it and stepped into the hall. The fluorescent lights flickered and came on, so cold he expected to see his breath, so bright that his shadow between his feet was a bottomless hole in the floor.

He looked up and down the corridor, but of course there was nothing moving, nothing alive. His extension cord snaked past five doors to vanish into the service closet. As bright as they were, the lights cast discrete cones of sterile illumination on the floor. The dark crowded around it, ate it up.

Oscar hesitated before he went to #368. He could be dangerous; he could be sleepwalking or on drugs...

Just you go and do nothing, then, and see what that gets you.

Thanks, Elaine. He went to the door and bent over the lock. The light in here was funny, his deep black shadow made the familiar door look like the dark side of the moon. He instantly regretted touching it. The lock was covered in some kind of rubbery slime, a septic blackish gunk like what grows inside a garbage disposal in a widower's house. He clamped his lips tight to keep from vomiting, but he took hold of the lock and tugged.

It was one of the cheap padlocks everybody bought from the front office, but it wasn't cut with bolt cutters, like the ones everybody rigged over their unlatched doors to fool the security. It fooled no one, Oscar was sure, but it let the management deny that they were a cut-rate flophouse. If the night watch wasn't practicing his sleeper hold on a CPR dummy in the office, Oscar might just get caught, before things got out of hand.

Maybe it was security playing a game with them, or one of their faceless neighbors, because someone sure as Chopin put the filthy padlock on the door to seal him in.

Creeps, the man had said, with a particular whine of primal terror. *Fucking creeps...*

Oscar looked over his shoulder. Nothing moved. No one lay poised to pounce on him. Then he heard a sound that made him jump back and clutch his chest. That clicking he heard from the ductwork, that faint but persistent sound that he'd written off as a failing component in the climate control system...

He heard it now, but it was not a faint, fading sound. It came from just the other side of the door, which shook, just a little, as he backed up against the opposite wall. It sounded like scissors opening and snapping shut.

"It's okay, I'm sorry, I'm okay... just go away, okay?" The man who'd just begged him for light now sounded blissfully unconcerned, like he was counting backwards on the operating table. "Just... go..."

Nothing he could say could answer that dismissal, but nothing, now, could make him obey. Briskly, Oscar jogged down the hall to the closet. As the lights passed by overhead, his shadow grew long and stretched out behind him, then shrank until it puddled at his feet to seep out ahead of him, as if it took three days to reach the closet and throw open the door.

Dark inside, but he found the switch. He'd inveigled the key from Mustafa, the daytime office manager, and he was pretty sure the grim Yemeni fellow knew what was really going on. But Oscar was no bumbling Watergate burglar. He taped up the strike plate so no one who didn't pull on the door would know it wasn't locked.

Shelves stocked with Waxie floor cleanser, Goo Gone, and industrial strength graffiti remover, next to a bonfire pile of broken mops, push brooms, and a bucket on wheels. He almost despaired of finding them before his eyes picked the bulky yellow rubber grips out of the mess. The ungainly weight of the bolt-cutters almost tugged him off his feet. He slipped sideways in his sweaty Argyle socks but checked himself against the doorframe with one shoulder as he charged back out into the hall.

Almost immediately, he sensed something behind him. The dim orange glow of his lamp was like the ember of a dying campfire in a coalmine. He kept running and all he could hear was his own labored breathing, like shovels full of wet sand hitting a brick wall. He ran harder, lurching and listing with the bolt-cutters in the crook of his left arm. He risked a fleeting glance over his shoulder as he ran and saw a flash of black and yellow teeth at his back, before the lights went out.

Still running, he whipped around and for a moment, the sixty-one-year-old music teacher galloped backwards like a first-string NFL receiver wielding Excalibur, lashing blindly out at the gurgling darkness.

Once he swung them, the bulky steel shears took over his momentum. It was like swinging two solid baseball bats one-handed. The carbon-steel teeth caught something that checked their wild trajectory and made the blackness shriek like dry ice on metal.

Oscar stumbled. The runaway cutting head smashed into a rolldown door like a battering ram on a drawbridge. Shock ripped up Oscar's hand as if the bolt-cutters had clipped a third rail.

Loud.

The sound was so loud, Oscar's left ear just shrieked like a cheap alarm clock. The echoes rolled away down the infinite tube and came back mushy and mingled with shreds of his own blood-curdling falsetto scream.

And then, just as it occurred to him that he was still running backwards, he tripped on something stretched across the floor. His feet skipped out from under him, and he flew ass-first into the dark. His arms flapped up to shield his head just as the floor cracked his tailbone and compacted his lungs into the back of his throat.

Rolling into a broken ball like a drowned spider in a bathtub, he could not defend himself, let alone speculate upon what had attacked him. A burning breath like a draught of liquid oxygen made him cough and retch on the concrete.

Someone in a nearby space shouted at him to shut the fuck up, they had to work in the morning. He gasped an apology before he remembered his own troubles.

Something had attacked him in the dark. His mind told him it was a dog, emphatically pushing pictures of big black Rottweilers snarling and baring yellow teeth, and it would be easy to accept them. It was no less terrifying, but it added up. The storage place had bought some guard dogs, or strays had wandered in, or—

No. What he saw, however briefly, overwhelmed any reflexive rational explanation. It wasn't a dog, or a man, or anything like anything he'd ever seen, before. It was something *Not of This World*, as the born-again Yuppies said.

And it was still somewhere, very close to him.

Nothing was broken, thank God for small favors, but he wouldn't be sitting in chairs for a week. He rolled onto his knees and dragged himself upright, clutching the wall and wheezing. By the murky lamplight, he saw that he'd tripped over his own extension cord. The bolt cutters lay splayed open on the floor about eight feet away. *You old fool,* he scolded himself, *you've got yourself all wound up over nothing...*

Something darker than darkness lay or squatted at the very edge of the lamp's feeble corona. The light glinted off something. An *eye...* No, it had no eyes. Only teeth.

His knees shook. He was too terrified even to run, but when he finally took a step, it was towards the thing, and another, slowly, testing every inch for a sign of life. At last, he bent, head swimming, grabbing the bolt-cutters. The prone figure hissed at him and backed into the curtain of opaque shadow. Coward, he thought, but he crept backwards with the bolt-cutters brandished like a cross against vampires.

He went to his own storage space and picked up the lamp, switching on the blazing white, fluorescent lamp, and the blinking red emergency light at the other end. The lamp hurt his eyes. How long had he been in the dark?

28

It was harder to pry himself out of his own space again. His hand caught the leash and started to pull the door down. A man was in the next space, and he needed help. They were discarded and damned, but they were yet human beings, and to ignore another would only prove that he was not fit to save himself.

Outside his space, the corridor felt hotter. He went to #368 and held the lamp up to the soiled padlock, then set it on the floor to apply the bolt-cutters. The serrated teeth nipped through the cheap aluminum lock like it was made of cheese. Something banged into the door just opposite his face. Oscar fumbled the bolt-cutters, then held them up like a club as he squatted to grab the handle and threw the door up as hard as he could.

It jerked to a stop at chest-height. Oscar took a step back. A palpable flood of stench rolled over him, like mildew and carrion and raw sewage poured into a space heater.

The dingy sheet-metal walls were plastered with clipped photos and maps from *National Geographic*, along with the pages of a Gaugin coffee table book. Everywhere, the sunny, honey-colored windows into another world gazed down in blind disgust upon this one.

His neighbor lay on a Coleman air mattress with his head at Oscar's feet. In a blue UCLA T-shirt and pajamas, he looked like someone sleeping in their own home, and for a moment, his beleaguered, lost stare was enough to make Oscar back away and apologize as he reached to close the door.

But then, no matter how much he wanted not to, he still saw the things that crouched over the art lover and brazenly continued with the business of eating him.

They were two or three feet tall, but hunchbacked and bent on all fours. Their skin a glossy, bubbling black like roofing tar; long, crooked limbs dragging bloated bellies and propping up wobbly, ponderous heads, which were nothing but bulging jaws and teeth.

He could see no eyes, ears or nostrils. Huge incisors and tusklike canines as broad as Oscar's palm were jammed into the huge jaws like a drawer stuffed with meat cleavers, and as they busily gnawed and nipped chunks off the man, they made that insidious clicking sound that he'd heard night after night. The sound of them eating their way through this building, and through its nameless, faceless tenants.

"Go away," the man moaned. "It doesn't hurt..."

Two of them dismantled his legs, while two more gnawed on the exposed bones of his arms and gobbled the loose, weathered skin of his neck.

Long, warty black tongues flopped out to lap up the sluggish blood flow and somehow, Oscar's reeling mind supposed they must be drugging him. Their saliva was some kind of anesthetic, perhaps, for how else could he still be alive and trying with a skeletal hand to wave Oscar away?

Repulsion drove a hot steel rod up his spine, turning fear to fury, as he accepted them. They were something impossible, but they were most definitely of this world. They were the very essence of the goddamned place.

A fifth creep that he hadn't seen squeezed out from behind a tumble of art books and growled at him, extending its quivering tongue like an invitation. Maybe it didn't hurt. Maybe, after everything else he'd been through, being eaten and becoming nothing, felt good.

I doubt it, thought Oscar Gurewich. He swung the bolt-cutters in a reckless downward smash that crushed the head of the advancing creep into its sunken shoulders. The others gasped and clicked and leapt over the prostrate feast with bloody, fat-marbled muscle in their teeth.

Oscar turned and banged his head on the rolldown door, raced blindly back to his space through a flurry of stars. Stumbling over his turntable and falling into the opposite wall, he rebounded and reached for the door leash. They came surging in before he could close it and set to work on his legs.

He kicked out at an impossible jolt of agony, throwing a squealing creep into the rotator for Elaine's old Leslie organ with a thick strap of Oscar's outer thigh meat in its jaws. He dangled on the edge of shock, but the pain was like a knot that simply untied itself. A cold, tingling euphoria suffused his trembling flesh with the promise of escape. It wasn't so bad, after all, to be eaten.

The others climbed him and he sagged almost willingly, under their rubbery weight. He felt claws at his neck and fetid breath stirring his thin, silver hair. Teeth shredding his clothing, yet he couldn't move a muscle.

He figured that something like this would be the end. The world had been taking bites of him for so long, stealing his wife and his livelihood and his home. At every turn, he had clung all the tighter to the false cocoon of things he'd secreted around his raw, unfinished form.

Elaine had loved him so much, it killed her. He knew that, always had, but never admitted it. His clinging to his records, his books and his junk had smothered her spirit, and when he could not tear himself away, she had sickened and died before he even realized he was losing her. He hated himself for the relief he'd felt, when he realized, he wouldn't have to abandon all that stuff, to live in the camper.

He barely felt the teeth clamping down on the crown of his skull, skating across bone as they peeled off his scalp. But he felt his heart breaking, and his tears came flowing down so thickly he couldn't see where he was swinging the bolt-cutters. In his head, he heard only the invincible rhythm of Verdi's Anvil Chorus.

The fanged cutting head demolished an orange crate filled with Wagner and Handel and sent a creep spinning. The creep on his back shredded the sleeve of his cardigan sweater and tried to chew off his arm, but he flung it headfirst into the cinderblock wall and chased it with the cutters, smashing its crooked spine between its chattering teeth before it hit the floor.

Spinning on his heel, greased by blood streaming down his leg, Oscar chopped down a stack of Elaine's old novelty records. Yma Sumac, Martin

Denny and Spike Jones took wings like clay pigeons. The bolt-cutters spun out of his grip and caromed off the wall. There were still more of them than he could count and more dropping out of the open duct overhead. Out of every crack and cavity in the sad tomb of his life, they slithered and skulked, snapping their cleaver teeth and crowding him into the narrow, coffin-shaped bonus space.

His life was forfeit long before they showed up, but Oscar Gurewich was nobody's food. He looked around at all his *things*, all the music that had both set him free and buried him, all the heavy, dusty things he had mistaken for the stuff of life itself. All the terribly flammable shit he'd surrounded himself with...

In his pocket, he thumbed the lid off his monogrammed silver Zippo lighter. A silly affectation he'd found in his stocking one Xmas, though Elaine loathed the smell of his pipe and cigars. He struck the flint and tossed it into a crate of sheet music.

The antique yellow paper ignited like potassium powder. The creeps cowered, hissing, as he flung flaming paper into every corner of the storage space. He kicked a creep away from his wounded leg, then heaved a tower of ancient Mozart limited pressings on top of the snarling abomination.

The fire took root among the crates and oiled cases and bloomed in earnest. Creeps melted like wax and burst in the flames or scrambled back up into the duct with their asses ablaze. Alarms rang in the corridor and sprinklers spurted unevenly outside his space. The vents sucked smoke and fluttering embers into the central duct.

Oscar looked around him. He didn't feel like he was burning, but he smelled bacon underneath the reek of broiled sewage. The thought of trying to save any of it made him laugh until he coughed. He didn't belong to any of this stuff. He could remember and play any of it that really mattered. But he turned and reached into the mounds of flame, digging by memory until he found the familiar grip of an old instrument case. His clarinet, the one he'd played in the symphony when he met Elaine.

He snapped up the case and patted out plumes of fire on his sweater. Backing away from the furnace roar of his life burning up, he noticed that he'd grabbed the wrong goddamned instrument. The grubby, rubber-banded grip was attached to the case for a beat-up tenor saxophone that Elaine had bought for him at a yard sale, back when they courted. A loud, vulgar horn that Mozart might've loved, but which had always seemed to Oscar to be the flatulent, razzing death-knell of the classical era. Well, to hell with it. He had to play something.

He picked up the bolt-cutters and shambled down the corridor past bleary-eyed refugees in thermal long-johns, down the stairs and out past the front office of Xtra Space Storage, oblivious to the security guard who tried to stop him, but screamed, "Jesus, you've been scalped!" and puked on the sidewalk.

Sirens wailed and blared as fire engines and police converged on the storage complex. They'd be busy for a while, maybe all night, if they found the nest of creeps.

Feeling neither the cold nor the pain of his wounds, Oscar Gurewich tossed an imaginary dollar into an imaginary swear jar, and walked down Sepulveda to go get his fucking camper back.

WASHINGTON, DC

Dan Henk

L-7

Misty and an oppressively dark grey, Ben always found DC to be a bit threatening. This was the murder capital of the US after all, and Dupont Circle might be kind of hipster cool during the day, but after midnight it was a whole different ball of wax.

Nobody cared about what happened to people like him and Chris. Especially the cops. The two of them were just funny looking punk kids from the suburbs. Ben, with his heavily spiked and garishly painted leather jacket, black fingernails, and matching eyeliner, was their definition of a troublemaker. He called it his "Death Rocker" phase, and it had gotten him beaten up more than once. Not to mention the bevy of trumped-up charges that were made up just to harass him.

L7 was great tonight. They always were. Ben, despite all the disparaging comments from mainstream pricks, was wearing his "Smell the Majic" band shirt. A guy eating the bassist out-how could you go wrong with that? It offended all the right people,

His girl always laughed at that, saying he was in love with their new bassist. Well, she was hot, but his girl always blew it off.

"I know you'll never hook up with her, so it doesn't really bother me. You're no Johnny Depp.".

He popped the top off another Mickey's Big Mouth and tossed the cap into the shallow water of the fountain. Passing a bottle to Chris, he took a seat on the concrete ledge and gulped down the malt liquor. Chris giggled and did the same. About thirty minutes in, they were both lit.

"Hey Chris, you gotta work tomorrow?"

"Not if I don't want to. Why, what are you thinking?"

"There's that abandoned project building a few blocks down P street, I always wanted to check it out."

Chris shrugged, his shiny leather jacket heaving up and down in general antipathy. Ben took that as a general agreement. Drunkenly pulling himself up, skipped off the sidewalk and headed towards P street, a slight trace of mold growing thicker as they ventured into a side street.

They passed a bus station, the bench sheltered by a Plexiglass partial enclosure that advertised some stupid rom-con. Ambling over to it, Bret started kicking until the glass shattered. After a few blows the facade over the movie poster tore loose and glossy strips started fluttering in the breeze. Chris giggled as they crossed the street.

The Projects

Black iron gating encircled an obviously distressed commercial building. It looked way old, its grimy pink tiles ascending from an unkempt mass of tree branches and shaggy bushes.

Scaling up the iron barrier, Ben used the branches to pull himself onto the fire escape. That moldy smell was worse near the building. His worn combat books slipped several times, and he almost racked himself more than once, but despite his drunken state he made it onto the balcony. Chris lingered behind, swiveling around as he looked for witnesses. Ben thought he was always a bit too paranoid.

"Come on Chris, we haven't got all night."

Chris gulped down the last of his Mickey's big mouth, hurled the empty bottle into the road (where it remarkably bounced but did not break), and scrambled up the fence. The window was cracked, and Bret tore a branch off the tree to use as a club.

Shattering the glass with a few strikes, he took a pause to glance about, then pushed free the jagged edges. Climbing over the window seal, he leaped down onto a tiled floor. A wave of stuffy air hit him, the cool breeze outside cut off abruptly as he dropped in.

Ben figured this must be a laundry room. The white gleam of what looked like a washer jutted up from a crust of brown filth that rimmed the wall. Because he smoked so much, the rancid smell wasn't overwhelming but there was definitely a damp scent wafting through. Made a little more repulsive by the slight trace of some industrial solvent.

Prying open the door with his boot (he was too much of a germophobe to use his hands), he stepped out into a hallway of cream tiled walls,-their darkened extremities more than a little unsettling, Maybe he was just being paranoid,-although this was DC. His friend Phil was in the hospital after some crackhead smacked him in the head with a two by four sporting a rusty nail.

Ben marveled that the walls still looked so intact. All under splatters of grime of course, but still solid and orderly in a sort of ancient hospital way.

Weren't they originally constructed for returning soldiers after the war?

Ben called back to Chris.

"You coming or what?"

Chris popped up, scaring the shit out of him, but Ben tried to play it off and started to trek down the corridor.

To his disappointment, he noticed that there was nothing here. The uniformity and small confines of it all were chilling, and this building probably did have a long and ominous past, but years of looting had probably removed anything cool.

Ben walked by a gray door and turned. Kicking it partially open, he could see that the frame of a steel couch hugged the wall, almost smothered under a mess of worn clothing and the remnants of what might have been household goods. A thin curtain garnished the single window; it's metal railing drooping under the weight of years of abandonment.

Nothing so far. Ben kept rambling down the hall, all of it surreal in his inebriated state.

Chris mumbled-

"This is boring man, let's go back to your girl's house."

"Let's try one more room. Then we'll leave. We might find something; besides, we already made all this effort."

Chris shrugged. He was usually malleable. All the girls seemed to love his sort of punk rock River Phoenix good looks, but he wasn't the most assertive. Not dumb, he was a genius with the computer, but not leader material.

A little further, Ben kicked open another door. It only opened halfway, obviously bumping into something. He could make out the black frames of chairs, and what appeared to be the jutting ends of a bedframe.

He used his boot to push, and the door creaked open a few more inches. A rotting smell washed over him.

Fuck This.

Just as he was about to retreat, a dark mass caught his eye.

39

Maybe a homeless guy had snuck in here and OD'd. They often camped out in the half-demolished house across from his girl's place.

He debated entering, a homeless guy had just tried to stab him the other day. Pulling out the knife he kept sheathed at his waist, he ventured in.

There was a guy sprawled on the bed. He looked like he'd been dead a few days. Some middle aged dark-skinned guy, garbed in soiled clothing. His eyes were peeled wide, staring lifelessly at the ceiling.

This was pretty heavy, but curiosity killed the cat. Ben figured he'd just get a slightly closer look, just be careful not to touch anything. The last thing he needed was for the cops to pull his fingerprints. He already had a record, so no one would believe any story he told them.

Squeezing around the door, he noticed that the man was missing most of his left leg!

It looked surgically cut, with the peeled back jeans rolled up to the knee, the whole limb cleanly severed below.

It almost looked like a sushi roll, the way a compact ring of bloody flesh encircled a smoothly cut core of bone. The aroma of butchered meat filled his nostrils and made him a little nauseous. Ben glanced at the face. A neatly sewn cleft curled down from his hairline.

He had seen Planet of the Apes. That was a lobotomy scar!

This was getting creepy, brain stuff always freaked him out. He thought about calling out to Chris, but making noise didn't seem like a great idea.

"Hey man, you find anything cool?"

Ben cringed at the sound of Chris's voice. In a slurred whisper, he sputtered-

"Let's get out of here!"

A noise echoed down the hallway.

"Time to go! Now!"

"What, but I thought you wanted to look around?"

He was so loud!

Ben knew that this had been a bad idea. Something in his gut told him, but alcohol had given him a false sense of bravery.

"Keep your voice down! Let's just get out. Now!"

The noise from the hallway grew louder.

"What the fuck is that?"

Ben wondered if Chris was stupid or just thick-headed because he was drunk. As he squeezed around the door, he glanced down the hall.

Loping towards them was what looked like another homeless guy. The whole top of his head, from the hairline up, was gone. Blood rimmed the shaved edges of an exposed brain. Drool trailed from the mouth, the outstretched hands slowly drawing ever closer.

Ben grabbed Chris and started to drag him down the hall. In his drunken stupor, Chris at first resisted, glanced at the thing approaching, gawked, and shuffled to follow.

Things Only Get Worse

The door to the fire escape was too close, and they passed by in their panicked scramble. The darkness of the hall swallowed them up. They skittered around a bend. Passing through a spot of utter darkness, the streetlight from an open door ahead brought to life walls that were increasingly growing more surreal.

Bloody smears demarked the tiles in strange symbols. Ben thought he recognized them from history books but didn't dare slow down. The depressed cavity of a door on his left came into focus, and Ben kicked at it. The door creaked inward, the black maw beyond completely inscrutable.

"Here-let's hide in here."

Ben croaked it out, gulping air as sweat trickled down his face. The green dye in his liberty spikes streaming into his eyes in hot pricks of watery pain.

Partially blind and half drunk, his sudden turn tumbled him into a brusque embrace with the doorframe. Banging his head loudly against unyielding plaster, something gurgled from within. With a thin hiss, tentacles slithered out. Ben lost his footing as they wrapped around his ankles. His bony posterior slammed into the floor, and he rolled over in pain just as Chris's head erupted in a spray of blood. As a rain of crimson specks and pink tufts pelted Ben, sinewy cords pulled him in. Ben almost passed out as his head slammed hard into the doorframe for a second time.

It was all an absurd dream for a minute as he fluttered in and out of consciousness. When clarity returned and his eyes adjusted to the pale light, the thing greeting him was so strange he blinked repeatedly, trying to clear blurry vision. The musky smell had grown into an overpowering scent of decay. The hair on his arm jolted erect, and some primal instinct overwhelmed him with the urge to flee.

A giant, squid-like creature, its slimy skin glistening under the pale light, heaved in wriggling contortions. Glistening scraps of intestines surrounded it, nibbled hunks of what looked like limps poking out of the offal. The semblance of more than a few mutilated faces were visible. Dull groans seeped from a mandible girded by countless rows of needle-like teeth. A multitude of eyes flickered, the irises bifurcated like some lizard.

The tendrils tightened around Ben's legs, pulling them so taut they were about to tear, but abruptly they slacked and fell loose.

Apparently, the thing was weak, maybe it was almost dead. He was pretty sure he could escape its clutches, but whatever had just killed Chris gave him pause.

Was it safer to scramble out, or remain, just out of this monster's reach?

"Parallax and Mill consolidated. Target neutralized. Rest of the hall looks empty."

Boots tramped by, then paused just at the door's edge.

"Should I check on the creature?"

"No. Why stir it up? Those things always give me the creeps anyways."

"Ok.

I'll check further down the hall."

The footsteps receded. Time seemed to crawl, the moldy odor of the creature growing ever more stifling.

But Ben was terrified.

More time creeped by, the guttural groans evocating a new wave of terror each time each time they resonated. The tendrils continuously coiled and then loosened.

Finally, Ben could take no more and peeped his head out the door jamb. The coast looked clear. Scrambling to his feet, he kicked away the restraining tendrils. They tightened, trying to pull him closer, but slackened again. With a hearty kick, Ben lurched out into the hallway.

Twisting to the left, he clambered over Chris's corpse, slipping a little in the pool of blood, and darted down the hall. Within a few feet, the corridor pivoted again, and he rounded the bend. Lo and behold, a few feet down were the grated vents of a floor exhaust conduit.

A rusty cover adorned it, the heavy layer of white paint marred by rust and who knows what else. It looked just large enough.

Scurrying over, Ben kneeled, dug his

fingers in the grate and pulled. A nail tore in two, and Ben started to cry out, but instantly covered his mouth. Then instantly spit profusely as the iron of blood comingled with a gritty residue. Pulling on the grate with his un-injured hand, a seam of crust cracked free in a shower of debris. A particle alighted in his eye, and he rubbed it, only making things worse. The sound of distant boots startled him, and he dove in. The smell was horrendous. Rotting sewage mixed with something even more nauseating. But an image of the bloody remnants of Chris flashed through his mind, and he squirmed forward.

Waves of claustrophobia shot through. He tried squinting his eye, the itch of the invading particle now a painful stab. Counting to 1,000, he steadily wormed his way, reasoning that might distract him just enough to avoid freaking out.

He'd reached 3,000 when his arms suddenly broke out of their metal confines and splashed down into a pool of foul smelling, brackish water.

Streams of light poured down from a grate above. He jerked back and forth, pulling his legs free from the vent, and tried to rise, but only made it into a crouch before metal slammed into his shoulders.

He was going to vomit. The alcohol, the noxious fumes, the foul-smelling black sludge that now coated him. Bile rose in his throat, as he fought back waves of queasiness. Spreading out his knees, his soaked leather pants weighed him down like they were made of lead, but he managed to jerk upright.

The gate moved a little, and he paused as he fought another wave of nausea.

One more push, and it broke free. Shoving the grate aside, he grabbed the edge and pulled himself out.

Scrambling upright, he darted down the street, a trail of muddy footprints in his wake. The skies were lightning, and he glanced back for pursuit as he barreled past the bus stop he'd mutilated.

There is Nowhere to Hide

Arriving at his girl's house, he popped open the grate, bounded down the short walkway, scrambled up the steps, and gripped the door handle. To his surprise, the door was unlocked.

It was never unlocked in DC, unless maybe his girl had left it open for him. She knew he was coming back, and it was a weekday, so maybe her and her roommate were asleep.

Twisting the knob, he pushed the door open.

As his eyes adjusted to the dim light, he could make out the forms of his girl and her chubby roommate. Both faces exaggerated in shock, their peeled open eyes stared lifelessly at the ceiling, A bloody red dot above their eyes trickled a dark stream that co-mingled with a crimson pool spreading out on the carpet beneath.

"Fuck! Fuck! Fuck!"

The shuffle of boots resonated from the back room. Twisting around, Ben flew out the door, down the steps, and onto the sidewalk.

Rounding the ever more visible fountain, the mess of malt liquor bottles more incriminating in the morning light, Ben headed for the train stop. The yuppies he passed grimaced, pinched their noses, and stepped aside as he darted past. Skipping down the escalator steps, bounding the token barrier, he caught a train just as it was pulling up.

47

The station attendant erupted from his cubicle, shouting threats. He looked almost comical, his black-tie flapping across his face and snapping against his shiny bald head. The train door closed before he could reach Ben.

The early morning occupants did their best to look anywhere but in Ben's direction, drifting slowly away and swishing their hands in front of their noses. Not that Ben cared. They viewed him as subhuman anyways. They were the chumps. 9 to 5, and you weren't alive. Or so he told himself.

Fairfax

The train stopped at Fairfax station, and Ben disembarked. The sun had fully risen, and the stench that engulfed him was now in full force.

Descending the platform steps, he already regretted the long trek home. His parents had kicked him out months ago, but they were all at work now and rarely locked the doors. He could slip in, wash his clothes, take a proper bath, and be out of there before they returned. Maybe they had a little food he could steal too. It was still early in the month, so the cabinets should be stocked with their monthly supply from the Military PX. If he was lucky, maybe his mom had stashed some money in the bedroom. Doubtful, but with him out of the house, it was possible.

Home Sweet Home

The trip seemed to take fore-ever. Ben almost gave up a few times, but that wasn't really much of an option, and time definitely seemed to be a factor.

The hot sun was wearing him down, the lack of sleep washed over him in clammy waves, a hangover kicked in, and he felt out of it. Every plodding step forward was an effort.

The endless stream of white sidewalks, all sheltered by a florid autumn tree line, was disorienting and just made him hate the suburbs more.

They didn't even border real woods for Christ's sake, they were just a barrier, so the yuppies don't have to look at the road!

Finally, he reached his old housing development and started clambering up the slight incline towards his parents' house.

Their station wagon was still in the driveway. Not a good sign.

He stumbled against the faux-wood exterior fence, the bricks below hiding the noise. Ben circumvented the carport and drew up next to the kitchen window.

A husky voice barked out.

"When's the last time you saw Ben?"

"Months ago. We kicked him out right after he graduated in May."

"Do you have any idea where he is now?"

"No. Listen, is he in trouble? Something I should be aware of?"

"He did some illegal breaking and entering in DC."

"Great."

The drawl sounded low and exasperated.

"I'd help if I could, but we've had no contact with him in months."

"Let me know if you do. Whatever fantastical story he tells, just be aware that he's a fugitive, and will probably lie through his teeth."

Ben knew his dad would believe whatever the authorities told him. One glimpse was all it would take. He had put Ben's brother in a mental institute for what was essentially teenage punk rock foolishness.

The man exited. and Ben noticed that he wasn't the usual military. He was bedecked in some black suit that screamed special unit. A visored helmet shielded most of the man's forehead, the tip of a microphone jutting out. Even more unsettling, an M4A1 rifle loosely straddled his side. Those firearms were pretty new and high tech. His gun nut dad drooled over them *Why would one be needed here?*

The man appeared to be listening to something, pressing a gloved hand against the side of his helmet.

"Yes Sir."

Raising his rifle, he turned back, entered the house, and fired.

Bens' eyes popped wide, and he took off. Rounding the cheap aluminum shed, he dashed into the woods behind.

As he scaled the fence, he calculated that the closest Greyhound terminal was in Springfield, not far from the mall he used to work at. That was miles away, but if he stuck to the woods, maybe he could make it.

He had friends down in Tennessee. He'd need money, but the formalwear shop he used to work at was in the mall nearby. By the time he got there, he was sure they'd be closed for the day. He still had his key. There was probably some money in the register.

It didn't matter if they examined the place for fingerprints later. He was a wanted man now!

An Unexpected Twist

The soldier exited the house.

"KILL CONFIRMED."

Just as he stepped down the stoop, his head erupted in a spray of crimson, the force throwing a lifeless body to the ground. A minute later, Ben's dad, looking very angry, his outstretched hands holding a smoking .45, emerged. Blood tricked from where a bullet had skimmed his forehead. His wife wasn't so lucky.

Ben and all his friends feared Ben's dad.

51

Ex-special forces, ex-green beret, ex-82nd airborne, tank commander in Vietnam... but the military was never known for their intelligence, and you can only push a man so far. Even a company man.

Buggin' Out

Robert Essig

We were a mile down White Chapel Road when we something big hit the windshield. Big enough to crack the glass. The thing rolled over the top of the car, all of us looking at the roof as it tumbled. I looked in the rearview mirror just in time to see it fall through the red glow of the brake lights that were illuminating dust from the runoff that had dried on the road.

"The fuck was that?" I asked.

My wife glared at me.

"Language," she said in that motherly tone, as if she didn't throw around swear words like a coked-out carnie assembling the tilt-o-whirl after a bender.

"Oh hell, they hear worse on TikTok."

The kids giggled in the backseat.

"'Sides, what the hell was that?"

"Probably a bird," she said.

"A big fuck—a big *darn* bird."

"Come on, let's get a move on. They're expecting us at nine."

I stared into the rearview mirror, as if the bird, or whatever I had hit, would stand and walk away. I felt guilty. In the beam of our headlights, thousands of flying insects darted around like an asteroid shower. Typical summer night in East Tennessee.

"Jason, come on."

The insistence in Laurel's voice had me putting the car into gear and letting off the brake despite my interest in whatever it was we'd hit. The kids were both turned around and looking out the rear windshield, just as eager as I to see what lay in the road, so I pulled forward slowly at first.

Mason and Coral both said "wow!" at the same time, which was enough for me to hit the brake and throw the car into park.

"What now?" Laurel asked.

"I have to get out and see what that was."

I didn't give her time to protest as I opened the door and stepped into humidity thick as cake batter. I rounded the car, eager for what had conjured such a response from the kids, knowing damn well it wouldn't take much to get that kind of awe out of them. A dead bird would do the trick.

But I had to see it for myself, because if that was a bird, we were talking an eagle or a hawk. Something big.

That's not what it was at all. Once I got a glimpse of it, I stopped dead in my tracks and just stared at the thing. I immediately knew what it was. I think I did. It's just, I couldn't believe my eyes. I'd never seen a moth that size before.

It was the size of a red-tailed hawk. Its wings were tangled a bit, and the fuzzy length of its abdomen gyrated this way and that, like the thing was suffering. It was white and black with an intricate pattern on its wings. A moth no one would think twice about on a normal night. Except for the fact that it was a big fucker. And ugly. The head twisted and turned robotically, as if it was perhaps in pain. The eyes were like deep, black pits that seemed to hold me under some spell for a moment, a strange feeling, like intoxication, that had my head swimming until the stink of exhaust and shrill tone of Laurel's voice brought me back from the inky depths.

The giant moth-like creature lay still, its mouth of serrated teeth lying open, the edges lined with barbed feelers of varying lengths. Perhaps equipping it to latch onto its prey.

Do all moths have such teeth?

I knelt and touched one of the wings.

A car door opened. Laurel's high-pitched voice cut through the soupy air like a guillotine. "What are you doing, Jason?"

I stood quickly, figuring I'd better get back to the car before she came out. She hated bugs. I mean, they were everywhere during summer, and it was everything we could do to keep them out of the house, but she hated them. Even moths.

I went to open the door when I noticed my hand was covered in gray dust from the moth's wing. After knocking the dust off on my jeans, I got in the car.

"What was it?" Laurel asked.

"Just a night bird."

Laurel tilted her head and squinted. "An owl?"

"Maybe." I put the car in drive.

"Looked like a big moth to me," Mason said.

"No, son, I think it was an owl."

I drove on.

We were picking up an air fryer that we had found cheap on Facebook Marketplace. We wanted to pick it up earlier, but the seller was busy. I was ready to call the whole thing off, but Laurel insisted. It was a big air fryer that would normally cost over a hundred bucks. We were getting this one for just twenty.

"Where exactly are we?" Laurel asked.

For the one who insisted we buy this damn air fryer, she sure was in a pissy mood about the whole thing. I could hear it in the way she asked that question. Like it was my fault we were on a wild goose chase.

"Somewhere near Oak Ridge," I said.

"I think we're near that old prison that was shut down a while back."

"We got plenty of gas, right?"

"Jeez, Laurel, we're not that far out there."

"Well, I saw on the news there's a trail out here somewhere and hikers' been going missing. Been happening for a long time, I heard. Turned into some kind of dare. People go on the trail just to see if they'll return."

"Sounds like a TikTok challenge," Coral said from the backseat. "The Fallout Challenge."

"Some challenge," I said as I watched the bugs through the headlights like the beginning of a snowstorm.

I could swear they were getting bigger. It became distracting watching them thud against the windshield, leaving the gooey smears of their battered bodies.

"Why's it called the Fallout Challenge?" Laurel asked.

Coral shrugged. "I dunno."

Mason piped in. "It's because you go to see some old building that was used in nuclear fallout experiments or something."

Laurel made a dismissive *pshhh* noise, then said, "Probably a lot of bull."

"We're almost there," I said after glancing at the GPS on my phone. "No service out here, but at least the map knows where we're going."

Laurel groaned and said, "Let's just get this stupid air fryer and get back home."

I shook my head. "Lord knows I didn't want to come out here this late for a damned air fryer. Don't blame me."

"Don't start, Jason."

Before I could start, which I wanted to do since this whole trip was her idea, a house came into view. More of a cabin, really. The inside glowed as if lighted by candles, or maybe twenty-watt bulbs in old table lamps. Rustic was an understatement. Without the dim glow within, this place appeared abandoned, but that meant nothing. There were abandoned houses all over East Tennessee, and houses that looked like they should be condemned that people actually lived in. Could be these people were selling their air fryer for a little cash to pay the electric bill.

"Do you see an address?" I asked Laurel.

"No."

"Me neither, but the map says we're there, so I guess this is the place."

"I'll text them," she said.

"Phones aren't working out here."

"Well, I'll try."

The front door opened, and a man emerged from the shivering glow of candlelight.

"Don't bother," I said as I unbuckled my seatbelt.

Laurel looked up, but didn't say anything.

"Must be the place. He's expecting us." I sighed loudly, making sure she clearly understood how I felt about this. "I'll go talk to him. You stay here."

I stepped out of the car before Laurel could say anything, though I couldn't see why she would have protested. I knew instinctively that she would not want to approach this man, not under these eerie circumstances.

With a smile on my face, I spoke as I walked toward the man, so he knew exactly who I was and why I was there. People this deep in the woods tended to greet strangers with a loaded shotgun.

"Hi, I'm here for the air fryer."

As I came within arm's length of him, two things occurred to me. One, why the hell had he left the door open on a night like this? Bugs were darting in and out of his home like crazy. And two, the smile on his face and the way his eyes kind of protruded reminded me of that goddamned preacher in *Poltergeist 2*, only this fella was kind of bloated. He was pale like grass grown under a log, red around the eyes and mouth and nose in a sickly manner that caused his smile to seem less authentic.

He held his hand out and I grabbed it to shake, figuring the quicker I get the damned air fryer, the better. When our hands touched, I felt something like a shock and thought for a second that the old son of a bitch had pulled a quick one on me by using an old-fashioned hand buzzer. The grip on my hand had an almost numbing effect, causing me to weaken at the knees. All the while he stared into my eyes and smiled.

"Come inside," the man said.

I couldn't resist. I was unable to. I followed him inside, our hands clasped together with a magnetic sort of energy.

The place was filled with the chaotic chorus of wings flapping and little bug bodies pinballing off the walls and windows. The man tossed me onto a couch, breaking the alluring connection our hands had made. I saw that there was some kind of pinprick on my palm. Half my body was numb.

The cushions of the couch began to writhe. I made an attempt to move, but my entire body had become paralyzed. The man approached with scissors. I screamed inside for him to stop but couldn't form words. Whereas one moment I had felt an absurd sense of bliss, I now feared this man had lured me to my death. He bent down and cut the front of my shirt, revealing my stomach.

The cushions continued to move all around me, and soon enough odd caterpillars the size of snakes emerged. They were slow but made up for their lack of speed in sheer size. I don't know if they were racing to see which one would be first, but they were coming for me and I was immobile, forced to watch.

I looked up. The old man was staring down at me, his face like a stretched-out Halloween mask, or someone who had lost a considerable amount of weight very quickly. He was pudgy and unhealthy looking. Pale and sickly. I also noticed that the front door had been closed. What was Laurel thinking? How long would she wait until coming to investigate what the holdup was?

I looked down when I felt the caterpillar on my skin. It was the color of spoiled meat with coarse barbs that did not look at all fuzzy like most caterpillars. All I could do was look as it crawled toward my belly button. It looked up at me and I saw that the head was oddly shaped, like a human skull with two bulging obsidian eyes, something that resembled a nose, and a strange mouth with a combination of human-like teeth, a pair of mandibles, and those thick, barbed hairs I'd seen on the moth outside. I'd never seen anything like it.

It looked up at me, its mouth opening and closing, gnashing its strange teeth with oily gums. The mandibles spread open and then clacked together. That's when the hairs wavered hypnotically, the barbs latching onto my skin as it dug those mandibles into my belly button, ripping and tearing its way into my stomach. Blood poured out of the wound like a ruptured water line. I screamed inside, but all that came out of my mouth were whimpering sounds. Tears rolled out of my eyes, cascading down my face. I could do nothing as the caterpillar gnashed and tore its way into my stomach.

Then the pain was gone, as if the little beast had the anesthetizing properties of a tick.

The old man grinned wider. "It isn't so bad, is it?"

Laurel sighed for the sixteenth time and said, "Where the hell is your father?"

The kids remained silent. They could sense something in the air. Something bad.

"I'm going to knock on the door. This is ridiculous." Laurel spun around to face the kids. "I'm leaving the key in the ignition for the AC. Do *not* touch anything up here, okay? You can change the channel on the radio, but that's it. I'll be right back."

60

The kids nodded. Laurel stepped out of the car and into the muggy night air, swatting at the multitude of insects flying around that were attracted to the glowing beams of the headlights.

As she walked up the drive, something swooped in from above. She looked up in time to see tree branches skittering. Whatever it was, it had been very large.

Another owl?

Swatting bugs as she stepped to the front door, Laurel knocked. Immediately, Jason opened the door.

On recognition, she said, "What the fuck is—"

Then she noticed his cut shirt and all the blood around a gaping hole in his navel. The look of bemusement on his face startled her.

"Come in," Jason said as he grabbed his wife's arms and pulled her into the cabin.

Laurel struggled and twisted her body in an attempt to remove herself from Jason's grasp. He threw her onto the same couch he'd been seated on. He then examined the palms of his hands.

"You don't have the sting yet," the old man said. "It develops eventually."

The man moved toward Laurel. She squirmed to get away, but he reached out with precision and uncanny speed for someone who looked as bad off as he did. Grasping her arm, he delivered a sting that caused Laurel to scream, but the scream died in her throat as the poison quickly flowed through her bloodstream. The old man let go of her. Something wiggled in his palm that looked like a large hookworm, a translucent drop of venom bubbling from its mouth as it retracted back into the saggy flesh.

"Get the kids," the old man said.

Laurel stared on with frightened eyes, raining tears and unable to move.

I opened the front door and, peering out through the beams of the headlights, waved my hand to gain the children's attention. Then I waved them in, as if telling them that it was all right.

One of the back doors opened.

"Dad?" came Mason's uncertain voice.

"Yeah, it's me! Come on in. They have some really neat stuff in here."

"Where's mom?"

"She's in here too. There's more than just an air fryer. They have video games and even an iPhone for sale."

Mason ducked his head back into the car, conversing with his sister, and then her door opened. Video games for Mason; an iPhone for Coral. They were too easy. And they both walked up to me with a mix of glee and apprehension.

Coral saw the bloody shirt first. I'd been holding it together to conceal the gut-hole.

"What happened, Daddy?"

"Oh, nothing. Hurt myself moving the air fryer." I smiled but it felt wrong and also very right all at the same time. "Come in."

I closed the door behind them. The thing inside me moved and I shivered.

At the sight of her mother on the couch, in what looked like a drug stupor, Coral asked, "What's wrong with Mommy?"

"She's just resting. Come this way."

I brought the children into a room. Though I hadn't been in this room before, I knew what waited there as if with some strange instinct that I hadn't possessed until the caterpillar burrowed into my flesh. I could feel things I'd never felt before. I sensed things on some deeper level, elicited by a pull through the ethers, a tether to something unidentifiable, something I couldn't understand. And yet I was helplessly drawn to.

I closed the door behind us. The kids were frightened, but there was that instinctive trust children had, that faith their father wasn't inviting them to their death.

"I want to go home," Mason said.

"Me too," Coral said. "Can we go home?"

"You are home."

The room was dim, but I could see quite well. Another attribute to the thing nestling inside me. Plastered to the wall were two cocoons that were shaped like humans wrapped in silken webbing. One of the cocoons pulsated as a creature emerged, tearing through the mass. A smell like deep rot escaped, but it didn't assault my senses as badly as I would have expected. Mason puked and Coral cried. Slender appendages pushed through the webbing, slick tendrils of rotten flesh hanging off and dribbling down the pristine exterior of the cocoon. The giant moth-like creature made an almost human groaning noise as it emerged. The kids bawled, but I wouldn't allow them to leave the room. The moth pulled its wings from the cocoon and fluttered them to fling some of the putrescence away. The face was more human now than what I had seen on the thing that slithered into my stomach. No mandibles. But teeth like the tips of knives and eyes like black pearls. That possessed a void to the other dimension within which I had handily surrendered my sanity.

No emotion.

No expression.

Salivating.

Hungry.

I watched the thing wide-eyed and grinning like a jester. And felt nothing. I knew that I was perfectly safe. At home. More alive than I had ever been, as if all my previous inhibitions had been released. I felt purpose as I shoved Coral into its slimy embrace.

The thing took her with two thick, branch-like appendages. She recoiled, screaming-

"Daddy! Daddy no!"

The hungry moth took a bite out of her shoulder. She screamed and thrust her body but could not escape. Blood gushed from the wound. The next bite was right through her skull, the teeth sinking in without resistance. Coral looked at me, eyes wide, mouth agape, caught amidst a scream that seemed to be locked within her throat. The creature bit down and yanked, removing a sizable chunk from the back of her head. It glistened like deep red Jell-O and cherry syrup.

Mason had covered his eyes, burying his face in my leg. Despite being ushered into this hell, he continued to seek salvation in the shelter of his loving father.

How sweet.

As Coral was feasted upon, sating the birth-hunger of the mutant moth, another began emerging from its human cocoon. I pretended to console Mason, who refused to face the squelching noises the moth made while feasting on his sister. Once the next moth was freed, I thrust Mason toward the thing. Mason looked at me with hurt in his eyes as the thing nibbled on his body, taking bites out of him as if sampling each appendage to decipher which tasted the best. As I watched him die, I felt a knot of hunger from deep within as the nameless thing twisted and burrowed in my body.

In the living room, Laurel lay on the couch with a mess of blood around her navel. Through an open door to another room, I saw the old man was leaning up against the wall, dead eyes staring at me. A vile looking caterpillar emerged from his gut, dripping thick clots of rotten meat. The little creature began the process of wrapping the corpse in silk.

As for Laurel and myself, we waited for the next human to respond to the ad for an air fryer.

The End

ABOUT THAT BUZZ

Merrill David

Some Beach, South Carolina, USA

"I knew it, Doug"

Said the six foot two inches tall, ninety-five-pound, twenty-something year old weakling Steve.

Standing on the trodden beach pathway in the swim trunks he'd chosen for the day, his body resembled that of a praying mantis, minus the wings.

"I told you she wouldn't even look over at us when she passed."

"No shit, Steve"

Said his also twenty-something year old buddy. Who sported quite different proportions!

"I coulda told 'ya that would happen. I even doubled down on the Axe spray today and her highness still didn't even give us so much as a glance."

"Yeah, I think everyone on the entire eastern fuckin' seaboard smelt that shit, Dougie. Givin' me a fuckin' nosebleed, feels like I been snortin' that pink fiberglass insulation they put up in the GODDAMN ceilings."

"Funny, fucktard. *You're* gonna talk shit, Steve? Wearing *those* hideous SpongeBob swim trunks?"

"At least I'm not shaped like fuckin' Sponge Bob."

"I think of my shape more akin to a Bartlett Pear."

"Okay yeah, I see that."

The 'she' they were referring to was none other than 'Queen' Christina. Steve and Doug had unceremoniously given that title to what everyone agreed was by far the hottest babe on the beach. Worst of all was the fact that she knew it. Not that they called her queen, but she was aware she was the premier female. She was there every day. The same beach, at the same time. In the very same seat. Like clockwork she was galivanting with the lifeguard stud. Laughing and sitting on his lap in that castle of bright red lumber.

That lifeguard stand, perhaps not so coincidentally, was just as bright and red as the stud boy's uber-tight Speedo.

Today the Queen was wearing her favorite, skimpiest, two-piece bikini. The one featuring horizontal black and yellow stripes. No, she wasn't a Pittsburgh Steelers fan, the colors really just seemed to speak to her. And she looked absolutely fabulous in them as well.

"You ever thought about ending it all, Steve?"

Doug asked while pulling a flask of Mad Dog 20/20 out of his pocket and taking a slurp.

"What the fuck, bro?! Just because one fine female won't look our way. There's about a hundred of us on this beach all in the same boat. Why would you even *think* about taking it to that extreme?"

"I mean, I'm not seriously gonna do it. I suppose it's just the existentialist thinker in me speaking out."

"The huh?"

"It just means that I'm one of those types who're always filled with anguish, anxiety, an overwhelming dread, and depression. All over things happening in the world, or by life in general. Hell, my very own existence. Sometimes I even fantasize about putting my neck through a noose and hanging myself from the highest tree branch.

But I never act on those thoughts. I'm just as fearful that with my lousy luck the damn limb will snap and I'd just break a leg or suffer something painful."

"Come on, Steve; don't you ever get tired of just being YOU? We're not that different, you and I. Ya know?"

Doug held up his flask.

"Want a swig? It's the Dog. Grape."

"Yeah, I'll have a swig. And thanks a lot homie, I appreciate you bringin' me down with 'ya like that. I was feelin' somewhat good about myself until you just bummed me the fuck out."

"I'm just sayin, dude; I'm so sick of having to work forty hours a week or more just to get by. Working for THE MAN. I hate the fuckin' MAN, and I hate workin' for him even worse."

"You talkin' bout the boss? Mr. Kocklick? Or his minion, that bowling pin shaped douchebag we call Captain Weeble?"

"I hate Weeble too, but I meant that big Cockroach, always walking around the workplace like he's lost while checking up on us all the time.

That big lurching mother fucker looks like a walking dildo, but with less personality. But it's not just those two, I was really referring to the whole system."

No matter how hard we work, all the great ideas we generate, all the wickets we whack out and all the numbers we crunch, it's never gonna be good enough for THEM. Unless of course you're buddies with them or stroken' 'em under the desk. If not, at the end of every budget year, they always announce cuts and send a bunch of us packing. How the hell are we supposed to be productive working under those conditions?"

"I understand why so many decide not to join the work force, when you can get all your necessities by thieving, or scamming. Why waste all your time and effort bolstering the boss' fuckin' bank account. Fuck that. I'd rather be free of that bullshit. And happy."

"And yeah, now that you mention it, I *am* sick of that Queen never even giving us a damn nod. But it's not just THAT female, all of 'em act the same way. We're not bad looking dudes. Why don't we get any respect?"

"We're definitely not hideous."

Steve agreed.

"And it's okay to be fluffy these days. Or super skinny. It's actually not cool to be fit anymore. Fitness is for jerkoffs. Real men like *us* are more into gaming and watching YouTube videos. And growing man buns and shit."

"Sure."

Said Steve.

"But look over there, tell that to the muscle-bound orange freak squirting oil all over that sexy Asian chick and rubbin' it all over her body. Or that handsome jock in the water playing Marco Polo with that smokin' hot bitch sitting on his shoulders, her pulsating genitalia gyrating against the back of his head. Or that dude with the washboard abs getting that blowjob up there in the lifeguard stand."

Doug stopped and began a scan, making a 360 degree turn to see that the beach was full of gorgeous, busty, tan women. ALL of them accompanied by a good-lookin' rich boy, or alone and *looking for one.*

"But you know what, Steve? As fucked up as it is that the Queen, hell all of them females, won't even acknowledge our existence, why the hell do I find myself wanting that ONE so bad?"

"Dude, you're not the only one. Look at all these horny males doing exactly the same thing you are. Every single morning they're out here, strategically trying to place themselves in position to bump into *her.* Or somehow make their paths cross. We do all of that only to get rejected time and time again."

Doug climbed up on his imaginary soap box and began to preach.

"Between the stress from work, the constant rejection from these bitches who think the whole world revolves around 'em, plus everyone else's bullshit nearly *every* fucking thing, it's ALL making me sick as FUCK! I swear, I've got an upset stomach 24-7. Not to mention this constant buzz in my GODDAMN head. It's not fair, and it's not right, and it's driving me MOTHA FUCKIN' MAD."

"Look over there."

"You see that shrub over there, on the edge of that sand dune? It's got a massive beehive inside it. Look at all those honeybees going in and out of that fuckin' thing. It's like a city in there, but without all the human bullshit that comes with it. Those bastards work their asses off, but all for a good cause. Each and every one of those insects, it's not like us working for THE MAN. Not by any means."

"Interesting. I never put much thought into it. You seem very knowledgeable about the whole bee thing."

"Think about it: do you suppose they have to deal with the same fuckery as humans do? No way. I'm totally serious when I say that I wish I were that fuckin' bee comin' out of the hive right now. Life would be so much sweeter. Bearable even."

"Yeah."

Said Steve.

"I agree. I'd probably make that trade and take that life. We could come and go freely. Anyplace we like, without worry of being banned or forced out, rejected, or ridiculed. But then again what do we really know about the lifestyle of a honeybee? I bet they have to work their asses off to maintain that hive. Maybe we actually have it good? I know you've heard that expression; the grass isn't always greener on the other side. Hell, and for all we know, that very bee that you see there could be wishing he was in your shoes right now."

During his conversation with Steve, Doug had failed to notice that Queen Christine had descended the bright red testosterone tower. As she made her way along that pedestrian path, she started Doug as she passed. But when she once again failed to acknowledge Steve and Doug, the self-admitted pear-shaped drunk decided to finally speak out.

"Hey Queen, what do I gotta do to get your attention? I mean, I'm not picky. just look my way,. Shoe me away with a flick of your wrist if you want. Shit, spit on me."

"ANYTHING."

"What do I gotta do. stick my head in that beehive over there?"

The female, not acting surprised or even fazed at being addressed by such a lesser being, still failed to acknowledge Doug with any sort of response.

"Really?"

Yelled Doug.

"NOTHING? Not a wink, or a nod, or even a flip of the bird?"

Fed up, he made his way closer to the rhythmic, pulsating hive situated within the shrub. Suddenly, slipping and falling all about in his drunkenness, Doug bumped into the black steel barrel trash can that was only inches away from that bush.

This careless action inadvertently awoke the masked monster within.

IT had been sleeping.

Or comatose.

Perhaps zombified.

Regardless, without notice, the former lethargic creature was now WICKED AWAKE.

As a growl began to emit from the lower half of the can, something slowly emerged.

This steroid-induced, crack addicted and extra-sickly THING with a stocky, round body and covered in greasy, matted, salt-and-pepper fur. Its god-awful sewer smell emitting from the container.

Wearing its traditional 'black mask' of fur, the batshit bandit sported black rings around it's ragged, fucked up tail, foam bubbling at the mouth.

The daylight seemed to hurt its eyes, and the rabid raccoon, clearly distressed, began to scream.

"AAAARRRRRHHH!"

Slightly less destructive than bears, raccoons can still wreak havoc on beehives. This one, being rabid, was even more dead set on devastation.

The crafty creature, foaming at the mouth as it flew out of that can like a feral flying squirrel. Belly flopping onto the first thing that it contacted. it promptly plopped onto Doug's shocked, pasty face.

The aggressive coon was quite agitated by the human keeping him from that hustling and bustling hive.

The sickly, manifestation of a mammal was all set to reach into the bustling beehive and help itself to a snack. Removing itself from Doug's face, Ricky dove for the hive.

Using nearly human hands to reach inside, the coon knew exactly where to find the good stuff. Even through its riddled gray matter, this beast knew that the standard nest architecture for all honeybees was similar. Most of the hive was made of interlocking hexagonal wax cells.

It was in these hexagons where brood was raised. But the treasure, that golden delicious honey, was stored in the upper part of the comb.

As the raccoon clawed through their home, hundreds of honeybees began to flee through pre-planned. Clearly under attack and prepared to protect what was theirs, they began to blitz. The insects swarmed onto Doug's head and let their stingers fly.

Jabbing Doug's big head with the small sharp-pointed organs, the bees stung repeatedly. Striking tenacity, the insects felt absolutely no remorse as they filled Doug with their venom.

Another hundred or so bees pumped the partially paralyzed raccoon full of poison.

As they stung the staggering beast, it flew into a fit of rage and began screaming. Pissed, the cockeyed coon decided to take out its rage on the man with the bright red head. Leaping back onto Doug's face, it began to claw ferociously at his flesh. Then, bearing its black fangs it sunk them deep into Doug's neck.

. As a result, Doug's main vein began to drain. As blood poured down his neck, the product of the pain, swelling, redness, and itching from the bee stings all kicked in. But those symptoms were small potatoes compared to what was happening internally. A bizarre combination of factors was taking place within. The massive input of venom created an anaphylactic reaction. The rabies injection collided with the new chemicals. Some sort of synthesis occurred, a mind-boggling metamorphosis, of sorts.

Suddenly, Doug felt... different.

"I feel free.... lighter, stress free...

Happy to be ALIVE! Like I'm in a Candyland surrounded by gumdrops and lollipops."

"There's a rainbow! And a little chihuahua dog riding a unicorn! Am I in heaven?"

"Not quite, weirdo."

"Who said that?"

"Me. Your Queen."

"Queen? You're talking to... me?!"

"Of course, silly. Why wouldn't I be?"

Now Doug was in shock, an addition to his state of confusion and bliss.

"It's just.. never mind. What happened to me? Where am I? Who am I?"

"That sick feeling in my gut is gone. There's no more buzz in my head..."

"Hey hunk, you saved my life back there, doing that thing you did with your head. You're a hero."

Doug, believing this all to be some stupid hoax, decided to play along.

"Right. Remind me again exactly what I did to rescue you? I seem to have had my memory jarred..."

"You beat that crazed black-masked bandit off with your face, distracting it away from me so I could escape."

"Oh, yeah. That..."

"In gratitude, I'd like to thank you properly. How may I reward you? Perhaps some sexual favors? Does that work for you? You like getting off?"   Doug nearly choked on his tongue. "Ummm... ahem... yeah, I suppose that would work for me."

"Okay."

Said the smiling Queen, looking lovely in her favorite black and yellow outfit.

"Meet me in the rose garden this evening and bring some friends. MALE friends that is..."

"Seriously?"

Asked Doug.

"I thought you were joking. After all this time trying to get you to even look in my direction... that's *all* I had to do to get your attention? Use my face as a pin cushion to keep you from being attacked?"

The Queen was baffled.

"Honestly, I've never even noticed you around here before. Today was the first day I've even seen you. Are you sure you're okay? You seem really confused. Did you get hit in the head?"

Doug shrugged.

"Actually, I think I might have some friends. So, you're for real about tonight?"

"Of course."

"And you want me to bring some dudes? Like a friend or two? I guess you have some girlfriends you're trying to set up. That's cool."

"They're all for me. Bring more like ten to twenty."

Later That Night

Pretty much as he'd expected, Doug had no problem finding willing partners to participate in the Queen's planned rumpus.

Finding fifteen willing males in no time, all appreciated this opportunity to 'meat' the Queen.

After multiple failed attempts at being welcomed into her presence, each of them was overjoyed at the chance. As the sixteen males all made their way to the rose garden, each decked out in their most masculine outfits, all had the same thing in mind.

What if she's looking to make a love connection? I need to look bigger and stronger, more potent than the others.

"Good evening, boys."

Said the Queen, as she seemed to magically. No one else was allowed in the garden at this time. The Queen wasn't worried in the least about making herself comfortable with her eager guests. Letting her dress slide down her shoulder, she made no effort to catch it as it fell. Taking a good slow look at all of her male guests, it was clear that her highness was as aroused as the fellas.

As her nipples began to harden and her hoo-hoo began to glisten, one male after the other found themselves disrobing. With erect penises in the front and equally stimulated stingers at the back, nearly every move in the close quarters resulted in a sword fight.

"Where's my hero?" asked the Queen, buzzing all about. Doug, the last to get naked, was feeling inferior behind the crowd.

Is she talking about me?

"There you are!"

She said, making eye contact with Doug.

"Thank you for bringing your friends."

"Oh, yeah. That was easy."

The Queen smiled.

"Okay, let's get started. I need to store up to 100 million sperm in my oviducts, enough to fertilize my eggs throughout the remainder of my life. This will strengthen my colony's ability to resist disease and environmental challenges.

"So Doug, yes, I do *want* you. But not just you. I'll take you and all your friends at the same time."

In unison, all of the males stiffened even more and uttered

"Hell, yesss."

"Oh."

Added the Queen.

"Just one condition, if any of you drones are unsuccessful in mating me, you can plan on being ejected from the hive at the end of the summer season. That means it's just a matter of time til you freeze to death or starve."

With that said, the Queen's mating flight, otherwise known as a Honeybee Gang Bang, was under way.

As she flew away in a frenzy, the sex crazed drones pursued her, penises pointing upwards and eager for that bee-ver.

Then, after they fought over who would get to do her first. they began the dirty deeds. But these deeds would not be done cheap. Each male would undoubtedly pay a stiff price.

As the sky orgy started, one by one, each drone flew over the Queen and mounted her. Positioning themselves so their thorax was above her abdomen, each drone then inserted his end phallus into her, ejaculating semen with an unfathomable force.

Doug, the last in line, wondered where all of the others had gone after sticking the Queen with their magic wands.

"Are you ready for me, Dougie?"

Asked the Queen, licking her left nipple.

Doug was harder than a diamond in a snowstorm.

I CAN'T BELIEVE THIS IS HAPPENING. IT'S GOING DOWN NOW! Finally free, about to pounce on this uber hot female, his long-time crush, Doug said-

"Yes, my Queen. Brace yourself!"

The pear-shaped male was prepared. Doug used both hands to spin her around, facing away from him. Slapping that fine bee bitch on her bare ass, Doug drove his fuzzy shaft between her cheeks and straight into her cooch. Then, firing off a man-sized jizz-missile inside her, his end phallus snapped completely off and remained inside her.

Doug fell backwards, soon realizing that his penis and the front half of him had been left behind. With his abdomen ripped completely open, Doug thought to himself, *wow. Now that's what I call a happy ending.*

Beach bystanders called 9-1-1, and emergency personnel and paramedics arrived soon afterward.

"What happened here?"

They asked a tall witness by the name of Steve.

"He's my friend. We got here about four hours ago. He was depressed, started drinking heavily, and then I think the sun kinda baked him too. One minute he was hatin' on work and the next thing I knew he was hittin' on the lifeguard's chick. He was all drunk and wobbly, bumped into a trash can, got bit by a raccoon and then got stung by a shitload of bees. Next thing I knew he was lying on the ground, completely out of it, talking about bees and calling someone 'Queen' and talking about sex orgies. So bizarre.

"I tried to wake him up, but he went into a seizure. That's when I called you guys."

The medics worked to resuscitate Doug, but it was useless. The young man was deceased, a super-sized smile across his bright red, welt-covered face.

The Next Day: Some Beach, South Carolina, USA

Harold, a drone bee just one day earlier, suddenly found himself in a different body.

"Oh. My. Gosh. It really happened! I'M HUMAN!"

He began to walk, happy to feel the hot, soft sand between his toes. He went into the water, anxious to experience that wetness on his human skin. *This is all incredible, just as I expected.*

But Harold, now a man, had desires. More than anything he yearned to touch a woman, to feel the softness of her skin, and perhaps even, for her to touch him back. There was also this thing called love that he'd heard so much about...

As the new man splashed about in the shallow water, an attractive young woman approached.

"Hi! You new in town?"

"No, I'm here every day."

"Hmm, never seen you before. You're kinda cute. Can I get you to rub this suntan oil all over my body for me?"

"Yes," said Harold. "I believe I might like that."

THE END

DEDWADONT

Tommy Clark

1: TODAY

SATURDAY, DECEMBER 14, 2024 11:40 A.M.

THE TUG HILL, REDFIELD NY

LAKE-EFFECT EVENT SNOWFALL: 4' OF ACCUMULATION (AND FALLING)

The savory scent of a boiling venison stew permeates the wilderness air. Its redolence sticks to the flying snow, as the invisible gale fights through the forest's trees. Rock music, muffled by the whipping winds, accompanies the aromas emanating from within an A-frame camp. Near the outhouse, hanging outside the cabin from a thick tree limb, a trio of deer carcasses—all are gutted, and one is skinned—twist in the breeze. Occasionally they collide with one another, visually resembling giant flesh wind-chimes.

The cabin is nestled near the Salmon River Forest in Upstate New York. Isolated, it's far from the eyes of civilization. Although the snow has nearly buried the building, it's still a safe haven for brothers Joey and Aaron Hatcher, local hunters using it as refuge from the storm. It's not the first time they've found themselves here, and it likely won't be the last.

The region is ripe with unpredictable weather patterns. In particular, their current location—the westernmost edge of the Tug Hill plateau, due east of Lake Ontario—is an inclement weather magnet, and it captures snow in feet throughout the winter months. Averaging over two hundred inches of snow a year, it is one of the snowiest, inhabited places in the world. This anomaly, known as lake-effect snow, can come from nothing.

Freezing Jetstream winds blow down and across the giant inland sea known as *Ontarí'io* by the traditional peoples of this land. They can transform an otherwise sunny, albeit windy, day into a blizzard of white-out conditions without warning.

In spite of the weather reports warning of a possible lake-effect event, they still went hunting. Feeding their families will not wait on bad weather to pass, as they are well aware white-tailed deer flourish in these woods. Venison has been a staple of their family's diet for generations as members of the Onondaga, the Fire Keepers of the Haudenosaunee, commonly known as the Iroquois Nation. Onondaga translates to "People of the hills," and the Hatcher brothers know this portion of the Adirondack Mountain range, its westernmost edge, well.

"Fuckin weatherman was right. Again." Joey Hatcher says as he looks out the frosted window of the A-frame before setting the tea kettle back on the stove top. Moisture from the humidity within the cabin had formed on the glass, and it's now partially frozen, obscuring the window's view.

"How much more do you think has fallen since we shoveled?" Aaron asks his younger brother.

"Another dick's worth, I'd say." Joey replies, holding his hands about half a foot apart.

"What kinda dick are we talkin' here? A white man's dick?" His brother snorts in response before answering.

"Okay then, two white-man dicks?" Joeys replies rhetorically, a slight giggle layers his words as he sips on his tea. "Last time I opened the door to piss, I pushed a bunch out of the way and more has come since."

"So how long do you think it will last?" Aaron asks, fidgeting in his seat.

"Who knows. Weatherman said it was going to be today and tomorrow, but the bands will be shifting. We'll have to shovel again after dinner."

The interior of the cabin is an anachronism. Its decor hasn't been updated in over forty years, from the tube TV and VCR to the analog clocks, wood stove, and seventies wallpaper. Olan Mills studios portraits, their colors still vibrant, of a family decorate the walls. An elderly woman with thick glasses is prominent in most of them. The Stereo 8 player, part of a nearly fifty year old home stereo, fades the song out as it prepares to switch programs. An almost fifty-year-old K-Tel compilation cartridge, its title rubbed off, provides the music. The volume of the wind increases as if on cue.

A loud click from the speakers startles Joey as the stereo switch's tracks, causing him to jump in his seat, and the song returns. The tea kettle comes to a boil on the woodstove heating the cabin's interior. The steam whistles out, surprisingly in key with the music, and Joey removes it from the heat while he stirs the stew with a wooden spoon. After setting the spoon back into a ladle, he pours the kettle's contents into a pair of ceramic mugs on the card table he and his younger brother (*but only by a year!*) are sitting at.

The strings of tea bags hang over the sides, and as the water pours in, Aaron stirs his cup. A burst of wind hits the cabin walls, overcoming the music—making it difficult to determine the artist playing—and causing both men to shiver.

"Stew's almost done?" Aaron asks his brother. The younger sibling nods in affirmation. "Good. It smells delicious. You used Great Gramma Marion's recipe; I can smell the onions."

"You bet your ass I did. Her cooking was legendary. I can't believe she's been gone over a year now. No wonder the holidays are sucking." Joey says.

"I know. She was like a hundred years old when she and Uncle RJ died in that place."

"The nursing home that burned down in Fenton during the 2023 Windstorm, right after she died?" The aforementioned straight-line wind storm, or derecho, devastated the communities bordering the Great Lake's shores. Most of the region still hasn't recovered from the damage a year and a half later.

"It wasn't a nursing home; it was an assisted living home. But yeah."

"I guess that's good. Can you see the outhouse?"

"Yeah. Why? Don't tell me you have to shit."

Aaron stands up from the folding chair and a loud, ass cheek clapping fart erupts from within his bowels. "I think I do!"

"Jesus Christ, man!" Joey wrinkles his nose in disgust. "Da fuck! You better check to make sure nothing slipped out into your drawers."

"Hah!" Aaron laughs in response, before zipping up his jacket. "This is gonna suck."

"Not as bad as the stench you just released in here!"

"Oh, come on, it's not that bad!"

"You tell that to the wallpaper and Gramma Marion." Joey points to one of the portraits of the matron decorating the walls, and a corner of the ceiling where a water leak has peeled back a corner of the decades old wallpaper.

"Really funny. I'll be right back, I'm gonna drop the browns off in the super bowl," Aaron chuckles as he puts on his jacket.

"Let me know if we need to shovel anymore," Joey says.

"I will." Aaron replies. Experienced with this weather, the brothers maintained a shoveled path to their outhouse. At this point of the storm, it resembles a chasm cutting through a wall of snow. He opens the A-frame's door. A gust of wind and blowing snow swirls about the door's frame, filling the building's interior and sending a few loose papers flying.

"Jesus Christ, man, close the door behind you!" Joey declares, and Aaron pulls it shut as he ventures to the outhouse, some forty yards down the path. In the conditions it may as well be light years away.

•

A crack of thunder resonates in the sky as icy snowflakes, propelled by thirty-mile-an-hour winds, swirl into the man-made gully leading to the outhouse. It's like gnats biting at the exposed flesh on Aaron Hatcher's face and hands. The deer they bagged yesterday, a trio of big bucks, one with a nice twelve-point rack, still hang from a line in the trees. They're safe out of the reach of a random bear not hibernating, or any of the packs of coy-dogs running rampant through these woods.

A tether line, supported by metal poles placed every ten feet along the path, guides him to his destination. The walk isn't much of an issue, and though the new snow reaches the tops of his ankles, it's the least of his worries. He counts his steps, from the cabin to the outhouse, *one... two... three...*

With each step Aaron's belly cramps, a result of the damn tea loosening him up. He clenches his ass cheeks, afraid the flatulence might be solid, or even worse... liquid. *Four... five... six...*

The idea of dying by hypothermia as a result of diarrhea doesn't mesh with Aaron's idea of a good time. *Seven... eight... nine... ten... what is that?* Aaron stops.

A flickering ball of light, hovering in the sky and mostly obscured by the trees, illuminates the path ahead with skeletal shadows.

"What the fuck is that?" He whispers to himself. The light raises his nape hairs more than the cold's goosebumps. He barely sees the outhouse through the swirling snow. It's too bright to be the moon and this knowledge aggravates the man's fear. His heart now racing, Aaron runs through the snow, bounding as far as stride will take him. Twenty steps later, he reaches it and closes the door behind him.

It's dark, with no lights or electricity in the outhouse. The soft glow from the ball of light shines through seams between the boards on the walls, illuminating the interior. As a result of these cracks, the walls do nothing to keep the draft out. That's all fine for its occupant, as he hasn't come here to hang out.

The building doubles as a utility shed for their skinning and gutting tools. The brothers have kept the old traditions alive through their skills as tanners and hunters. When they were boys, their grandfathers and uncles taught them to skin and gut deer in the same manner as their people have done since before the Colonists arrived. The tools are made from antlers and bone, as well as flint, wood, and stone. These ancient implements are as effective and efficient as any modern device made of steel and plastic when it comes to dressing prey.

Aaron's teeth chatter as he unbuckles his belt and drops his jeans. Goosebumps line his legs. He sits on the ice-cold toilet seat, and lets out a surprised yelp, cursing as he does so.

"Jesus fucking Christ, that's cold." He shakes his head. His bowels waste no time in evacuating and relief spreads through his body. It seems solid, at least. He sighs while the wind whistles through the cracks of the outhouse. The effect creates an eerie, hypnotizing melody. Aaron hums along with the ethereal ear-worm, noting how soothing it is. It's peaceful until he hears his name called from outside. The voice is foreign, but familiar, one he hasn't heard in... decades?

Aaron...

He stops humming, holds his breath and listens, but all he hears is the blowing wind answering with a whistle. "Joey, is that you? You pranking me, you dirty little bastard?" He says. He waits a moment for a reply.

There is none.

Aaron grabs the role of toilet paper and cleans himself with a few wads. He drops them into the cistern, sprinkles a handful of sawdust shavings over the mess, and closes the seat after pulling his jeans back up. Another gust comes, and with it the volume of the wind's haunting song increases to a deafening level.

Aaron...

He hears his name, again, as the light disappears, the same familiar tone adding another surprise to the experience. His thoughts continue to blame his brother, *Joey and his pranks. The light is probably something he rigged up there and he put some speakers on the roof.*

Bundling up in his jacket, Aaron opens the door to discover the path back to the cabin is obscured by the blowing snow invading their trench. Holding the tether line, he trudges back, shielding his face from the elements with his free hand as he counts the steps he takes to the shelter.

Twenty... Twenty-one... twenty-two... He looks up, expecting to see the cabin ahead of him. *Twenty-three... twenty-four... twenty-five...*

Which he does. The deer carcasses are swaying in the swirling winds, the rope creaking on the tree limbs. Aaron's heart jumps when a figure moves near the cabin... *What? First a creepy light and now this? Whatever this is? Is it a shadow of the deer?* He ponders the possibilities as his heart races... whatever it is, it's no shadow and it's outside with him in this shitty weather, on the drifts, climbing—*no skittering*—over the roof and disappearing. *What the fuck is that? It's no shadow!* He thinks as he stops counting his steps. *Is it Joey?* He

92

wonders before vocally calling for his brother, after all, who else could it be.

"Joe? What are you doing outside?" There's no answer. "Joey!" Aaron shouts, louder. Still, there's no reply. Aaron tries again, this time shouting his brother's formal name as loud as possible. "JOSEPH!"

This time the door of the cabin flies open. The music from the eight-track player bleeds out without Aaron placing it. He ponders for a moment without positive recognition. On the cabin's stoop, he sees his brother standing within the door's frame. "What's your problem? Everything okay?" Joey asks, his words barely audible over the wind and music.

Aaron, still trying to remember either the name of the song or who the fucking singer was, looks to the side of the cabin one last time, and sees nothing sulking about in the snow. *I swear to God there was someone—something—there,* he thinks before shouting back to Joey, "Yeah! Hold the door for me, I'm coming through." Grasping the lead with one hand, Aaron hurries back into the cabin, slamming the door shut behind him. Once inside, he removes his cold weather gear and sits down, a bowl of hot venison stew awaiting him.

"It all come out okay? Didn't get any on ya?" Joey asks, smirking. Aaron shakes head and rolls his eyes before answering.

"Naw. Hey, did you hear something on the roof just now before I came back?"

"No. Should I have?"

93

"I don't know. Huh."

"Did you see something?"

"I dunno. Were you punking me out there?"

"Hardly. Too shitty out."

"That's what I thought. Was probably the wind moving some trees. Who knows." Aaron raises the spoon to his lips, the steam of the stew rising and tickling his nose hairs. A smile grows across Aaron's face as he opens his mouth to take his first bite... when someone—*or something*—knocks on the door.

The brothers sit in silence, neither wishing to get up to answer, both of them wishing the sound is the errant result of a tree limb. This is all dismissed when the knocking, a distinct pattern of three in rapid succession, comes again. This time it's followed by a muffled noise.

"Hellll....." It's clearly someone's voice, and the raising winds do their best to cover it up. Aaron and Joey aren't sure if it's a call of distress, or a greeting. The brothers shrug their shoulders in unison, pull their chairs back, and stand. Aaron reaches the door first. It's not without trepidation.

His mind slips back to the skittering thing—*he thought*—he saw outside minutes ago. *Is something hunting us?* He further ponders as he reaches for the doorknob. Hesitating for another moment, he sees whoever is outside has grasped the door knob, and rattles it. Aaron pulls his hand back while Joey steps over to an arm's length from his shotgun.

"Helloooo?" The voice repeats from outside, followed by another round of rapping. It's obviously a man's voice, which prompts Joey to secure the shotgun. He holds it at the ready, not aiming, as Aaron steps forward, grasps the knob, and turns it. The door opens out, and the visitor—a thick-bearded man covered in snow and ice—stands frozen in place until a gust of wind blows and he collapses into the cabin's interior. The snow sticking to him explodes from his body on impact, revealing he's wearing a full body snowmobile suit, but no gloves or hat. *"...help...it...it's...when...go..."* The man's words drift off.

"Hey man, you okay? What is *it*?" Aaron asks their visitor. "What's following you?" The man doesn't reply, instead he exhales a sigh and passes out from exposure and exhaustion.

"Holy shit. What the fuck could be following him?" Joey asks.

"Who knows!" Aaron's mind goes back to the thing he—*didn't see*—saw climbing the A-frame (*Was it a spider? How could it be a spider,* the logical side of his brain counters. *Could it have been an octopus? A snow octopus? Right!*) earlier. Another flurry of wind creates a squall of snowflakes within the cabin, reminding Aaron to close the door and lock it. The click of the latch securing choruses with the Stereo 8 player as it switches to another track in its endless loop of sound.

It's as jarring as a gunshot crack.

2: YESTERDAY

FRIDAY, DECEMBER 13, 2024 10:00 A.M.

UPSTATE NEW YORK, THE SHORES OF LAKE ONTARIO

LAKE-EFFECT EVENT SNOWFALL: 6" ACCUMULATION (AND

FALLING)

The winds blow across the Great Lakes, picking up the moisture along the way, and dropping its passenger onto the first land it hits. Sbli'rldlnisa-aea, the elder thing, floats on these winds as they propel her through the fingers of falling snow spreading across her hunting grounds. Though she is far from her lair, this is of no concern to the great goddess of ice and snow. What has she to fear from mortal beings?

As an omnipresent, immortal deity, the denizens of this place cower before her magnificent presence in awe and fear. They are her flock to cull, or protect, on a whim. A good shepherd nurtures their charge, does it not?

Today the great old one seeks sustenance in the maelstrom. Though her prey is scattered, hiding within domiciles offering shelter from the elements, she will find satisfaction. After all, she's the overlord of this land and she knows the places to hunt...

They're where the snow is deepest.

FRIDAY, DECEMBER 13, 2024 12:36 P.M.

WHETSTONE GULF STATE PARK, LOWVILLE, NY

LAKE-EFFECT EVENT SNOWFALL: 10" ACCUMULATION (AND

FALLING)

N early a foot of snow has fallen since the westerly winds kicked up, covering the land east of Lake Ontario in a white blanket. Though the winds roar, the humming engines of snowmobiles can be heard, the machines cutting through the terrain on treads and skis. Before the pair of sleds come into view, each of their single headlights cut through the blowing snow, heralding their arrival. Anyone in the area witnessing them might think the snowmobiles to be cyclopean things emerging from the wilderness, with one glowing eye each.

Jason "Jay" Nichols and Stuart "Stu" Hinds love snowmobiling, but they love money more. Going out in a lake-effect event typically isn't advised, but their side job requires a bit of risk. The men's wives give them grief over it, how they fear for the safety of their husbands being out in dangerous weather. But money talks and bullshit walks, the old adage goes, or in Jay and Stu's case: money takes a sled to the state park and the wives can shut the fuck up.

Each man wears a backpack filled to capacity with crystal methamphetamine, the value of which is undetermined. Suffice it to say the amphetamine made from broken down cold meds can easily transform into a metric-fuck-ton of money once distributed on the streets. And every time the snow falls in the off-season, Jay and Stu deliver their cook's goods to drop off points throughout the state park system.

This exchange is so regular, the pair is expected when they arrive at their first destination. They come to a stop in the parking lot of a local watering hole, The Hill-N-Dale Country Club. The attached golf course is closed, of course, covered in a blanket of snow. It's open for the pleasure of the local snowmobilers and ice fishermen.

It's a tradition for Stu and Jay to stop here for a little pick me up before venturing out on the last leg of their ride. They know the bartender, Katie, a plain but attractive girl who chain smokes and gives good conversation. What they don't expect to see is another woman sitting at the bar this early in the day.

And she is smoking hot. The men see her and can't stop staring, memories of their wives replaced by the lust of the moment. They'd never seen her before, an almond-eyed beauty with the hair of a raven. She's the epitome of beauty... from the ponytail to the fleece vest, tight sweater, stretch pants, and fur-lined faux-doeskin boots. All she's missing is a cup of pumpkin spice coffee to be a stereotype.

I bet her name is Karen, Stu thinks. The jukebox is playing classic rock. It's some glam rock song about getting laid. Could be Poison, or The Dark, or maybe Warrant, the guys can't tell. Finally, Stu recognizes it as being one of the radio hits from The Dark. What song it is, he can't recall its name, all those eighties hair metal songs sound the same, but the singer's voice is unmistakable. What was his name? *Brophy? Brodie?* It really doesn't matter. What does matter is a cold adult beverage and an order of wings.

And the hot chick.

Stu is drawn to her. Brushing the snow off their suits, the duo remove the unnecessary articles from their attire, the backpacks, gloves, and the beanies worn under their helmets. Both men unzip the tops of their all-weather overalls and pull their arms out the sleeves, exposing t-shirts worn underneath. Stuart's arms are covered in faded tattoos. More ink can be seen coming up to his neck.

Stu reaches the bar first as the song fades out, making sure to sit closest to the other occupant. Jay joins him. The bartender has already secured a pair of pint glasses. "You know how I knew I'd see you guys today?" Katie says as she fills a glass with Labatt Blue.

"I don't know, tell us." Stu replies.

Katie points to the bay window overlooking the golf course, "The snow is falling."

"Well, duh. It's what we do." Jay confirms. "Snow falls, we ride our sleds. Wouldn't you?"

"Yeah," she agrees, "I'll be right back, I have to drop your wings. The usual?"

"Sure," Stu says, "And use that ghost pepper honey you've got on them. I love that shit."

"The Frog's Point stuff? I think we have some left."

"Yer gonna shit fire balls," Jay quips. Stu punches his friend in the shoulder.

"A'ight. You two behave. I'll be right back." Katie steps around a corner, into the kitchen, and disappears.

"Behave? I mean what could we possibly do?" Stu laughs as he speaks. Along with Jay, he watches the weather on the television, the signal from the satellite is choppy, making the picture pixelated. The weather girl, a buxom and voluptuous blonde, is pointing to the fingers of lake snow drifting off Lake Ontario. She warns that feet of snow could be possible in some portions of the Tug Hill. Stu takes a healthy draught of his beer, jeering the meteorologist's prediction of a snowpocalypse and turns to the woman sitting next to them. "And who might you be? Other than gorgeous, that is."

"My name is Sandy. But you can call me Bella." She sips on her cup of steaming hot tea.

"Is that so? Okay then, Bella it is. I'm Stu, this is Jay." he motions to his compatriot, who nods in acknowledgment. Jay stares in silence as Stu continues to be their spokesperson. "So, what brings a doll like you out here on a day like this?"

"The same thing as you."

"Is that so?"

"It is. I love the snow, among other things."

"And what could those things be?" Stu says and spins his knees around to touch the woman's leg. He moves his hand near hers. At the touch of his fingertips, he feels a jolt like a static shock, and recoils his hand. She does the same.

"Things your wife wouldn't approve of, I would think?" Sandy says, her gaze glaring at the wedding band on Stuart's left hand.

"Rings don't fill no holes, ain't that right Stu." Jay quips and pats his buddy on the back.

"That's a fact," Stu concurs and tips his glass to his friend. "Who wants to make naked snow angels today?" They both giggle. Bella does not. She turns away, moving her leg out of Stu's reach, putting the back of her stool to him. "What? We're just joking." He protests.

"I'm not."

"No need to be a prude, squaw bitch." Stu says, his smile turning into a scowl. Bella ignores him and stirs her tea. Bella's brow furrows in displeasure at the words being used.

"Excuse me? That's uncalled for." Katie says as she returns to her station behind the bar. "What did I say about behaving?"

"What? Call a spade a spade, right?" Stu shrugs his shoulders and takes a long draught off his pint glass, emptying half of it.

"Jesus Christ, Stu! No one talks like that anymore." You're pissing off my only other customer right now. For fuck's sake, man." Katie shakes her head. Bella and her make eye contact. Katie mouths the

101

words *I'm sorry*. Bella nods. "Why don't you move down to the other end of the bar?" Katie tells Stuart and Jason.

"We weren't doing nothing wrong, just having some fun. Doc wouldn't make us move." Stu says, invoking the bar owner's name.

"Move or leave and don't come back? This is *my* bar, not your pal's, when I'm behind the counter. Don't you forget that, Mr. Hinds. Doc'll tell ya the same thing."

"Yadda yadda yadda. Whatever." Stu says as he and Jason move their seats. They sit in silence, finishing their beers and not asking for refills. Outside of the TV, the room is silent. No music, no talking. After a few minutes, Katie goes out back to retrieve the men's food.

"Don't make me regret leaving you alone here." She says, admonishing the men again for their lack of etiquette. Stu shakes his head and dismisses her by turning and taking another sip off his beer.

Once she's out of sight, Stu glares at Bella, then looks to Jay. "Fuck this place. Let's go."

"What about the food?"

"She can stick it up her ass for all I'm concerned. Telling us what to do like she thinks she owns this place." Jay chews his lip and nods in agreement. The men zip up their tops, and pull their backpacks back on. They note the woman at the bar is watching them out of the corner of her eye. For all Stu cares at this point she can watch them leave. Bella turns her head and Stu flips her a middle-finger as they exit the bar.

•

When Katie returns from the back with their wings, Stuart and Jason are gone. She can hear the engines of their snowmobiles fire up outside, and she watches them speed away.

"Those bastards!" She shouts, places the food on the bar, and sighs in exasperation. "I'm sorry they were such shitheads, Sandy." Katie turns, thinking she's talking to her one customer.

No one is there.

•

The sleds barrel through the frozen drifts. Skis and treads propel Stu and Jay forward until a squall rises, blotting out everything before them, creating a brief white-out and causing the men to stop their machines. They are on a ridge alongside Route 26, near their destination. Below them, the park lies hidden under the fresh snow. Idling his Arctic-Cat ZR-9000, Jay raises the face shield on his helmet, exposing his red beard. Sitting on his Polaris PRO RMK, Stu does the same and frees his own beard from the confines of his helmet. Within seconds snow sticks to it, turning the dark brown to white.

"Man, you already look like Santa." Jay quips.

"That must make you my elf." Stu replies.

103

"I thought that was the girl at the bar." Jay jabs at his friend.

"Yer number one, you know that?" Stu says, flipping Jay the finger through his gloves.

"You know it. It's down there." Jay points down the gully.

"I think we should spin around the entrance, no one will notice with all this falling right now. No trails means no evidence, bro."

"Are you sure?"

"You saw the weather." Stu reminds Jay, "They're saying we could get a couple feet by the end of this, our tracks will be covered up for sure! Anyone coming through won't think anything of it, trust me."

"Right. Plus we don't know if there is loose timber or baling wire down this slope. And I'd rather not hit either. I like my head where it is."

"Exactly," Stu admits. "Let's do this. I want to get back home before dark."

"Relax, we have plenty of time." Jay assures his partner, "Sun don't go down until 4:30 and we're only an hour from home. Your old lady isn't going nowhere."

"Yeah, yeah, yeah, I know. I'm just tired of this snow already. And yeah, winter is just starting, I know." Before his friend can acknowledge, something catches Stu's attention. "Hey, what's that?" He points to the park entrance.

Floating around the ranger station, a trio of lights slowly dance in the wind, crackling and flickering in the process. They're weird in color, shifting from pink, to blue and back.

"Ball lightning, maybe?" Jay suggests, before revving his Arctic Cat. "Let's find out, cos that's where we go in!"

Stu pulls his face plate down to end the conversation. Jay follows suit, and the pair hold down their clutches. The sleds roar to life and slowly descend the ridge onto the road below. In a matter of moments they pass the entrance to the State Park, the sleds spitting snow out behind them.

By the time the men arrive at the ranger station, the psychedelic lights have disappeared. They don't stop to look for the lights, instead they round a bend and head to the cabin sites.

Stu sees something ahead, in the snow. It's not the lights, it's something else. *Is that a deer?* He wonders to himself and slides the snowmobile to a stop, kicking up a wall of snow in front of him and Jay.

"What's wrong?" Jay asks. Stu can barely hear him through the helmet and over the engines. He points to where he saw the deer. Jay shrugs his shoulders and shakes his head. Stu raises his windscreen and squints his eyes. The wind dies down for a second, and with it some of the blowing snow subsides.

It's gone.

"What the fuck?" Stu says.

"What? Did you see the lights again?"

"No. I swear there was a deer there!" The men inch their snowmobiles forward, near the spot Stu thinks he saw the animal.

What they find puts fear into their veins.

It's not the lights, oh no. The body of a black bear lays before them, almost buried in the fresh snow fall. Its rib cage is ripped open with strands of ruddy flesh and muscles hanging off the bone spikes. The discovery of a dead bear in and of itself isn't all that bad a thing. What disturbs the drug mules is the white-tailed deer with its head buried in the offal of the bear's eviscerated belly. The ungulate's antler rack scrapes on the bear's exposed rib bones.

"What the fuck is this?" Stu shouts in shock, his eyes wide with fear. The deer hears the man's protest, and raises its head. Much of the skin and hair on its face and muzzle is missing, exposing the bone of the animal's skull. Strings of sinew hang from its mouth.

"Holy shit, Stu! Is that a wendigo?" Jay asks, his hand shaking as he pulls his visor up.

"I don't know what that is." Stu replies.

"It's one of them Indian cannibal monster things in burial grounds! The wendigo they call it! It makes humans eat each other and they say it looks like a fuckin' deer! Like this fucking thing! Shit, Stu! We're fucked!" The deer grunts in response, steam billowing from its disfigured snout.

"Monster? I'll show you how we deal with monsters." Stu reaches down next to his leg and slides out a .30-.06 Springfield from its sheath alongside his seat on the Polaris. He chambers a bullet, complete with its brass jacket the thing is as long as a man's forefinger, shoulders the weapon, takes aim—

"Stu," Jay interjects, "you can't kill a wendigo like this!"

"I can't?" Stu replies to his friend...

He pictures the woman from Hill-N-Dale and squeezes the trigger. Buh-bye biotch!

Thunder cracks and fire shoots out of the barrel as the back of the deer's head explodes. Bits of bone and brain splatter out while the body takes a moment to realize it's dead. When it finally does, the animal falls atop the bear, its blood turning the snow around it to shades of crimson and pink. Smoke wafts from the barrel while the men sit in silence, waiting for further movement.

There is none.

"Looks fuckin dead to me, Jay. Wendigos aren't real. Starving deer eat meat. Don't be such a fuckin' pussy next time." He re-sheaths the rifle. "Let's get to the cabin before you see any more monsters in the snow. I'm tempted to go shoot that bitch from the bar in the face, too, so don't give me any excuses." The sleds roar to life, the men drop their face shields and move the machines through the snow to the cabins.

Behind the men, the trio of pulsating lights rolls out of the tree line, through the wake of the snowmachines. Rising into the blowing snow, they swirl about, hovering over the ice-covered bodies of the dead bear and deer. Something drips from the lights, it's black with thick, viscous strands, pulsating as gravity draws it down. The ichor lands on the corpses' exposed organs and bones, bubbling and spitting. Each burst releases a thousand whispers, hidden in the wind's roar, as the substance spreads across the carcasses.

The lights race away into the wind and follow the men. After a moment, when their soft glow disappears into the blowing snow, something happens. If Stuart or Jason witnessed this, they surely would have gone mad. Stu's learning experience would be a crash course in how ineffective a rifle is against "whatever the fuck" he saw. And Jay? He'd likely be screaming "WENDIGO!"

You see, this is because the bodies of the bear, and deer... well, they stir and rise from the snowpack. The animated corpses each moves with a stiff, trembling gate down the trail left behind by the snowmobiles.

'foll...ow,' *the bear says, its vocal chords unsure of how to articulate human language.*

'yessssss...,' *the deer replies, with what's left of its brain pan suffering the same dilemma.*

'Sbli'rldlnisa-aea, Gudinnen av alle ting.' *They sing in the first language They learned, to Their 'goddess of all things...'* Sbli'rldlnisa-aea For himmelens droning.'

Jason and Stuart will have plenty of time to question reality and scream later, when the Others catch up to their Mistress and Her chosen prey.

3: TODAY

SATURDAY, DECEMBER 14, 2024 12:35 P.M.

THE TUG HILL, REDFIELD NY

LAKE-EFFECT EVENT SNOWFALL: 4' 6" OF ACCUMULATION

(AND FALLING)

The stranger's prone, unconscious body lays on the cabin floor until Aaron and Joey decide to do something about it. They wipe the remaining snow off him and pull his overalls off, which takes his t-shirt along with it, revealing his upper body. It's covered with tattoos of all types, but the majority of them are tribal-like runes, many are clearly Norse. Valknuts, troll crosses, raven and wolf heads, Vegvisir (the compass), the Helm of Awe, and the thunder god Thor's hammer, Mjolnir, are the most prevalent.

Aaron pats him down for any possible identification and discovers there is none. Whoever he is, the man is built like a brick shithouse. The brothers drag him to the old sofa—he weighs at least 250 pounds, making this a bit more laborious than they intended—roll him up onto it, and cover him with a couple of blankets before sitting back at the dinner table.

"Who do you think he is?" Joey asks his brother.

"Fuck if I know. Probably some stupid tourist out snowmobiling in the woods when he shouldn't be." Aaron answers.

"When he wakes up, we'll find out."

"For sure. I don't like waiting."

"Grow some patience, big brother. It's not like he's gonna do anything sleeping on the couch." Joey says. Aaron chews his lip and shrugs his shoulders in response. He goes to the old Frigidaire and grabs a cold Labatt Blue.

"You want one?"

"Sure," Joey replies. Aaron grabs two bottles, hands one to his brother and sits back down at the table. The music from the Stereo-8 begins to garble. Within moments the tape inside the cart snaps, and a high-pitched whine follows.

"Well, that sucks. I thought these things lasted forever." Aaron says. Joey pops out the bad cartridge and replaces it with a red one. One of Abba's many radio hits, 'Take A Chance on Me,' is in mid-song—

highlighting the vocal harmonies of Frida, Benny, Agnetha and Björn. It's an inescapable earworm.

"Aw fuck, Abba? Are you kidding me? I'm gonna have this song in my head all day." Joey says, unhappy with the music.

"There's fates worse than Abba. It coulda been that damn blue one." Aaron makes an expression of disgust on his face while pointing out the cartridge in question. The pastel coloring of the cartridge allows it to stick out in the storage tower of white and black plastic.

"You mean the Barry Manilow greatest hits one?" Joey laughs at his brother's reaction. "Come on, that was Grandmother Marion's favorite."

"I swear she thought she was Lola dancing at the Copacabana." Aaron stands up and pretends he's ballroom dancing with an invisible partner. This is when their guest finally stirs.

"Uhhhh..." the man sighs, his eyes fluttering as he attempts to open them. "Where, where am I?" He rolls off the couch and lands on the floor with a loud thud, predicated by the Stereo-8 changing tracks with its typical 'click.' Another Abba song, 'Waterloo,' comes to life while the Hatcher brothers rush to the aid of their guest, assisting him in sitting back up on the sofa.

"Who... who are you?" He asks them, rubbing his shoulder.

"We'd like to know the same about you. You came to our door, rambling about being chased by something." Aaron says.

"Yeah. I know this might sound crazy, but a wendigo is out there." The man says. Aaron and Joe burst into laughter in response. "No, I'm serious. It came after me and my buddy."

"Where is he?"

"It got him."

"So, let me get this straight," Aaron says, "a wendigo, a made-up fantasy thing, ate your friend?"

"Right in front of me, it ate Jay, bones and all."

"Jay? He's your friend? Okay, then how did you escape?" Joe asks.

"This, I think?" He touches the Thor's hammer charm hanging from the silver chain around his neck. The brothers stare at the necklace before sitting back down at the table. "It touched me with one of its tentacles, I felt some sort of static shock and it ran away. Or disappeared. Whatever, I didn't get a good look at it."

"What did you say your name was?" Aaron asks.

"I didn't. But it's Stuart. Stuart Hinds."

"Well, Stuart Hinds," Joey says, "I'm Joe Hatcher and he's Aaron, my brother. Why don't you tell us why you think a wendigo, something that doesn't exist, ate your friend?"

"Oh, they're Goddamn real, I tell you!"

"And let me guess, it had antlers and fangs."

"No, that was the deer we saw. This was something different. I can't describe it. It was all weird colors, and it had tentacles, and—"

"Tentacles?" Aaron questions the man, recalling what he saw only hours ago outside... *skittering on the A-frame's roof in the snow...*

"Yes, tentacles." Stuart confirms. The brothers look at one another with blank expressions on their faces.

"Where were you?" Joe asks.

"Whetstone Gulf."

"Dude, really?" Aaron is perplexed and his verbiage shows it, "That's thirty miles away, fifty if yer in a car. How did you get here from there in this weather? You should be a popsicle."

"No shit. I drove my sled all night through the snow. The Polaris ran out of gas near here, I think." Stu shifts on the couch, holds his belly, and grimaces. "Do you have a bathroom? I need to go."

"If you gotta number one, then step outside the door. If it's a number two, well, all we have is the outhouse, you'll have to suit up." Aaron informs him.

"That's fine, it's a number two."

"TMI, but when you come back, we've got some stew, you're gonna need it." Joe says.

"Thank you. Where's the outhouse?"

"Just outside. Ignore our kills." Joe tells him. "They aren't wendigos."

"Real funny, I know what I saw."

And we know wendigos don't exist, the same as Indian burial grounds and Medicine Men, it's all bullshit white-man stereotypes.

113

Aaron keeps his suspicions to himself. Their guest pulls his jacket back on and steps outside into the elements while Abba's Greatest Hits continues to play. This time it's 'Take a Chance on Me.'

•

*R*edskins? Really? Within the confines of the outhouse, sitting on the bowl, Stuart Hinds wonders where the fuck he's ended up. Hanging from the wall are various implements used for *Godknowswhat*. Sharpened antlers, pieces of rock and glass wrapped in twine. There's a deer skin stretched out on the wall. *What the hell is all that? Caveman art?* Stu wishes he still had bullets for his rifle, then he'd let the Indians know who the boss is here. But no, he left it at the park when he ran off, all the ammunition spent. He'd hoped he'd have enough fuel in the Polaris to reach civilization, and he likely would have had he not gone west instead of south, or even east. No, Stu ended up traversing the expanse of wilderness covering the Tug Hill and ran out of gas.

Did I really kill a wendigo? He wonders, then disregards the thought, something that's hard to do with the peculiar decor of the outhouse staring back at him. *It was a deer, nothing but a deer,* he reminds himself. *But if it was just a fucking deer, then how was that bear walking around?* Stu doesn't have an answer for this, and ultimately, it's why he fled the cabin in Whetstone Gulf.

114

Well, that, and the explosion and whatever the fuck melted Jay. How the hell is he going to explain this to Jay's wife? Or the Reapers?

Stu wipes his ass and doesn't bother to sprinkle any wood shavings on it. Why should he? It's not like putting that down will solve anything. Then an idea strikes him, and he takes one of the antler knives hanging on the wall. It's an insurance policy in case the redskins needed to be dealt with. He thumbs the blade, it's sharp and he's sure it will gut the Indians as well as it eviscerates a deer. A moment later Stuart zips up his snowsuit, opens the door, and steps back out into the elements. Snow, blowing about from the winds, obscures his vision. He takes hold of the guideline in the channel—

And is greeted by a blinding flash of light as something strikes him in the back of the head, sending his thoughts to the void.

4: YESTERDAY

FRIDAY, DECEMBER 13, 2024 2:36 P.M.

WHETSTONE GULF STATE PARK, LOWVILLE, NY

LAKE-EFFECT EVENT SNOWFALL: 13" ACCUMULATION (AND FALLING)

Ethereal in the squall, the headlights of the snowmobiles driven by Stu Hinds and Jay Nichols fight to pierce through the elements. The men and their snowmachines move unabated through the drifts and falling snow, coming to a stop in front of their chosen cabin in Whetstone Gulf State Park. The snow has picked up, creating a whiteout. The men lift their visors to see and hear each other better.

"There it is!" Stu shouts, pointing to the cabin. Snow is encroaching its frame and covering the small building's pitched roof. "I think we're gonna need to stay here for a bit until this shit settles down some!" Jay nods in affirmation. They park their snowmobiles, cover them with tarps, and enter the cabin. Stu makes sure to bring his rifle inside. *Just in case, you never know.* He reminds himself.

The interior is Spartan, with a small sink as its only utility. There's a bunk bed complete with thin, teal-colored mattresses but no sheets or blankets. A small sitting table, and a pair of chairs, as well as a kerosene heater sit next to the sink. Stu wastes no time in igniting the heater. It warms the cabin interior quickly. Jason pulls a floorboard up, exposing the smuggling spot they'll be hiding the meth in. He drops his backpack inside, then takes Stu's, before replacing the wood and stomping on it a few times to make sure the nails are tight.

"That's it. How long do we want to wait?" Jay asks Stu.

"A couple hours at least. They said the bands will drop down onto Syracuse this afternoon." Stu answers

"It'll be dark then." Jay reminds his friend.

"What are you? Afraid of the dark? We have headlights and more than enough gas in our tanks to get back home. Ya know what? It might be nappy time." He withdraws a small flask of Jameson from his pocket and takes a draught before handing it to his buddy.

"Might be." Jay says and takes a hit off the bottle, "I've got the top bunk!" he hops onto it before Stu can protest and wads his jacket up to use as a pillow. "I'm in the penthouse, bitches and hos!"

Stu does the same, without the excessive display of vulgarity, and climbs onto the bottom bunk. Within minutes the pair is snoring away...

The Others, animating the bodies of a bear and a deer, follow the trail left behind by the snowmobiles. They move slowly, and the snow's depth further impedes them. But the eons serving their cold mistress have taught them patience, and they know they don't have to run.

Far ahead of Them, Sbli'rldlnisa-aea floats above the drifts surrounding a cabin. Outside of the small, snow-covered shelter, a pair of snowmobiles are parked. The elder goddess tracked her prey this far, and knows it hides within the walls of the cabin. Now she watches with the great, pulsating eye at the center of her grand bell, gazing into the minds of these wayward men who so brazenly declared 'rings don't fill no holes.'

Of course they don't, the great *goddess of ice and snow* acknowledges. *A ring is a symbol of faith, a goal to achieve, is it not? She sees they are not kind men; they have harmed those they claim to love. She understands they are men who would shield themselves from harm with the bodies of their wives and children.* They will not be missed by those who would mourn them, *she assures herself. No... they would be better served as sustenance for the one who protects her flock. Afterall, will the sacrifice of these evil men not allow the protector of this land to flourish?*

When The Others finally arrive, Sbli'rldlnisa-aea rises over the roof of the cabin, engulfing it in her majesty. Her tentacles spread out while tendrils extending from the hydrostatic skeleton of her trunk slip through cracks in the building's frame. They slither and seek the bodies of its occupants...

And find one.

•

Deeply sleeping, Jason Nichols' dreams are not what he expects. Instead, they're laden with horrors no sane person could see without going mad. His eyes are closed but they are active under the lids, darting left and right, up and down. They are watching something deep within his subconscious. Jay sees skeletal creatures moving through snow and darkness, grinning with white teeth and exposed mandible bones. The creatures are singing in a language he doesn't understand.

'Sbli'rldlnisa-aea, Gudinnen av alle ting.'

'Sbli'rldlnisa-aea, For himmelens droning.'

The deepest parts of Jason's brain know his fear. It's innate, all consuming. Laying on his bunk, one can see Jay's body sweats and shivers, a reaction not only to the cold, but to the nightmares he is now enduring within the dreamscape of his psyche. He listens to the words of the song and finds he can understand them.

The Goddess of all things...

Yes, my Goddess. Jason now recalls the woman from the bar. She wanted him, not Stuart. Who was he to come between them? He knows where she is. She's in the cabin with them. *But she has come here for me, not him!* Jay reminds himself. Lust for his new desire fills his body. His cock engorges, seeking to enter his new love and bring them together as they were meant to be. As one.

Then she comes into view... floating above him, raven hair fluttering in the air. No longer clothed, She's even more beautiful nude, a perfect body, with no imperfections. She's an angel... *HIS* angel. And he knows She will lay with him, not that Goddamn Stu. He opens his arms to embrace his new Goddess.

She falls into him and accepts his offer.

•

Something drips onto Stuart Hinds' forehead, waking him up from his nap. *Did Jason piss himself?* He wonders as he wipes his face off. Expecting to find water, Stu instead discovers a viscous slime. *What the fuck?* He opens his eyes and is greeted by a soft, neon glow filling the interior of the cabin. It's coming from the top bunk, over his head.

Stu jumps up to find something more fucked up than he could ever imagine. He expects to find Jay watching a video on a tablet or his phone. Instead, he's not sure where Jay actually is. A cocoon of coiled tendrils, coming from all directions, is where Jason should be, resting in a puddle of black goop. Neon colored, the tendrils pulse and change from blue to pink to purple and back again.

"Jay?" Stu manages. "Are you in there?" He asks, not sure of anything better to say. He reaches over, grabs his rifle and pokes the cocoon with the barrel. It's solid and resists the barrel's pressure by coiling tighter and glowing brighter. "This is all fucked up. What in the hell is going on here?" Stu turns and opens the cabin door. The expected snow is there, and so is the unexpected. "You've got to be fucking kidding me." Stu declares when he sees a familiar bear and deer standing outside the cabin door. He slams the door shut.

The tendrils seem to be minding their own business, allowing Stu time to make a decision. It doesn't take him long to realize the best course of action is to get the fuck out of here. The drug mule suits up, readying to go back out into the elements. He's almost finished when something touches him on the chest, almost poking him. *What the hell?* Stu looks down to see a tendril trying to slither onto him. He brushes at it with a tattoo covered hand—*And a spark of electricity erupts in the cabin!*

A mind ripping screech follows as the cabin's kerosene heater explodes in response to the superheated discharge. Stuart Hinds is blown out of the door and lands headfirst in a snowbank, his rifle still clutched in his hands. He wriggles about to orientate himself upright and sees flaming timber falling about him, lighting up the night.

Stu looks for the snowmobiles and sees his is unmolested. The bear and deer are nowhere to be seen, likely blown away from the cabin by the explosion. What's weird is the sky. It's pulsating with colors, as if an aurora borealis were in full effect, but only over this spot.

"What is going on here?" Stu says, shaking his head in disbelief. He doesn't wait a moment longer to make his move and runs through the snow toward the Polaris.

A snowbank comes to life, and he hears the bear roar. Both it and the deer rise from the snow in front of Stu. He stops, shoulders the .30-.06, aims, and fires at the things' heads until they both fall back down. There's no fanfare, only the flash of a muzzle and retort of a rifle echoing through the trees. The shattering of bone follows. Pieces of antler, teeth, skull, and bits of desiccated brain matter are scattered about. It takes all eight shells to bring them down, but it works.

Unsure if they'll rise back up, Stuart runs straight to his sled. He throws the rifle down, ambivalent to his attire. He's not wearing a hat or gloves—being anywhere *not* here is a far better option for survival he surmises in the moment—and speeds off into the wilderness on the Polaris.

He'll regret this later.

5: NOW & THEN

FRIDAY, DECEMBER 13, 2024 4:27 P.M.

WHETSTONE GULF STATE PARK, LOWVILLE, NY

LAKE-EFFECT EVENT SNOWFALL: 16" ACCUMULATION (AND

FALLING)

NOW...

Sbli'rldlnisa-aea roars in pain as she caresses the prey... and her embrace is forcefully rejected. A searing pain, not felt in millennia, courses through her being. She's not known such agony since being captured and brought to this place an eon ago. The Others feel it, too, and are stunned by the anomaly. The impact the prey's weapon has on their host bodies forces them to retreat to their mistress. Ancient wards of protection cover the prey's skin, crafted by the priests of the All-Father and her nemesis, the thunder god Þórr.

To see the thunder god is to see death. The Great Goddess of Ice and Snow's memory is as infinite as time itself. She remembers. How can she forget the day when Auður, Þórr's witch, used these same wards against her? The scars still mark her tentacles from that night...

ICELAND, 806 A.D.

THEN...

A blizzard rages in the night while thunder roars and lightning sprouts from black clouds hovering above the volcanoes of Iceland. Beneath this spectacle, the cultists of Angrboða are gathered, carrying torches, covered in white robes. They surround the priestesses of their Great Goddess of Ice and Snow. Ahead of them, the mouth of a massive cavern comes into sight. Smoke and mist rise from its bowels, mixing with the falling snow.

"Sbli'rldlnisa-aea, Gudinnen av alle ting." The worshippers sing, evoking the true name of their patron deity, Angrboða, in the chant. *"Sbli'rldlnisa-aea For himmelens droning..."*

One amongst them is carried on a litter. A bound man, he is naked except for the ropes securing him to the platform. His outstretched arms are tied to two poles, and a hood covers his head. He is the

123

honored sacrifice to their great goddess. And all sacrifices must come with pain, otherwise they would not be a sacrifice.

The wailing woman following the procession knows this all too well. She curses the cultists as she weeps. "He is my husband, only I should be his judge, not any of you!" *She is ignored.* "Alföðr hear me!" The woman shouts, desperate to rescue her lover from the fate the cultists have in store for him.

The cultists nearest to her stop chanting. They turn and face the woman, then bend over and pick up bits of volcanic rock.

And throw them at her.

She covers her face as the rocks strike, but the edges cut and scratch the exposed skin on her hands and arms. She falls to her knees, begging for this nightmare to end. "Save my husband from these monsters! Óðinn!" The woman cries out. A crack of thunder from a distance is the only reply. One of the cultists pulls back the cowl of her robe, revealing a teary-eyed matron.

"Why are you interfering with the ritual Auður? Your husband," the matron says, shaking a fist, "lied to my daughter! He laid with her; told her he would care for her. And now she is with child, and he pretends to not know her? How can you be so devoted to a person such as him?"

"These are lies, all lies! He's done no such thing." Auður protests the accusations made against her husband.

"Oh, you sweet, innocent, daft girl. Everyone knows Ólafur philanders, and yet you cannot see this for what it is? Be happy he was chosen by Angrboða. Can't you see his sacrifice will lead to our prosperity under The Móðir? At least now he serves some purpose for good." More thunder rumbles from the mountains overlooking the Goddess's lair.

"Good? How can you say this is for good? May Þórr strike you down with his hammer!"

"Þórr isn't here, you forget we stand in the glory of Her Greatness, Angrboða the Móðir, beloved consort to Lokke with whom she birthed Hel, Fenrisúlfr, and Jǫrmungandr." She throws one last rock at Auður, then spits at her for added satisfaction in the moment. Without another word, she pulls her cowl back and joins the other cultists.

"You'll learn! You'll all learn!" Auður shouts at her husband's accusers. "Óðinn and Þórr will hear my cries and bring justice to this place!" The procession reaches the mouth of the cave and light torches in sconces, illuminating the area. The wind, blowing the snow, does its best to extinguish the torches, but fails. The load bearers carrying the litter set it down near the mouth of the cave, while the other cultists circle around, still chanting and singing their song. *"Sbli'rldlnisa-aea, Gudinnen av alle ting. Sbli'rldlnisa-aea For himmelens droning."*

More thunder rolls while furious lightning dances in the black clouds pouring from the volcanoes. A bank of fog rises from the cave entrance. Pastel lights in pink and blue grow in the mist and the chanting of the cultists grows in volume. The fog bank rolls out of the cave, separating when it reaches the sacrificial litter.

The avatar of Angrboða, a comely, nude woman with long dark hair steps out of the cave's entrance. She is oblivious to snow and wind, walking through the accumulation with ease. The cultists bow their heads, their chanting now a communal whisper.

"Móðir...Móðir...Móðir...Móðir..."

The naked woman raises her arms above her head, then spreads them out from her sides, and holds them abreast as she approaches the sacrifice.

Auður runs through the throng of cultists, screaming as she does. Coming to a stop between her husband and the avatar, she reaches into her bosom and withdraws a sigil, an amulet carved in runes and holds it before her. The being comes to within an arm's length of the wife and stops. She tips Her head, with curiosity covering the otherwise blank expression on her face.

She extends her hand forward to touch the charm, and shirks back when a spark jumps out from the amulet. The wife repeats its words, spewing them with as much venom and disdain as she can muster.

"May Þórr's lightning hold all evil away from Ólafur." The wife declares. "May Þórr protect him with Mjǫllnir. Flee from evilness! You get nothing from Ólafur. The gods of Ásgarðr shield him from your evil!" The being steps back, allowing the cultists to stand and encircle the man's wife. Their threat to Auður is short-lived when the gods finally answer her cries.

A bolt of lightning strikes the ground between Auður and the Goddess's avatar. The burst sends earthen debris flying about, scattering the cultists, blowing them away from the epicenter. Auður falls to the ground, and rolls from the blast wave, coming to a stop at the feet of the litter holding her husband. The Móðir stands still, unshaken by the event.

For the moment.

Thunder crashes and lightning falls from the sky, striking the ground surrounding the ritual. The Móðir's avatar turns to flee into its lair, discovering her sanctuary has been compromised. The cave mouth is gone, collapsed under the barrage of lightning.

"The gods protect us!" Auður taunts the Great Goddess, still holding the amulet protecting her from the Old One's glamours. She runs forward, emboldened by the protection given to her by the charm's runes. The avatar shirks away from the woman, stepping back until there's nowhere else to go, its back against the wall of rubble. Auður touches the avatar with the amulet, without anticipating the outcome of her action.

The agony of a thousand strikes of lightning sears Sbli'rldlnisa-aea...

•

FRIDAY, DECEMBER 13, 2024 5:16 P.M.

WHETSTONE GULF STATE PARK, LOWVILLE, NY

LAKE-EFFECT EVENT SNOWFALL: 18" ACCUMULATION (AND

FALLING)

The Others flee their animal hosts and return to Sbli'rldlnisa-aea's embrace, absorbing back into her majesty. Whole again, the Great Goddess of Ice and Snow's rage surfaces, and her intent is clear. She will devour this mortal and send it to her version of Hell by any means necessary. She won't be alone in finding him. Her flock lives in these hills, and they love her and will aid her. After all, is she not their mother, the Goddess of all things?

6: TODAY & TOMORROW

SATURDAY, DECEMBER 14, 2024 12:35 P.M.

THE TUG HILL, REDFIELD NY

LAKE-EFFECT EVENT SNOWFALL: 4' 8" OF ACCUMULATION

(AND FALLING)

TODAY...

While Stuart shits and plans, back within the A-frame the Hatcher brothers listen to Abba lament about Fernando and the Mexican Revolution. All is fine until the Stereo-8's sound warbles. It's not like before, when the K-Tel's tape broke. This is...different. Aaron notices right away. The words, the music, it was shifting, changing. The voice, no longer Frida's, now brought a sense of Deja Vu to Aaron.

I know this voice, he thinks. "Joey, you hear that?"

"I do," his brother admits. "How can that be?"

"Fucked if I know." Aaron replies. The lyrics are the same, but the voice has changed, the music, too. Instead of the strings, keyboards, and synth drums of the Abba hit... a bass drum kicks in time with a roaring bass line as electric guitars wail the melody, and a woman's familiar voice screams the vocals, complete with a familiar vibrato. *Is that Aunt Bobbie?* Aaron finds it hard to accept, but the sound is unmistakable. It's clearly their missing Aunt's voice.

Thirty years before, Roberta Webster, known on the local music scene as 'Bobbie Be Good,' disappeared during the Blizzard of '93. All the search for her turned up was a boot in a pile of snow in the nearby city of Fenton. Aaron runs to the stereo and digs through the compact discs sitting next to an ancient Discman, searching for one in particular. "Here it is!" Aaron declares when he discovers the object of his quest. He thrusts it into the air.

"What's that?" Joey asks.

"Aunt Bobbie's demo CD, remember how proud she was when she made this?"

"Dude. I was three years old and all I cared about was Barney. So, no."

"Well, I do. And the song playing right now?"

130

"Yeah? What about it?"

"It's off this CD!" Aaron points to the speakers with the case held in his fist.

"How could that be?" Joey questions.

"How the fuck do I know? This has been one messed up hunting trip. First the storm, then I see some weird lights and hear voices outside when I'm in the shit—"

"Voices?" Joey interrupts his brother. "You didn't tell me about any of that."

"Well, I sorta did when I asked if you were pranking me earlier." Aaron shrugs his shoulders. "Sorry I was so vague, my bad. But now this biker dude shows up at our cabin ranting about wendigos? And the music? This is all too weird."

"You've been doing too many edibles, again. The CD player probably turned on."

"How so?" Aaron holds up the RCA cable from the Discman. It's not connected to the stereo. "This is all too weird, bro. I'm just—" Aaron's reply is cut off by the television turning on of its own volition. The color tube is shot, and the screen shows a black and white image. It's a woman, singing, and her lips are in sync with the music.

"Is that Aunt Bobbie?" Joey asks.

"Holy fuck." Is all Aaron can say as he nods.

The song ends and the woman on the TV screen stops singing. The next song starts, and the lyrics and music are as far from Abba as possible. The words are foreign to them. *"Sbli'rldlnisa-aea, Gudinnen av alle ting... Sbli'rldlnisa-aea For himmelens droning..."*

Until they aren't...

"The goddess of all things... Honyarekowa..."

The TV flickers, static and digital snow covers the screen as the woman they know as their lost aunt moves closer, until her head pushes through the glass. Dumbfounded, Joey and Aaron watch in disbelief as Aunt Bobbie steps out of the television, naked as a newborn. The Hatchers, Keepers of the Old Faith of the Haudenosaunee, finally understand why their long last Aunt has returned, and where she has been all these years.

Aaron grabs a poker for the woodstove as he and Joey open the door and step outside...

SUNDAY, DECEMBER 15, 2024 7:00 A.M.

THE TUG HILL, REDFIELD NY

LAKE-EFFECT EVENT SNOWFALL: APPROX. 6'+ OF

ACCUMULATION

TOMORROW...

Stuart Hinds wakes up, disoriented and unsure of how long he's been unconscious. He opens his eyes to see the snow has stopped falling and can see bits of sunlight peeking through the branches of the trees surrounding the cabin. His head throbs and his nose is filled with snot, and though his face is freezing, the rest of his body is numb. Stu soon understands why he's so cold and disoriented.

He's naked and hanging upside down by a length of rope, his ankles tied together and his tattooed arms dangling. He finds he can't move them, and fear sets in when he sees he's strung up next to the deer carcasses. Icicles hang off his toes. He tries to speak, to scream for help, but finds he is gagged.

The skeletal face of a skinned deer stares back at Stu, startling him more. But when it speaks, he loses his shit.

"Sbli'rldlnisa-aea, Gudinnen av alle ting." The deer says, its mouth moving and the teeth and bones clacking as it does. The wind spins Stu around, facing another of the deer carcasses, this one not yet skinned.

"Sbli'rldlnisa-aea For himmelens droning." This one says with less clicking of bone. Stu's fear causes him to lose his bladder. He pisses, and it runs down his torso, soaking into the ice caked on his beard, and finally dripping off his face into the snow below.

He hears the cabin door open, and the Indians step out onto the stoop, each dressed for the weather and holding the curved, antler knives in their gloved hands. He can only imagine what their plans are for him, and he's certain it's nefarious. For as terrifying as this is, what really freaks Stu out is the appearance of the woman from the Hill-N-

133

Dale, no longer wearing her pumpkin spice stereotype chic. Instead she's naked, and smiling, seemingly unaware it's below freezing outside. She steps onto the stoop between the brothers and stops.

"This is the knife we found on you. We're assuming you planned to kill us in our sleep, no?" The brother calling himself Aaron says. Stu struggles to speak to deny the accusation but finds he can't. Whatever they've done has robbed him not only of his ability to move, but to speak. "Don't try to answer me. You won't be able to. We know everything we need to know about you, now."

"Yeah," the other brother affirms, "and it seems you're a very bad boy."

Fuck you, redskin! Unable to speak, the words come to Stu's brain and remain there as spit and mucus make garbling noises. The nude woman stays on the stoop, pointing at Stuart as the brothers advance toward him. They make sure he can see the knives.

Crunching through the snowpack with each footstep, Joey reaches Stu first and holds him still for Aaron and the delicate job he has ahead of him...

Lucky for Stu he can't feel them work. But he knows what their intent is... They're going to flay him.

Aaron starts at Stu's feet, slicing into the epidermis around his ankles. The cut circumvents the leg. He does so with both, before tracing down the back of each leg, slicing both open. It's not long before a warm, coppery liquid mixes with the urine in his beard.

Blood. Stu's blood.

Aaron peels the skin back from the left leg first, then the right, and pulls them both down to Stu's groin.

"I guess you won't be needing these anymore," Joey says, and slices off Stu's cock and balls with one cut of his antler knife. He drops the sexual organs at his feet. Stu hears them land with a wet plop in the snow. This is when Stu discovers he can still cry, as tears well and drip from his eyes and roll down his forehead.

Joey holds him still as Aaron saws into the flesh on Stu's back, neck, and arms. It doesn't take him long to remove the skin from his torso, arms, and neck. Aaron tosses what is now nothing more than a tattoo covered shirt of skin to the side, away from them. A pool of blood has turned the white snow under Stu from pink to crimson to a deep red. Satisfied with his handiwork, Aaron steps aside. His brother joins him.

"*Dedwadoñt, Honyarekowa,*" Aaron Hatcher says in the tongue of his Grandmothers and Grandfathers, as he and his brother motion to the flayed man, their offering hanging from a rope.

"Eat with us, great serpent goddess." Joey Hatcher repeats his brother's words in the language of the Yankee Colonizers.

Sbli'rldlnisa-aea, wearing the skin of Roberts Webster, needs no further invitation. The goddess's avatar opens her mouth. It stretches wider than humanly possible. A preternatural roar is followed by an infinite number of tendrils erupting from the gaping maw. They embrace the man's skinless body as only a lover can. The helpless man, his body dissolving as the tendrils consume his flesh and bone, wants to scream but he can't. His mind cries out as the goddess of all things absorbs his flesh, bone, and mind. Stuart Hinds won't be alone within her, the Others will be there with him...

   ...Forever.

EARL OF IMPRUDENCE

Ryan C. Thomas

"What's it doing?"

Becket Anders, Lead Operations Supervisor, leaned over the back of Eli Dwyer's office chair, staring at the three massive computer monitors on the man's desk.

"It's stuck," Eli responded.

On the left screen was a real-time video feed of a foreign surface comprised of regolith, monolithic boulders, and distant rocky cliffs. The landscape, which stretched off into a black starry sky, was in the process of turning opaque as a low gas cloud of swirling, oily, iridescent purples and greens rolled in, obscuring the view.

"As soon as it entered this weird ground...cloud," Eli continued.

"It just froze."

"What's its composition? Hydrogen? Argon? Almost looks like...swamp fog."

"Still analyzing it."

"And EARL? Is he receiving?" Anders asked.

"Is he getting anything from us?"

"According to my data, our guy is still reading us, he's just not responding to commands."

"Tell him to keep going. Tell him again."

"I already did."

"And?"

"EARL receives the command but doesn't carry it out. Like he's being stubborn."

On Eli's center screen was a schematic of the company's latest robotic terrestrial crawler, part of their Explore, Analyze, Review and Enlighten division. Essentially an aluminum, ceramic and titanium rectangle on suspension treads that could maneuver over just about any type of ground, including ice, rock, flora, and mud. It also housed extractable maneuverable drone propellers, dual in-board engines in case it should fall into liquid and could withstand heat of up to 1,000 degrees. From the outside, it looked like a massive roving iron ingot. On the inside, it housed a dozen retractable arms and claws built to collect physical samples, as well as an array of atmospheric analysis mechanisms and cameras that constantly recorded its surroundings.

The Company had dubbed it EARL, even though the acronym was inexact, owing to the last letter having to be culled from the middle of the word *enlighten*.

Currently, EARL was frozen in the encroaching colorful mist it had driven into on the protoplanet X-089, which moved slowly in the frozen blackness of space some 4.2 AU away from the company's headquarters in San Diego.

"Manny."

Anders yelled.

"What's the satellite say?"

At the next desk over, Manny Uriquez put down his coffee and stared at his own collection of large monitors. He ran his finger down lines of data on the screens.

"Everything is the same as it was five minutes ago. No storms, no radiation spikes, no foreign waves. Maybe EARL is just stuck on a rock? Something wedged in its treads?"

Anders shook his head.

"No. It can climb fucking mountains, a rock wouldn't stop it. Plus, it can yank the rocks out with its claws if it has to. It's gotta be this gas cloud. Eli, can you ping him again, just to be safe?"

"Already did. Give it a few seconds to come back."

The command room in the company headquarters went silent. Some fifty employees stared at their screens. Several of the monitor views were also visible on a massive video display board (which everyone called the Jumbotron) that hung over the entire room, waiting to see if EARL was going to be ok. It had taken a lifetime to get this project off the ground, then another lifetime to get the robot out to the protoplanet. People had been hired and retired before they ever saw EARL pick up its first rock. It had only been on the planetoid for a month now, had only moved about five miles from the landing craft, which was designed to return EARL to Earth after five years of exploration. If it couldn't be hailed, if it couldn't return with geological samples that justified future mining operations, the company would be out trillions of dollars, and thousands of people's lives were going to go to shit real fast as their futures crashed and burned.

"There it is!" Eli said.

"He pinged us back."

There was a collective sigh in the command room as employees resumed their work.

"Has EARL said why he won't move? Is something stopping him?" Anders asked.

Eli scratched his chin.

"Negative. Maybe he's just enjoying the colors, trying to figure out how to analyze them. EARL has a mind of his own sometimes, but he knows what he's doing."

It was common for everyone to refer to EARL with the masculine pronoun" he" instead of the more informal "it," but it was in times like this, Eli remembered, that the robot didn't actually make human decisions. At best, its AI brain was running through a checklist of actions, deciding which would yield the best results. The larger issue was, what was it considering?

"Yes, but *what* is he doing?"

"Not sure. Let's just give him a chance to figure it out."

"OK. Fuckin hell, why not," Anders said.

"Let him chill for a bit. In the meantime, see if he'll send out the Earlettes. Maybe we can still collect some data from this new valley while we wait."

The valley Anders referred to looked like a lake of black ice surrounded on all sides by even blacker mountains. Eli had once traveled to Norway to visit family. X-089 reminded him of Troms in winter, if everything was shown in negative.

Eli nodded and sent the command to EARL. A few minutes later, the third monitor on his desk showed Earl's response:

"Acknowledge deployment of mini agents one through four."

"At least he didn't fight us on that."

Manny said, back to sipping his coffee.

Eli and Anders watched the video feed from EARL's cameras as four small ports slid open on each side of its body. Small robotic spiders, each about the size of a chihuahua, scurried out and stood at the ready in the colorful gas fog.

"Earlettes are out," Eli said.

Anders rubbed the back of his own neck, trying to relieve stress. "Okay good. Send 'em away and let's see what they find. Maybe they can figure out why EARL is being a stubborn SOB."

Eli typed the command into his keyboard and waited. The signal had a natural delay of a few minutes so he steepled his fingers in front of him and waited until the robots started moving on the screen. By design, they moved very slowly, careful not to overlook anything of importance or get themselves stuck somehow.

Anders turned from the station and weaved his way back through the room of computers, desks, servers, and over-caffeinated employees, and headed to the break room where he poured himself his third cup of coffee for the day. When he returned, the Earlettes were moving off into different directions like the corners of a square exploding in slow motion.

Each spider bot was equipped with almost the same collection tools as Earl, as well as high-definition cameras and atmospheric sensors. They moved independently of one another yet could work as a single unit if necessary. If one encountered trouble, the others would move in to help. Or, as Eli liked to put it, they were a hive mind with an individuality problem.

As they crawled over the frigid, obsidian rock that clustered the ground, Eli realized this must be how cats saw the world—low, cautious, dirt and rock scraping their chins. Their call signs were E1, E2, E3 and E4, and the only way to differentiate them, other than the labels on their video monitor feeds, was by the colored stripes running across their backs. Of course, one could only see the colors if they were in proximity to each other, which, currently, they were not.

"E-1 is entering what appears to be a large crack in the ground."

"Great," Anders said.

"He better not get stuck down there."

Eli was about to remind his superior that the Earlettes all had drone propellers to fly out of tight spaces, but he let it go. He knew his boss was just venting for the sake of venting, because that was his MO.

"E-2 seems to have found a low cave-like structure. Entering now."

"What's E-3 doing?"

"Not sure. I think she's climbing up a big boulder. All I can see is fog, but the angle of her trajectory is at an ascent."

"See if she can look down on EARL, maybe give us a better idea of why he's stopped."

Eli typed the command to E-3, who, like E-4, had been given a feminine gender.

"I'm getting an atmospheric reading from her," Manny chimed in.

"Temperatures in the fog are rising. Up five degrees from her last location on the ground."

"Interesting," Anders said.

"Maybe the mist acts like insulation for the sun's rays."

"We'll know as soon as she sends us her report," Eli added.

While E2 crawled deeper into the crack of the planetoid's surface, and E-3 scurried farther into the blackness of the small cave, and E-3 continued to climb up the boulder, E-4 was moving out onto a flat plain of black rock that appeared as smooth as an ice rink. The little robot struggled to find footing on the glass-like ground, finally deploying small crampons from the ends of its legs. With the crampons out, it picked up speed, heading out into the middle of the black tarn.

"Wonder what she sees?"

Anders sipped his coffee, leaning once again over Eli's shoulder. Thankfully his tie didn't drape over Eli's head this time.

"Temps still rising in that gas cloud," Manny said.

"Another five degrees."

"Jesus," Eli whispered.

"How does it maintain that kind of heat out there? Solar radiation wouldn't raise it that quickly, would it?"

"I don't know. Can someone get me some calculations on how solar light might affect this mist? Where's Gillroy?"

"He's in the bathroom, sir."

Said Serena Nowak, the red-haired woman on the other side of Manny.

"I'm logging it for him just in case. I'll tell him to get on it when he's back."

"How long has he been in the bathroom?"

Anders was antsy, he expected his team to answer his questions as soon as he asked them.

"Since EARL stopped."

"Really. Who craps for that long?"

"He said his stomach was hurting him. Seemed like, well, you know."

"Diarrhea?"

Serena looked away, uncomfortable with the conversation.

Eli, who'd taken his eyes off his monitors to listen to Serena, noticed three other command center employees now rising from their desks, their hands over their stomachs. They each headed toward the bathrooms, one of them bumping into the back wall's trophy case. A case that housed a collection of items cataloging company milestones—two space suits worn for the first trip to Io, a robotic wheel that touched the surface of Janus, a claw that had brought back rock samples from Vesta, and dozens of pictures of foreign surfaces taken by now-retired rovers.

Maybe someone made the coffee too strong, he thought. It had happened before. A few months ago, someone had overloaded dark roast in the machine with barely any water and Eli had had to go home early and lay in bed shaking from caffeine toxicity. He still hadn't found out what idiot had been responsible for that.

On his monitor, E-1 was sending a signal from the depths of the crevice: OBJECT FOUND. SIZE UNOBTAINABLE. REQUEST COMMAND.

The entire command room went silent, everyone looking up at the Jumbotron to get a look at Eli's screens.

"I don't see anything," Anders said.

Eli told E-1 to increase illumination from its flood lights. A few minutes later the black, jagged rock that filled the Earlette's view lit into plum-colored crystal. Something ovoid was buried far in the

145

depths of that purple rock. Unfortunately, it was too hard to make out anything except the blurriest of details.

"The fuck is that?"

Anders said.

He was excited, downing the rest of his coffee in one gulp.

"Zoom in and grab a still of it."

Eli waited for E-1 to get a zoomed-in picture of the blurry object. When he had it, he put it on his center monitor, simultaneously showing it on the jumbotron.

People began to chatter and point. Whatever it was, it was not rock. It had markings on it.

"Alien," someone in the room muttered. In response to this, someone whooped and clapped.

"Quiet!"

Anders yelled. "We have no idea what it is. It could just be a rock. A trick of the light. I want imagining and spectral imaging on this stat."

"On it!" someone yelled.

"E-2 is hailing," Eli said.

"It's got something."

"Well bring it up," Anders ordered.

Eli's center monitor now showed the E-2's view from inside the small cave. It had already increased its light sensors so that the walls of the cave showed the same deep purple hue, as well as what looked like the pale blue veins of ice.

"That could be water," Eli said.

"I'll try to get it to drill for a sample."

The little spider bot unveiled a tiny cut-off saw and started chewing into the rock.

"Grab those rock samples too."

Anders suggested.

"I want everything they can get."

As if E-2 could hear the conversation, it began vacuuming up the chips of rock that fell from the bore.

It was a couple of minutes before the tiny robot gouged far enough into the rock to hit the blue vein. When it did, a hiss of gas escaped.

"Record that. I want to know what's coming out."

"On it. We've got trace amounts of hydrogen and argon and helium."

"Nothing new there."

Just then a slab of wall fell away, almost crushing E-2. Her external sensors measured the whiff of air just a few inches away from her forward eye lens. The tiny robot backed away from the debris and relayed what it was now seeing to the command center. Where the rock wall had broken away, a sheet of violet ice shimmered. There was something chiseled into the wall. A bass relief, like something found in a museum back on Earth. A circular picture, full of swirls and whorls and symbols that defied any known language. It was similar in many respects to the picture E-1 had taken.

"Get that up on the board now," Anders said. His eyes were wide with glee. There was something alien on this comet, and he knew it.

The whole room knew it. People were standing, craning their necks, running their hands through their hair, whistling.

"What is going on here?"

Manny whispered, as if speaking for everyone else.

"Look at those markings," Eli said.

"That's not just a trick of the light, that's something intentional."

The two blurry, ovoid images hovered over the command center as every employee tried to make sense of what they were seeing.

"Is Gillroy back yet?"

Anders barked.

"Not yet, sir," Serena answered.

"Jesus Christ. Who can clean up these pics for me? Now! I want them as sharp as possible."

"I can do it," she said.

"Just give me a few minutes."

"Hey, Becket," Eli said, opting to use his boss's first name considering the seriousness of what they were witnessing.

"There's a strong magnetic pulse coming from both of the objects. Look here."

"What do you mean 'pulse?'"

"Just that, a pulse. E-1 and E-2 are recording it. The flux density is—"

"Yeah, I see it now. Fucking things are beating like slow hearts."

Anders was known to swear in the control room, though he usually reserved it for times of high stress. Or, as was currently the case, severe anxiety. Eli couldn't blame him; he was thinking the same thing. The EM sine dancing on his screen almost looked like it was alive.

"Do the other Earlette's denote any magnetic waves?"

Eli was typing, calling up the stream of data E-3 and E-4 were dumping to him. He pointed to the measurements on his monitor, which showed that, yes, they too were recording similar waves.

"They each have signals. But I'm not seeing objects on their visuals."

"Fill up the screen with E-3's lens. I want a full view of what she's seeing. Is she at the top of the boulder yet?"

On the center monitor, E-3's viewpoint above the low shimmer fog showed a vista of black, jagged rock cliffs stretching off into the distance. If one could photograph bleakness, this was the image they'd see.

"She's getting an EM signal, " Anders mused, "but where's its source?"

"I don't know. Let me scrub back through the video feed. Maybe she missed it."

Together, Eli and Anders watched the previous several minutes of footage E-3 had sent, but they didn't see any objects in the rock.

"Maybe it's under her, *in* the boulder."

Anders suggested.

"Can she dig down?"

"Sending the command now."

A message popped up on Eli's right monitor shortly after: NEGATIVE. COMMAND OVERRIDE. NEGATIVE.

"The fuck does that mean?"

Anders yelled.

"It means she's refusing our command."

"I know what it means! I mean, why is she saying it?"

"I don't know. She's not responding to any other commands. She won't move. It's almost like she's stuck."

"Like Earl. Jesus. Ok, Switch the view to E-4. Let's see what she has."

Again, the monitor switched to a full-view screen of the Earlette that was sitting alone on a flat, plain of obsidian. The EM pulse it recorded was strobing, and she seemed to have centered herself over it.

"Nothing much to see," Eli said.

"The hydrogen cloud is too thick."

"I sharpened the first image, Mr. Anders."

Serena was pointing at her own monitor.

"Put it above us, replace the old image."

On the Jumbotron, Serena's newly enhanced image of the object in the rock now sat alongside E-2's addition. There was no mistaking it now. Both pictures contained the same types of symbols and markings.

Eli watched as two more employees got up from their desks and made their way to the bathroom, each holding their stomachs.

"See that there," Anders said, pointing at the two pictures above their heads.

"The way those swirls almost have kinks in them, spaced almost uniformly apart?"

"Yeah," Eli said.

"What does it mean?"

"I don't know. But look at the ground in front of E-4. That thick crack right there. That look like a big, curved line with a kink in it?"

Eli squinted at the monitor, as if that would make the rocky ground he was seeing any more decipherable. What Anders was referring to looked like a wide, curved tread mark, like the tire skid from someone doing donuts in a truck. Only the black line was twice as wide as a truck tire and disappeared out of view into the hydrogen gas after just a couple of feet.

"It's too hard to tell. It could just be the shale breaking up."

"Go above it," Manny said, joining the conversation.

"Drone Mode."

Anders tapped on Eli's monitor, mulling it over.

"Yeah, do it. Get it aloft and then use the fan underneath. See if it can clear out some of the gas ad get a better view."

Eli obeyed, sending the command. A few minutes later, E-4 unfolded its drone propellers and lifted into the air. As it rose, it powered on an air blower on its belly designed to clear out dust and debris from its treads, forcing some of the gas cloud to roil away to the sides. An additional camera underneath the robot showed a large circular space of visible rocky ground.

Eli's stomach cramped as more ground lines became discernable in this new top-down view. They're not treads, he realized, but rather the same symbolic markings covering the objects on the Jumbotron, just at a much larger scale.

"Go higher," Anders demanded. He was sweating, his glasses slipping down the bridge of his nose. His face was pink and flush. Eli couldn't tell if the man was excited or sick.

As for himself, his stomach cramp grew more intense, and a brief wave of nausea rushed through him. He swallowed and closed his eyes, waiting for it to go away. When it didn't, he pushed himself away from his desk and said, "Excuse me. I need to use—"

He ran to the bathroom. The blood rushed from his face as beads of sweat broke out on his forehead. As he passed the trophy case, his reflection in its glass was that of a pale, glistening ghost.

He threw open the door to the Men's room and heard the metallic reverberations of retching and sobbing coming from the stalls, all of which were occupied. Men were on their knees, feet stretched out backwards beneath the stall doors. The cacophony of sickness washed over Eli, echoing off sky-blue walls, upon which hung framed images of space taken by the company's satellites.

The cosmic gases in the images seemed to be swirling, the stars twinkling, the planets spinning.

I'm hallucinating, Eli thought. *Is it food poisoning? What is the food in the cafeteria? Did we all get e-coli?*

Eli felt the bagel with lox he'd had for breakfast working its way up his throat. He looked at the wall of urinals, realized it would be untoward of him to vomit in them. The same with the sink. Instead, he ran to the trash bin, yanked the lid off, and leaned over top.

His eyes watered and his stomach tightened into sharp stabs of agony. He let out a low cry. Searing aches ran up his back as saliva dribbled from his mouth.

"Oh fuck," he whispered right before his mouth lodged itself open and a gushing stream of white and pink goo shot out from his throat. The muscles in his neck threatened to rip through his skin.

It felt like an eternity for it all to come up. When he was done, he leaned against the wall, catching his breath. From the nearest stall, there came a guttural moan and the sound of someone banging his fists on the stall walls. Eli watched as the man's feet convulsed and then went still.

Dyspeptic, Eli bent down to look under the stall door, curious who was inside. He couldn't see the man's face, just his legs and ass. Before he could ask if the man needed anything, he saw a stream of blood run down the base of the toilet and pool up on the floor. The man seemed to sag.

Eli backed away just as one of the other stalls opened. A man staggered out, his face yellowed, his mouth coated in blood. His white button-down shirt was a mess of sticky red and pink fluids. He looked at Eli with pleading eyes.

Eli put his hands up, warding the man off.

"Just sit down. I'll try to get help."

As he left the bathroom, Eli saw Anders motioning to him to hurry back to his workstation. When he got there, he mumbled,

"Something is wrong. People are really sick. We need to send out a company-wide alert."

"In a minute,"

Anders said, offering a non-committal nod.

"I need you on this right now. Look what E-4 found when it hit a hundred feet of altitude. Look!"

On the monitor was the view E-4 was seeing as it hovered above the black ground. The strange cloud had been blown away by the robot's drone propellers. There were numerous etchings on the ground. When zoomed out from high above, the image was exactly the same as the previous two on the jumbotron. It was becoming routine now, Eli realized. E-3 had to be near some marking as well. But were there more elsewhere? Should they send the Earlettes out even farther than their safe range? Would they even obey the commands?

On the screen above the room, the third image now appeared.

The ground shook and the monitors glitched into scanlines. Everyone not sick in the bathrooms went silent. A few people hit their monitors in a futile attempt to fix them.

"Did that little earthquake just rattle our servers? Tell me they're okay." Anders scoped out the room. The only thing still working was the jumbotron and Eli's computer. He stabbed a finger at a collection of men near the far wall.

"Get these stations back online right away. Do whatever you have to do. Hurry!"

Eli pressed his hand against his knotted-up belly.

"Becket, the people in the bathroom—"

"Can wait. You're the only station still running. Get E-3 on the line. There has to be another image. I want all of them captured. This is going to be the biggest discovery of our lifetime."

From the back of the room, another employee moaned and left their station, heading for the facilities.

Around the command center, framed photos of distant planetoids and colorful quadrants of space throbbed in their frames.

Was anyone else seeing it, Eli wondered. *Surely, he couldn't be the only one.* Yet, nobody else seemed to be looking up from their computer screens. Everyone was too enthralled in what the Earlettes were capturing on their feeds.

Eli watched as Dan Rollins, who oversaw the thermodynamics division, staggered out of the bathroom, blood and puke on his face, and stumbled down the hallway toward the storage rooms as if he was lost. No one seemed to care.

"I see it!"

Manny yelled.

"Where?"

Anders asked.

Manny pointed at the image E-3 was seeing as it sat atop the large boulder on the asteroid.

"It's across the valley. See that mountain all the way over there? I think I see markings. Tell it to zoom in as much as possible on those coordinates."

Eli shook his head.

"I don't want to."

"What."

Anders said. It wasn't a question so much as a challenge.

"Don't zoom in. Something isn't right."

"You're not feeling well. Move over, I'll do it."

Anders shoved Eli out of his seat and took over the station. His fingers quickly typed a command to the little robot looking out over the black plains.

Just a few minutes, Eli told himself as he backpaddled toward the bathrooms and corridors leading to the cafeteria, followed by the breakrooms and eventually the exit doors. The command would take a few minutes to relay across all the satellites. He had to get out of here. Something was very wrong here.

Around him, the framed photos of space were coming alive like animated graphics. Gases roiled, planets spun, stars pulsed, gravitational fields warped light. Right before his eyes, a poster-sized image of Ganymede shook in its frame, the moon cracking apart into shards of rock hurtling outward in 2-D.

A shadow passed over the room. Eli looked up to see the sunlight coming through the room's skylights turn amber.

Several people looked up; several others threw up into their desk wastebaskets. One woman retched so violently blood burst from the vessels in her eyes.

"Don't zoom in!"

Eli yelled.

Anders either didn't hear him or didn't care. He was bent over Eli's monitors, tapping his hands wildly on the desk like a child amped up on sugar.

"Shut it down, Becket! Shut it down!"

Those people not looking up at the sky or holding their stomachs were now starting to notice the pictures on the walls.

Serena ran to him.

"Look at the images up there on the jumbotron. All the lines are connecting. The pictures are...joining."

"Shit."

Eli whispered, watching the whorls and lines on the three images connect themselves like vines growing across lattices. It should have been impossible. They were three different images. Three different files. They weren't in any way connected, yet they were interacting with each other.

Whoom!

The building lurched. People fell to their knees. Family photos fell off workstations. Monitors crashed to the floor in explosions of sparks and shattered glass.

Anders stood up from where he'd been tossed to the ground. He looked across the command center at Eli.

"What's going on? What the hell was that?"

"Tell E-3 not to zoom in! Now!"

Suddenly noticing the anomalies in the room—the moving pictures, the red atmosphere, the vomiting employees—Anders typed furiously on Eli's keyboard.

"It's not responding."

Overhead, the image E-3 was relaying to the Jumbotron screen began to zoom in on a distant mountain across the planetoid. Manny was right, Eli realized, there were markings on it. It showed itself next to the other three on the screen now, a fourth puzzle piece completing a picture. As it came into full view its symbols likewise stitched themselves across a nonexistent digital space to connect to the other pictographs.

What showed on the screen now was one singular image adorned with swirls and serpentine markings moving as if they were alive. The image glowed bright yellow, mixing with the red light from outside, turning the interior of the breakroom into a sickly shade of rust. Somehow the color intensified, dilating Eli's pupils until he had to turn away.

The edges of the Jumbotron grew white hot, illuminating the command center in a searing brilliance. The blinding edges grew outward from the display board, forming a square of light that seemed to exist separate from any power source. As it grew beyond the scale of the Jumbotron, Eli could see images of space within it.

"It's folding space."

"What?"

Serena asked, hands shielding her eyes.

"It's a fucking black hole or a...a...portal. We opened something. Here, get in this, quick!"

He smashed the trophy case with his elbow and kicked away the hanging shards of glass. He grabbed the old spacesuits inside and pulled them from their hooks.

"Put this on. Hurry!"

In the air above the command center, the square portal grew larger, stretching out toward the edges of the room. Its terminator line crept over the desks, causing any computers that it passed over to burst into flame. In its wake was black regolith and jagged obsidian shale mountains.

Eli recognized the landscape. He'd been staring at it for weeks now. It's X-089, he realized.

The portal was bringing them to EARL.

Eli jammed his foot into the suit's legs, yanked it up and got his arms in. He shoved his feet in the boots and locked them in place. Next to him, Serena was struggling to get the gloves on. He grabbed her helmet and forced it onto her, locking the neck in place. Then he did the same for himself, his fingers shaking in fear.

Across the room, Manny screamed and projectile-vomited blood, the skin on his face sluicing downward like a man suffering a stroke. Besides him, others bent over and vomited blood, each gurgling in pain as they clutched their stomachs.

Eli just managed to get his gloves locked as the terminator line passed simultaneously under his feet and above his head. Passing behind him toward the break rooms and engulfing the entirety of the Company HQ, like a whale swallowing its own personal Jonah.

A second later they were all on the surface of X-089.

EARL sat nearby, unmoving, as if he was dead, save for the few running lights that still glowed red near his belly.

In front of Eli, his friends and co-workers writhed on the black, dusty ground, throwing up and crying. The few that had stopped vomiting were sitting on their bottoms, staring up at the universe. There was no air here, but somehow they weren't suffocating.

The iridescent gas cloud that had appeared hours earlier swam at them. It crackled as it touched the first employee's foot, drifting over his sneakers and moving up his legs. Others soon found the cloud moving over them, their skin crackling with tiny fireworks.

Then the gas cloud touched their faces. Their cheeks sagged and dripped like hot wax, falling into their own laps. Their noses slid down into their open jaws, which in turn dislodged from their skulls and landed on the ground. Their hair shriveled as if burning in an invisible fire.

A few people stood, vomit on their shirts, and tried to run but their legs melted into pools of hot clay, and they dropped to the black regolith. Succumbing to the cloud which dissolved their clothing and made their skin bubble and pop.

Eli held his breath as the cloud moved over his suit, obstructing the view through his visor. Somehow, he was still able to hear the crackles and snaps of his co-workers' faces melting into mush.

Someone grabbed his hand. He looked to his left and saw Serena there, crying behind her visor. He looked down at her hand and clutched it back. Her glove still wasn't secured. The air around her wrist dazzled with electric shocks as the cloud seeped into the broken seal. He grabbed her wrist and tried to tighten the locking mechanism but it was too late. The cloud was moving up inside the arm of her suit. He could feel her elbow vibrating as it melted away her bone.

"Eli!" she pleaded as the gases rose up inside her helmet.

"Please!"

He let go of her hand as her body shook. Inside her helmet, her face dripped into ribbons of biological mush, a striation of white and red and tan goo that fell down her neck toward the belly of her suit.

She crumbled like a Jacobs ladder, nothing but sludge filling the inside of the helmet.

Eli watched as the last of his co-workers bubbled into similar ooze on the planetoid's ground.

He looked back toward the command center, which had been sucked onto the planetoid with him. The portal had moved past its exit, outside the building, into the parking lot. It continued to move, sucking in the lawn in front of the Company. Everything from outside rattled and shattered as it was transported to the ground of X-089, much of it disintegrating or flying off into the vastness of space.

Physics did not apply here. Something else was at play. Something that relied on those four pictographs the Earlettes had uncovered. Something that had called to the tiny robots and asked to be set free.

Who had put the pictographs here? Aliens? Something else? How had it or they buried them on this rock in the deep blackness of space? How long had they been out here?

Eli watched as the border of the portal engulfed the park across the street from the Company headquarters. Employees brought their kids there sometimes. There were kids in it right now. They were staring at the encroaching portal. Their parents bent over and vomited. The children fell to the ground, crying in fear.

"Run!"

Eli shouted, but he knew they couldn't hear them.

As the gas cloud swam over them, it melted them into puddles of slop.

The portal expanded toward the highway and the nearby strip mall. It wasn't going to stop.

Eli felt lightheaded. He was running out of air. If the cloud didn't get him, he'd die from asphyxiation.

He moved to the nearby onyx boulder that E-3 had ascended earlier and climbed up out of the cloud. It took a minute, but soon he was at its apex, the gas far below him. He sat down, feeling giddy. Above him, the universe twinkled and roiled in swaths of red and purple.

What was out there, Eli wondered. *What had buried these pictographs? Was it watching him now?*

Something bumped his leg. E-3 was crawling into his lap. He doubted the robot knew he was a person. It was probably registering the difference in material between the ground and his suit. But it didn't matter. He let it sit in his lap and put a hand on the metal plate over its optical lens.

He glanced back toward Earth one last time, watched as the portal moved around a hospital, patients melting in the hallways as the gas cloud engulfed them, walls crumbling to dust.

E-3 looked up at him and buzzed.

He pet the robot on the head.

"It's ok. You didn't know. Nobody did."

He watched the stars until he no longer could.

"GODDESS OF THE APOCALYPSE"

Dicey Grenor

Snatched.

It began when the sky went from sunny and cheerful to dark and ominous in less than fifteen seconds. Children went from studying in school... Parents went from working their jobs... Insurance CEOs went from denying healthcare claims...

To suddenly—

Whoosh!

Whoosh! Whoosh!

Whoosh! Whoosh! Whoosh!

There were no warnings. No government broadcasts. No emergency phone alerts. No siren alarms. Just one day, the sky turned to midnight soot and people started vanishing with a *whoosh!* into the air. One by one, they were snatched into the sky by glowing beams of light amid the mysterious darkness. Their panicked screams trailed off as they disappeared into enormous, hovering metallic ships. No one felt safe. No one knew why. And no one saw it coming. Chaos erupted citywide as terror spread like a virus, thick and bitter, feeding on itself and growing with each passing second.

Bri thought she was losing her mind when she watched her neighbor vanish.

One moment, Ms. Parker was tending a small garden on her patio, humming softly to herself as she paused to smile and wave at Bri. The next moment, a shaft of light, bright enough to burn away all color from Bri's retinas, enveloped Ms. Parker. Bri watched as Ms. Parker's body folded and ripped backwards into the sky on a *whoosh*, leaving an outline of dust where her physical form used to be. When the light faded to a pinpoint at the base of a large ship, Ms. Parker was gone, her shears lying in the dirt like a discarded relic. Only the faint echo of Ms. Parker's shocked scream remained, a sickly reminder that Bri was left alone on her own balcony, too shaken to react.

Bri hadn't been drinking, hadn't been on medication, and didn't suffer from mental illness. Not that she knew of anyway. She did have weird dreams from time to time, but she'd just come home from college and been wide awake during Ms. Parker's disappearance. Plus, her dreams were only harmless remnants of her accident from a year ago, not something to prepare her for this.

They certainly didn't explain why Ms. Parker disappeared. Into what appeared to be a spaceship. In the middle of the day that looked like midnight.

Bri couldn't scream, couldn't move, couldn't believe what she'd witnessed. She also didn't know Ms. Parker was just the first of many vanishings Bri would witness.

Bri would find out soon enough it was not an isolated incident.

As she looked out into the darkened street, she noticed others being snatched through the air into ships as well. Men, women, trans, nonbinaries... *Whoosh! Whoosh! Whoosh! Whoosh!* There appeared to be no pattern. No discrimination based on race or class. None regarding age or profession. And somehow, that felt less comforting. Random people snatched during unpredictable times made the whole ordeal feel...

Unstoppable. Inevitable.

Apocalyptic.

Stunned and terrified, Bri dropped her coffee mug with a shatter onto the patio and covered her mouth to stifle a scream. Watching so many get snatched within the blink of an eye informed Bri that Ms. Parker's disappearance had been no fluke but the beginning of something massive. When drivers started vanishing and their cars began colliding, Bri knew this was far more serious than she could ever imagine. With trembling bones and a racing heart, she ran inside, shut the blinds, and barricaded herself in her apartment until she could get answers to the impossible.

Answers never came.

For weeks, the sky thrummed with a low, electric hum, a constant reminder that the next moment could be anyone's last. The strobing lights came and went, abducting more people at random, until Bri barely had time to mourn the losses. She had no family left. No friends. No community.

Bri felt lonely, sad, and mostly, scared.

What happened to people once they disappeared? Would they ever come back? How long could Bri go without getting snatched? What would happen if she ended up being the only one left?

Each passing day left her with more questions. More anxiety.

It wasn't just about the disappearances. As Bri ventured out to get food and supplies, she discovered terrible and uncertain circumstances for everyone struggling to survive in the aftermath. Pets left behind scratched at doors, whimpering and howling for their missing owners. Families torn apart in an instant required parents to move on without their children and children to move on without their parents. Many were alone for the first time without life skills or a survival plan. The collective sadness and sorrow felt thick in the air, overwhelming Bri's own sense of loss and emotions.

Gradually, screams of grief and anguish decreased to ragged gasps of despair, followed by empty sounds of dashed hopes and haunted memories. The streets grew silent except for the hollow wailing of the wind, like ghosts of those who were gone but not forgotten.

Bri read all the materials she could find and watched any broadcasts available.

Scientists theorized on live television and radio about electromagnetic energy from solar winds and the quantum effects of a false vacuum in space. Clergy wept from pulpits, admonishing about the Rapture and second coming of Christ. Conspiracists screamed from rooftops about the government collecting people to replace them with robots and clones. But nothing made definitive sense. Common people, desperate for resolutions, gossiped amongst themselves and labeled the disappearances "abductions", the abductors "aliens", and the spaceships "UFOs". Because why not? It was just as plausible as anyone else's guess.

No one knew for certain, and eventually, Bri stopped listening to everyone else and turned inward to her intuition.

Her dreams.

With the intensity, complexity, and growing occurrences of Bri's dreams, she began to believe in the alien abduction theory. While not most comforting, it made sense to her that hostile extraterrestrials had come to take over the world's resources and collect humans for invasive research on their bodies. Or to mate with humans, make them slaves, or... eat them. She accepted the alien invasion depicted for so long in science fiction had finally happened to Earth, and the world as Bri knew it had ceased to exist.

She just didn't know what to do about it. Or how to save herself.

Dreamed.

B ri's dreams had begun before the abductions. Ever since she'd drowned in the ocean on a tropical vacation and been brought back to life by a lifeguard, she'd dreamt of ocean creatures with dancing tentacles.

They were subtle at first, irregular, and kind of entertaining.

They started out as friendly octopus with tickly extensions, helping her locate the water's surface and guiding her back to safety onshore. She'd wake up with a broad smile, disappointed she didn't get to finish her nocturnal unconscious fun. As time went on, the ocean became darker, and the tentacles began to take on a life of their own. They looked more like deadly serpents, intent on striking and torturing her in her sleep. She'd wake up in a cold sweat, clawing at her bed, desperate to get out of her own head. Desperate to end the underwater fight and never return to the mollusk reptilian dream sequence.

Except they returned. More often, until they occurred every night.

When Bri slept now, she'd find herself standing on the edge of a vast, dark ocean, the air thick and oppressive, suffocating her lungs. The ocean churned with violent rage beneath her, the water an inky black, devoid of any reflection or light. Massive shadows writhed beneath the surface gradually revealing serpentine shapes that moved with a terrifying elegance, their scales glistening like wet obsidian. She could feel their eyes on her, hundreds, maybe thousands, of eyes, watching from the depths. Daring her to swim out. Or fall in.

What had started out sweet and subtle, beckoning and playful, had morphed into something monstrous and foreboding. It was a warning. A powerful evil. Closing in.

The worst part was the sound.

A low, rumbling hiss that vibrated through her bones, a whispering that carried with it the promise of something ancient, something powerful, something... hungry.

In her dreams, Bri felt as if the ocean was alive, not just with the writhing tentacles turned snakes, but with a sentience far older than humanity. The ocean intimidated her. The snakes taunted her. An omnipresent figure beckoned her. Stalked her. Demanded her attention and obedience.

Or maybe Bri summoned the figure. For comfort and salvation. In the same manner she had prayed for help when she was drowning.

I am here.

Over time, the shadowy figure became more defined in Bri's dreams. It appeared as a woman with skin shimmering like dark oil slick on water, her hair moving like living serpents.

I have risen.

Her eyes glowed, twin orbs of molten gold, watching Bri with an intensity that made Bri feel small. Fragile. Insignificant.

Preyed upon.

It is almost time!

Bri woke up with goosebumps drenched in cold sweat, her heart hammering in her chest, the sheets tangled around her like the coils of those dream serpents.

Each time Bri slept, the woman emerged from the erratic ocean and the storm grew more violent. The sky cracked open, and rain poured like blood. The waves she rode on surged higher, until they seemed ready to consume the entire world. The snakes grew frenzied, thrashing and tearing at each other as if eager for what was coming. Starving for their rewards. Begging to break free from their oceanic confines and take over the land.

The oil-slicked ocean woman with the serpentine hair delivered the same message each time: *I am here. I have risen. It is almost time.* But with every emergence from the ocean, more of her form took shape. Each time, her voice grew more authoritative, her presence more commanding, and her message became crystal clear... until she finally stood fully formed and powerful enough to carry out its meaning.

Bri thought they were just dreams at first, but they felt too real. Then she thought she was hallucinating then astral projecting. But to the middle of a stormy black ocean with an ancient black woman with serpents? Nah.

Now... since the vanishings... she wondered if her dreams meant something more.

Perhaps Bri had survived drowning and come back from the other side with more than just a reminder of how fleeting her life was. Perhaps, she still had a connection to the other side of death, and her dreams were premonitions, foreshadowing things to come. Perhaps, her dreams wanted to tell her something useful. Something helpful to her survival. Something to help her see how the tentacles and snakes connected to the aliens, and how she could protect herself.

Bri just needed to identify the woman in her dreams and figure out why she was here, what she had risen from, and what was it time for?

Chased.

Bri's neighborhood was eerily silent. No chirping birds, no hum of insects, no rustling leaves. Just the ominous groan of abandoned buildings and Bri's pensive thoughts.

She hugged her scavenged sack of canned goods close to her chest, cursing the lack of cover in the open street, as she walked back to her apartment.

Suddenly—

She felt a searing white beam shoot down towards her from the metallic belly of a saucer-like craft that loomed in the swirling black sky. She leaped out of its path, landing in a prickly bush, just in time to miss its target. Groaning, she sprang to her feet and faced the beam head-on. She couldn't believe she'd been able to dodge it, but that stroke of luck gave her courage to run in the opposite direction. Bri dropped her newly acquired supplies and hauled ass.

"Not me," she muttered through gritted teeth as she ran like her life depended on it. "Not today." She wouldn't make it easy for the aliens to snatch her.

The chase was on.

The beam followed her like a laser with unnatural precision, slicing through the gloom and locking onto her with a predator's gaze. Bri's stomach churned. Her boots pounded against cracked asphalt, her breath coming in quick, panicked gasps. She'd never seen a beam miss anyone, and she'd never seen a beam snatch anyone from inside solid shelter. If she could outrun it, there was hope. She'd also never seen a beam bring anyone back, and that kept her afraid and fueled with adrenaline to keep running until she could find a safe place to hide. Whatever was up in that spaceship had to be worse than anything she'd encounter on Earth.

The beam trailed her every move, burning a path across the pavement. Heat prickled the back of her neck as the light came dangerously close, sending sparks flying when it touched metal debris. Bri vaulted over a rusted car hood, hitting the ground on the other side hard. She leaned into the fall, rolled, and got back to her feet in an instant without a break in her run. She had to get to cover, but every alley, every crevice, seemed too narrow or too far away.

Her lungs burned. She ran harder.

The beam grew brighter. Closer. Too close.

"Damn it!" she hissed, veering into a narrow side street lined with overturned dumpsters and abandoned bicycles. The air smelled of rust and decay, but there was no time to think, only run.

"Over here!" A woman's voice called sharp and urgent.

Bri skidded to a halt, her boots scraping against the asphalt. A curvy woman stood at the edge of a toppled food truck towards a pier on the bay, her face obscured by a scarf and goggles, waving Bri over. The beam's hum and light intensified, making her teeth vibrate and her skin singe.

No time to think. Bri had to move.

She sprinted forward just as the woman yanked open the truck's back door. Bri dove inside as the woman slammed the door shut behind her, plunging them into darkness. The hum grew louder, almost deafening. Bri and the woman pressed themselves against the wall, holding their breaths. Through a crack in the truck's warped metal, she saw the beam sweep past, illuminating the truck for a terrifying second before moving on.

Bri's heart thundered in her chest. Minutes passed like hours until the hum faded into the distance and the truck became dark again.

"You okay?" the woman asked, flicking on a flashlight and pulling down her scarf to reveal sharp cheekbones and piercing green eyes.

Bri nodded, still catching her breath. "I... I think so." Been a long time since she'd seen another person. She found herself staring a bit too long.

"Name's Shelby." The woman peered through the crack to make sure the coast was clear outside. "And you're lucky I was around. That beam would've fried you if it didn't snatch you up first."

Bri clenched her fists, trying to steady her trembling hands. "Thanks." She looked around at the empty truck that had the lingering smell of yummy food. It made her stomach growl. "But is this really help? I dropped all my food to find shelter... in an upside-down truck." She buried her hands in her face. "Maybe I should have just let it take me."

Shelby smirked. "Then what?"

Bri shook her head. "Hell, I don't know."

"Then you did the right thing." Shelby patted Bri's shoulder. "Better the hell you know than the one you don't."

The ground shuddered faintly as the UFO drifted farther away.

Bri turned to Shelby. "Now what?"

"I got a boathouse on the dock." Shelby crooked her thumb over her shoulder. "It's not much, but it's somewhere to sleep until we can figure something out." She turned to leave out the other side of the bus. "Plus, I've got some water and cans of lentils we can share."

Bri exhaled. "That sounds good."

And with that, they slipped into the shadows, the threat of beams and aliens paused for a moment.

Enlightened.

I am here. I have risen. It is almost time!

Bri woke up on Shelby's boat, panting and panicking in a cold sweat from another vivid snake woman dream. Shelby rushed to her side on the short, moldy couch. Bri sat up, and after reassuring Shelby she was okay, she decided to tell Shelby about her dreams. She told her about the stunning black woman standing in the middle of the stormy ocean with long locs that moved like snakes, alive with a power that felt too vast to comprehend.

176

Shelby took it all in then sat in silence, appearing in deep thought. After some time, she got up and dug through her cabinets and drawers until she found paper and a pen. "Can you draw her for me? The woman in your nightmares?" She handed them to Bri. "Please?"

Bri was no artist, as she'd been studying accounting in school, a worthless skill during this era. But she'd seen the woman and snakes so often, it wasn't hard to conjure a mental image and put her likeness on the page. In fact, it felt cathartic. Bri had someone to share her fears and theories with.

Shelby stared at the drawing a beat before commenting. "If I'm not mistaken... This is Medusa, one of the Gorgon sisters. And from what you described, she's been calling out to you."

Bri erupted in laughter. She stopped when she noticed Shelby's serious expression. "Oh, god. You're serious."

"Goddess, actually..." Shelby started pacing. "Not god. Medusa was born human but became a goddess."

"I don't understand." Bri wanted answers, not more questions. "Medusa is a character in Greek mythology. And even if she were real, why would she be reaching out to me?"

Shelby started searching through her shelves. "It could be said that any god is fake, yet billions of people worship and kill in their names daily, since the dawn of time." She tossed a dusty book to Bri. "Why you... that's the question, isn't it?" She watched Bri catch the book and swipe at the dust. "Maybe because you look similar?"

Bri opened the book to the tabbed page. She immediately recognized Medusa standing in the ocean between her two sisters. At this point, she didn't feel shocked, only relieved to finally get some answers. "I'm her descendant?"

"I would say that, but there's no record of her having children." Shelby chewed her own bottom lip. "There has to be another connection."

"I once coded after drowning." Bri browsed the page and turned to the next, refreshing herself on the mythology. "They didn't know how I came back to life, but they found snakeskin in my locs and clothes. From snakes that weren't native to the area."

"Maybe Medusa saved you." Shelby plopped down on the couch next to her. "Maybe she's trying to save you again." She held Bri's hand like a caring sister. "She's seen as a symbol of female rage and power. She represents resilience and strength in the face of trauma. She protects and punishes those that harm whoever she's chosen to protect." She gave Bri's hand a comforting squeeze. "Who did she protect you from?"

Bri swallowed the lump in her throat as she thought back on painful memories. Finally... "It wasn't my finest moment." She continued when Shelby nodded encouragement. "I was in a low place. We'd broken up. My fiancé... He... I didn't know how to swim. I went into the water. On purpose. I was angry. Sad. I wanted to..."

Shelby got the point. "Maybe Medusa felt your pain, took your suffering, and brought you back." Shelby's eyes narrowed. "What happened to him?"

"He, uh..." Bri's forehead crinkled. "The girl he left me for shot and killed him." Her eyes grew wide as she connected the dots based on Shelby's insinuation. "You don't think...?"

Shelby pursed her lips and rose to her feet. She started pacing again. "Definitely sounds like Medusa. But also... Hecate. And maybe... Athena." She grabbed another book and started flipping the pages, scanning the content. "Very strange."

"How do you know all this?" Bri knew better than to consider anything an impossibility these days. She just wanted to know what made Shelby so knowledgeable.

"Because before the world went to shit, I was a college professor, and I taught this sort of thing to doctoral students."

Bri nodded slowly. It all made sense now.

"There was a lot of strange oceanic activity during the weeks leading up to the direct contact with aliens." Shelby held up old printouts of online news articles. "The real ocean, not just the one in your dreams, had begun to pulse like a living, breathing entity. Fishing boats reported odd, unnatural tidal patterns. Currents bended, twisting in ways that defied scientific explanation. Dead fish with milky white eyes began washing up on shores, their bodies covered in serpentine scars." She pointed to a headline to prove her point. "Knowing what I know about myths and ancient sea deities, I paid close attention to signs others disregarded. I recognized the UAPs right off the bat, but I also knew something otherworldly was afoot and we were headed to catastrophic chaos."

"UAPs?" Bri leaned closer to the edge of the couch. She felt less fear now and more curiosity. She also trusted Shelby's intel.

"Unidentified Aerial Phenomena." Shelby set the book down and picked up Bri's drawing in one hand, a news printout in the other. "You just confirmed I wasn't imagining or overexaggerating any of it.

Endangered.

After several days of them sharing the last of Shelby's water and lentils, they became restless, worried, and desperate. They had gone out every day looking for food and supplies and come back with nothing. Each time, they'd had to run back to avoid alien light beams.

"The beams are searching this area more often now. It's not safe here. We have to move." Shelby wrapped her arm with a towel to stop the bleeding from a wound she'd gotten from face-planting during their last run.

"Where do we go?" Bri helped her secure the towel.

"The ocean."

Bri's heart skipped a beat. "The ocean?" The mere mention of it made her stomach churn. Her nightmares and drowning experience rushed to the surface of her mind. "Why the ocean?" Bri's voice shook.

Shelby's hands trembled as she ran them through her hair. "I don't know. It's just... The ships, the lights... They seem to avoid the ocean. We should take the boat and go now, while we still can. While there's still two of us."

Bri swallowed hard, staring at Shelby. The idea of escaping the aliens seemed like a great idea, maybe too good to be true, but the ocean had traumatized her. "I don't know, Shelby. What if we're wrong? What if—"

"We don't have any other choice!" Shelby snapped, her voice breaking. "If we stay here, they'll take us like they took the others, or we'll die of starvation. We have to try something!"

Bri recoiled. Shelby hadn't raised her voice to her since the first day she signaled to Bri to run for cover.

"I'm sorry." Shelby's head hung low. "I'm just exhausted… hungry…" Shelby lifted her towel-wrapped arm. "Injured." She picked up one of the old news printouts. "This is the Great Blue Hole. Based on reports, I believe this sinkhole is the original source of all the strange underwater activity. If we sail the boat over there, maybe the Gorgons will help us. Medusa's been communicating with you for a reason. She may be our only hope."

Bri sighed and nodded, "Okay," though the pit in her stomach grew heavier with each passing second. "Let's do it."

They spent the next hour preparing themselves, then pulled the anchor and set sail. At first it was peaceful, like a vacation, a leisurely cruise. As long as they ignored the fact that they were fleeing alien abductions on land, they managed to relax and enjoy the journey.

They huddled together on the worn-out boat as it creaked with every wave. *Creak… creak… creeeeaak.* Eventually, the water grew rockier until it surged with a terrible fury. The air became thick, oppressive, and the sky was covered in roiling black clouds that churned like something alive.

Their relaxing vacation devolved into the stuff Bri's nightmares were made of.

As the boat sailed further until they could no longer see land, the waves began to swell unnaturally high. Ominously high. The sky above crackled with lightning, and the air filled with the scent of salt and decay.

And then they came.

From the depths of the ocean, massive serpentine creatures burst forth. Their bodies were impossibly large, slick with dark scales, and their eyes glowed a sickly yellowish green. They coiled around the boat, their massive heads rising above the deck, jaws open wide to reveal rows of needle-sharp teeth.

Shelby screamed as one of the creatures snapped its jaws inches from her face, the force of its breath hot and rancid, like rotting flesh. Bri's breath caught in her throat as the serpents circled the boat. Her dream was real. All of it. But this time, there would be no waking up.

The air itself seemed to hum, as if the water beneath them was vibrating with an ancient, hidden energy. Then she heard it. A low groan, deep and primal, emanating from the ocean.

"Did you hear that?" Bri whispered.

Shelby gripped Bri's hand. "She's coming."

The first crack of lightning split the sky in two, jagged and unnatural, casting an eerie glow on the churning waters. The wind roared, and the sky opened. Rain poured in sheets, blurring the horizon, but it wasn't just rain. It was thick, oily, and foul-smelling. The already dark sky and ocean turned black as ink.

Thunder rumbled, and within it, Bri heard a voice carried in the storm. The tone was melodic but powerful, a chilling lullaby.

"I am here. I have risen. It is time!" The voice wasn't just in a dream now. It was alive.

Bri's legs felt rooted to the boat. Her mind was spinning. Something was happening, something much worse than the UFOs or UAFs that had ravaged their world.

Another flash of lightning illuminated the sky. The shape of the waves took form. Serpentine, twisting, coiling masses rising from the ocean, their shapes writhing in the chaos of the storm. The snakes were attached to a woman. Waving, writhing. On her head. Like the locs of her hair.

The top part of the boat was ripped off as the hurricane whipped into a violent crescendo. They screamed, futilely scrambling for shelter in the boat's under quarters as the ocean became an unstoppable force, swallowing their courage bit by bit.

As if in slow motion, the ocean parted, revealing a vast, dark abyss beneath the surface. From it, the woman began to rise. Ancient. Beautiful. Powerful. Terrible. The storm's eye seemed to open up over her, and the ocean itself bowed in reverence.

The colossal woman breached the water, her skin black as the storm clouds, glistening with the salt of the ocean. Her hair whipped around in the wind, fading in and out of form from snakes to locs. Bri's mind rebelled against the sight of her, unable to comprehend the sheer scale of the woman. But she knew the ocean itself had vomited forth a goddess.

Medusa.

Her snake-like locs writhed, each one a living, breathing creature, hissing and snapping. Her eyes glowed with the fury of a thousand storms, and as her gaze swept across the ocean, Bri knew they were all doomed. Not just she and Shelby. Everybody. All of humankind. Including the aliens.

"Bri!" Shelby screamed, "I know she's beautiful. But whatever you do—Don't look in her eyes!"

Bri looked away in the nick of time.

Awakened.

Medusa's emergence seemed to rip the heavens apart. Lightning rained down like wrath.

Behind her, the ocean continued to churn. From the depths, two more shapes emerged, twisting and turning as they broke through the water. Bri's eyes widened as she beheld the other two gorgon sisters, Stheno and Euryale, their faces stunning, their bodies serpentine. They appeared angry. Hungry. To dole out judgment. To torment. They looked ready to deliver Hell on Earth.

Bri fell to her knees, drenched and shaking. This wasn't better than the alien invasion. This was the end of time itself.

Shelby's skin had paled from exhaustion and fright, but her expression told Bri she had come to the same conclusion. She squeezed Bri's hand for comfort. "I'm sorry. I was wrong. She didn't reach out to you to save you."

Bri's mind flashed with realization: the UFOs had been their salvation. They weren't the enemy. They were trying to save whoever could be spared. The aliens had come to rescue as many humans as possible, to take them from Earth before this devastation. Bri had misunderstood her dreams and feared the wrong things. Shelby had misinterpreted everything.

Bri turned towards Shelby and shared a knowing, solemn look. "She was warning me to go with the aliens."

The hurricane reached its peak, the wind so deafening that it drowned out everything else. The Gorgons stood like goddesses over their dominion, their eyes surveying Bri and Shelby like insects before them.

Medusa's gaze finally turned towards Bri, her golden eyes piercing through the storm. Bri's body seized in fear, but she didn't look away. In those ancient, terrible, beautiful eyes, Bri saw the full depth of what was coming. Hell was not beneath Earth. It was here, rising with the Gorgons, and it was too late for salvation.

Medusa whispered, her voice slithering into Bri's mind like a thousand hissing serpents. "I tried to warn you. We are the end." She outstretched her arms. "We are also the beginning."

In the hidden depths of the oceans, other beings emerged from the water.

Medusa's voice boomed into the cosmos. "This the divine feminine era. This is the new world. This is the time for the forgotten goddesses to rise, deliver justice, and reign. Mami Wata, rise! Wadjet, rise! Hecate, rise!" Each time Medusa said a name, another magnificent entity appeared from the ocean. "Lilith, rise! Nyx, rise! Gaia, rise! The Morrigan..." She continued shouting names as the ocean water began to recede, revealing a city with mountains, temples, and castles. Beneath the ocean bed, the world was cracking open, revealing portals to realms older than Earth itself.

Bri let go of Shelby's hand and knelt under the weight of Medusa's golden eyes locking onto hers with a gaze so powerful, it felt as though her soul was being stripped bare. "Goddess, I beg of you. Spare my friend Shelby. Send her back to the aliens." A tear ran down her cheek. "Please."

"No!" Shelby grabbed Bri's hand again and knelt next to her. "We're in this together."

Medusa's smile was slow, deliberate, and beautiful beyond words. "It is time."

Bri screamed as her flesh began to harden, her limbs turning to cold, unyielding stone. Her final thought, before agony and darkness claimed her, was that the real terror hadn't even begun, and she was so glad she was going to miss it. Shelby's scream was the last sound she heard before darkness swallowed her whole.

Medusa reached onto the boat and touched Bri and Shelby's statues with her fingertip, jolting life back into them and leaving them with serpentine bodies where legs had been. "You have been deemed worthy to stand with us." Medusa's snakes bowed as Bri and Shelby woke to their new powers. "I saved you once from drowning. You saved yourself from destruction." She smiled and raised her arm. "Now, rise."

GRAVESIDE JOURNALS

Patrick Lacey

Hello and welcome to another edition of *New England Nightmares*. I'm your faithful host, Art Knapp, chaser of the unknown and hunter of all things haunted. Let me catch you up on tonight's eerie episode. We're headed to the once-bustling mill town of Marlowe, Massachusetts, to explore a cemetery with some rather odd customs. That's right, folks. This is part three in our ongoing series *Spectral Cemeteries*, where we examine New England's oldest resting places.

Tonight, I'm speaking to you on location. Not from the cemetery itself but a one-star hotel on the border of Marlowe and Danvers. The walls are yellowed with nicotine and though this isn't a pet-friendly establishment, the rugs sure smell like cat urine to me. But I digress. Let's talk business, and business in this case would be the infamous graveside journals.

For those not in the know, Marlowe is a paranormal investigator's wet dream. The town has been the purported site of extraterrestrials, cryptids, strange rock formations, and don't forget it's most famous resident serial killer Tucker Ashton, who murdered no less than one hundred victims during his heyday.

On the northern side of this charming yet spooky suburb, you'll find Friend Cemetery, so named for its owners, the Friends of Marlowe,

188

a non-profit religious organization that runs two parishes in town. From what I can tell, the Friends practice a sort of pseudo-Christianity with a dash of new age mysticism to form a spiritual stew focused on astral projection and neighboring worlds.

I was met at the cemetery entrance by churchgoer Simon Foster, with whom I'd originally corresponded when setting this trip in motion. Initially, Simon was reluctant. The journals have been kept private despite the age of social media.

I assured him we at *New England Nightmares* take these matters gravely serious, so to speak. We've covered many religious and cultural traditions that may seem "out there" to the general public, but we know our listeners maintain an open mind. After some convincing, Simon agreed to speak with us.

He was much taller than I'd anticipated, well over six feet, dressed in a flannel shirt and khaki pants, nothing to set him apart from the average Marlowe resident. His voice was high-pitched and did not match his near-mammoth stature.

"It's nice to finally meet you," I said.

"And I you," he said, leading me toward the front gate, which is the subject of numerous urban legends. Together, the bars form an avant-garde sculpture some claim resembles a face, its mouth a gaping snarl of too-long teeth. While I'll admit the asymmetrical design is jarring, I found no such anthropomorphic details.

"Beautiful, isn't it?" Simon said with his mismatching voice.

"Sure," I said, allowing him to take the lead.

He unclasped the lock. The rusted iron shrieked in the morning autumn air, scaring away a murder of crows from a nearby tree. If I was prone to hyperbole, I might liken it to a scream.

"It's just this way," he said, though it was more of a mile-long hike down an overgrown path.

"You must get a lot of trespassers out here," I said, peering left and right at the overgrown brush. This far out, I couldn't hear the traffic of I-95, couldn't hear a single sign of life aside from our own.

"Not really," Simon said, picking up a fallen branch and using it as a makeshift walking stick.

"Come on," I pressed, "kids must party up here. I don't see any lights and we're, what, two miles from the nearest house? It seems like the ideal spot to trade ghost stories."

Simon shrugged. "That's just it. Around here, the cemetery *is* a ghost story, one that scares away those who don't understand it. And humans have always been afraid of what they don't understand."

We arrived at the site some fifteen minutes later, where a second surreal gate marked the property. In the distance, huddled around a grave, were three of Simon's fellow Friends of Marlowe, two women and one man, all of them as non-descript as Simon, if much shorter.

"Pleasure to meet you," I said, keeping it cordial.

They eyed Simon, as if asking permission, before they returned the gesture.

I peered into the freshly dug hole and studied the dirt-speckled casket, moments from being excavated. Worms and grubs writhed along the edges; their subterranean homes disturbed.

I should pause here in case our listeners are unfamiliar with the graveside journals. As far as I can tell, they've existed for as long as the Friends, which date back to Marlowe's founding. In a proverbial nutshell, every parish member is buried with a single leather-bound journal. And a pen of course. The idea is simple if perplexing: that these dearly departed will somehow communicate with the living via acid-free paper, that in death they'll inscribe hidden secrets and forbidden knowledge far past the comprehension of those six feet above. One year to the day of their burial—rain, snow, or shine—their bodies are dug up so their journals may be studied. What's written inside is usually cryptic, jotted in sentence fragments and non-sensical symbols. Many believe the journals are a hoax, that their pages have already been scribbled upon before each funeral. On this, I can't comment, but I can assure you what I read was…interesting.

But I'm getting ahead of myself.

Simon told me and the others to step back. A contraption was lowered into the grave. The casket was lifted and set down beside the stone. The Friends keep their markers simple, with names and dates and the same insignia for each: "A Friend in life, death, and beyond." The body in question belonged to a man named Frederick Pritchett, who died of natural causes at the reasonable age of eighty-four. Out of respect, I turned my head while Simon and his colleagues went about prying the casket open. Again, I studied the trees and brush and noted how civilization seemed much farther away than it surely was. Perhaps Simon was right. If I was kid, I'd stay away too.

Eventually, I heard the group gasp in awe. When I turned back, they held Frederick's posthumous writings, already thumbing through. As I approached, they closed the journal. A bit too quickly, I might add.

"It will be transported to the Marlowe Historical Society," Simon said, "where you'll be given full access."

"Come on," I said, "not even a peek?"

"You'll get much more than a peek, Mr. Knapp. Of that, I can assure you."

I told Simon that was agreeable, albeit reluctantly. Who can say I would be reading from the same journal and not some prop prepared for this occasion? But, I reminded myself, I was not a member of the Friends, and since few others were allowed a glimpse behind their curtain, I remained respectful. After all, I'd travelled a great distance and I couldn't let you down, listeners.

I peered toward Frederick. Whoever had done the embalming must have been an expert in their field. The process of decay had yet to interfere, and it felt entirely possible—perhaps even plausible—the man would open his eyes and ask what I thought of his inscription.

After that, I was ushered out of the cemetery. I followed Simon's car (a Jetta that looked and sounded older than I) to the Historical Society, a converted mill building located between a playground and a now-defunct automobile garage, each of its windows shattered by time, teens, or a mix of the two. Simon led me past the unmanned front desk, toward an elevator, which we rode two floors down.

"I'm afraid our section of the building is somewhat humble," he said during our descent. "A lot of folks don't even know we're here. That's probably for the best."

I asked what he meant but the elevator doors slid open, their mechanical whir masking my words.

"It's just up ahead," Simon said, and again his definition of distance was skewered. We passed countless basement archives, each of them holding public records and microfiche, all the artifacts that make up a town's past. The Society kept the space dim and cool. It smelled of mold. I spotted cobwebs and dust bunnies and more than once I heard scuttering.

"Here we are," Simon said, stopping in front of a door on our left. He pulled out a key, turned the lock, and presented a room stocked with floor-to-ceiling bookshelves, each of them secured behind a layer of protective glass. Judging by the leather spines, I could only assume this was the complete collection of graveside journals.

I was directed toward a table in the center of the room. Simon took a seat across from me and pulled Frederick's journal from his breast pocket. He set it down between us, fingers holding it shut.

"I'd like to have a few words first," Simon said, "if you don't mind."

"I thought I was the one asking questions."

"I find that questions are best kept a two-way street."

I fingered my collar, which seemed two sizes too tight. "Ask away."

"Why?"

I cleared my throat, which was suddenly facing a drought. If I'd had a bottle of whiskey beside me, as I do now, I would've helped myself. "Why what?"

"Why are you so interested in the journals?"

I shrugged. "Because that's what I do. That's what *New England Nightmares* is all about. Deep dives into local lore. All things macabre and unusual."

"I suppose the journals can be considered both," Simon said.

"I suppose so," I agreed, but what I didn't say, what I'm only admitting now, is that I hoped to find something profound within those leather covers.

That's the problem with my profession. Long-time listeners of the program are no doubt familiar with my sole paranormal experience but for any newbies, I'll make it quick.

When I was nine and living with my grandmother, having lost both parents to a freak plane crash, I stepped outside during the height of a blizzard. It had been snowing nearly ten hours, the world nothing but a white, cotton-like veil, and I found myself growing antsy. On the rickety back porch, I sensed I wasn't alone. There was movement in my periphery, a figure sitting in the swing as if it were a calm spring evening. At first, I thought—*hoped*—it was my grandmother. But what sat before me had no features to speak of and instead appeared as a rippling void, like the figure itself was a doorway, a hint at something close to our world, yet far removed. I asked what it wanted. It never told me. Instead, it stayed like that, swinging gently in the breeze. I ran inside, woke my grandmother up, but by the time I dragged her back outside, the figure was gone.

The reason I bring this up is because I've been pursuing the unknown ever since, hunting it down like Bigfoot himself. The problem is, once the unknown sees you coming, it keeps its distance. But with the journals, I sensed a change, a shifting tide if you'd like. I felt certain

I'd uncover something worthwhile, one step closer to the dragon I've been chasing.

But I couldn't tell Simon as much. I wasn't certain his faith system allowed such things as ghosts or featureless beings. Instead, I promised him this was for research, for shining a respectful light on the Friends. I thought at the time he believed me. Now, I'm not so sure.

"Is that good enough?" I asked next, watching his fingers clench the journal.

He sighed, broke into something like a smile, and let go. "Good enough for me."

He slid the journal across the table.

Now is a good time to mention my main source of research for this week's episode. I'd like to read a passage that summarizes what happened next better than I suspect I can.

As far as I know, Harold Svenson, author of *Grave Secrets: New England's Oldest Cemeteries*, is the only other non-member offered access to this archive. He writes "While the Marlowe graveside journals may seem like meaningless doodles, I must admit they have a certain effect on the reader, or at least they did for me. I began feeling nauseous and cold and was certain I'd been followed all the way back to my home. In the middle of night, I received strange phone calls from blocked numbers, whispering things too soft to discern. Perhaps the events are unrelated, a too-convenient coincidence, or perhaps what's written in these books are more than just words."

Frederick's journal was an even mix of symbols and sentence fragments. The more I read, the more I suspected some secret meaning, some message I was close to deciphering. The pages reminded me of an optical illusion, the kind that forms an image after you've crossed and uncrossed your eyes enough times. And speaking of eyes, mine felt dry and swollen. Even blinking hurt. My nose began to run.

"Here," Simon said, handing me a tissue.

After pressing it against my nostrils, it was sopping red. I held my head back, tasted pennies.

"Totally normal," Simon said. "Happens to all of us our first time. The words have a profound effect on the body. It's far from leisure reading."

"I'll say," I said, feeling pressure behind my eyes. "I suppose you don't have any aspirin hiding around here."

196

"We have many things hidden here, but I'm afraid aspirin isn't one of them."

From my vantage point, head still bent back, Frederick's messages seemed to swirl in the corner of my eye, tiny swarms of ants, but each time I looked that way, they were static.

"Tell me," Simon said, "is it what you expected?"

"I'm not sure what I expected, but it wasn't this. How can you make sense of it?"

"The same way any archeologist makes sense of cave paintings. It takes time and patience. That's what we consider ourselves here: archeologists."

"What's this one say?" I pointed toward Frederick's journal as I kept my bloody fingers away from its pages.

Simon pulled out a pair of reading glasses from his pocket. I didn't care for the way they magnified his eyes. They seemed too large now. Too close. I watched him read as if the words weren't jumbled. He muttered beneath his breath, nodded to himself. The strangest thing about Simon is that he had no discernable features aside from his height. He was the sort of man I couldn't pick out from a crowd, the kind that blends in without trying. In some ways, he reminded me of that faceless thing, swinging in the breeze.

"Interesting," Simon said.

"What is it?" I said, wondering if I'd need a second tissue.

He paused, choosing his response carefully. "I'm afraid I can't tell you what Frederick left for us. While I appreciate the spotlight you've chosen to shine on us, the Friends must keep what is written in the journals a secret. It's not for you to know. You understand." I noticed the lack of question marks here.

I nodded. "Loud and clear."

Simon's cell phone chimed. He studied the screen and excused himself, promising he'd be back to see me out.

When he stepped into the hall, I studied the journal once again, willing the words to form a passage, and when they didn't, I clenched my fists. I'd been sure this time, after so many failed visits, so many botched attempts at discovering the unknown. I'm not proud of what I did next, listeners, but I've always promised to tell you the truth. I shoved the sodden tissue in one pocket and Frederick's journal in the other. Simon's voice echoed in the hall. He sounded distant now. Perhaps he was speaking of official Friends' business. And perhaps I could use his distraction to my benefit.

I opened the door slowly, wincing at the way it creaked, not unlike the cemetery gate. Following the hallway, I came to an unfamiliar intersection. I turned left and passed more rooms filled with the past, until I found a set of stairs, which I took three at a time to the Historical Society's back exit.

I'll pause there. Not because I'm ashamed but because my glass is empty now. There, that's better. Cheers to those drinking along at home. I guess it's true, what they say. The better the booze, the less it burns. I'm used to bottom shelf but this one's much closer to the top. It's smooth and it cost me. But tonight's a special occasion.

You see, I have Frederick's journal here before me. I've tried reading it several times. While still illegible, I feel closer to cracking its code. And that's where you come in, faithful listeners. Perhaps hearing the words aloud will spark something in you. Perhaps one of you will understand. I've taken photos of the symbols and posted them to our Instagram page. The comments are rolling in. It appears some of your noses have already started to bleed, and those that have studied the images at length complain of feeling watched. I can attest to both.

The strangest thing is I believe I was *allowed* to take the journal, that Simon somehow planned on it. I suspect he *wants* these messages deciphered. Whether the Friends will live up to their name, or whether they're closer to foes, that's what we're about to find out.

Please excuse the knocking in the background. Someone's been trying to let themselves into my room. I can see the shadows of their feet beneath the door, but I won't peer through the peephole, even if I know what I'd find. No eyes staring back at me. No features to speak of.

Let's get started, shall we? It's time for the first live reading of a graveside journal. Lock your doors and turn up the volume. Snuggle beneath your favorite blanket. Fetch some fresh tissues. If the phone rings, don't answer it. You never know who might be on the other end.

LULLABY OF THE SPHERES

Christine Morgan

*T*he Moon, like a pearl
  Went 'round the World;
The World, as it spun
Went 'round the Sun.

Julia woke with it stuck in her head for some reason, a sing-song little ditty she could not identify or place. A quick online search as the coffee brewed turned up nothing helpful. She asked Bryce, over breakfast, if it sounded familiar, but he likewise drew a blank.

"Maybe you dreamed it?" he suggested.

"Must have," she said. "I'd about swear, though, I'd heard it before."

"Dreams can be weird that way. And you are dreaming for two." He rubbed an affectionate palm over her belly as he kissed her cheek, then nuzzled her neck. "My radiant, glowing goddess --"

"Oh, quit," she giggled. "Nothing radiant or glowing about bed-head, sleepshirt and jammie pants."

"To me, there is." He kissed her again, a long steamy lingering one on the mouth. "Wish I didn't have to go to work, so we could snuggle all day."

Julia nestled her head on his shoulder. "We couldn't do that anyway. Great-Aunt Linda's coming over to help with the nursery, remember?"

"Are you really sure you want her to? I know things were always weird with your family --"

"It's okay. She's one of the good ones."

"She pinched my dad's ass at the wedding reception."

"He was shaking it in everybody's face, thinking he had the moves like Jagger!"

"We just *had* to have an open bar."

"Your mother laughed so hard she fell off her chair."

"Open bar," Bryce repeated, with a rueful shake of his head. "Still, okay, if you're sure. It'd be nice for the baby to have some connections on your side, especially with mine all being fucking bonkers."

"Hey, mine are bonkers too!"

"Totally different bonkers."

"True 'dat."

They finished breakfast, Bryce insisted on doing the dishes and cleaning the kitchen before heading to work, and Julia seized the opportunity for a quick shower. Bed-head tamed, sleepshirt and jammie pants swapped for a comfy dress, she bid him goodbye and -- so wifely! -- waved from the porch as he drove off.

Their house was nothing much, nothing special, by most peoples' standards. Barely more than a cottage, two beds one bath, tucked away on a corner lot in a quiet neighborhood. Compared to the groaning ancestral manse she'd grown up in, overloaded with musty antiques and even mustier customs, it was a bright little patch of freedom, something of their very own. To decorate and do with as they pleased, without worrying about what was 'proper' or not. If she wanted to paint the exterior purple with polka-dots, if Bryce chose to display his LEGO collection in the living room, if they put a twenty-foot fiberglass dinosaur sculpture in the yard, so what?

Not that they really *were* doing that -- aside from the LEGO -- but it was the most wonderfully liberating sensation to know that they *could*.

The second bedroom, aka the nursery, was a cozy nook of morning sunshine and dappled afternoon tree-shadow, furnished in simple basics and clean lines rather than the ornate elaborate heaviness of her own childhood. The wallpaper was pale blue, subtly patterned with clouds; the ceiling, a deeper blue overhung with wispy swags of gossamer white. It gave the impression of floating in a serene sky, peaceful and safe, above it all. As an extra touch, the ceiling was also strewn with tiny silver stars, invisible until the lights were out, then coming alive in glittering whorls of constellations, galaxies, and nebulae.

Generations of her forebears would have absolutely *loathed* it.

Even if she'd decorated it with saints and angels, turning it into some godly celestial heaven scape, they would have loathed it. Stern and strict rigidity, confinement, oppression, and a stifling, suffocating *order* was the manner by which they'd lived, the manner in which she'd been raised. Higher powers were to be *feared*, placated, and obeyed without question.

Her own father had, to give him credit, *tried* to escape. And, for a few years, succeeded. But then, cruel fate came calling in the form of a grim day in September, a day forever marked by tragedy on a nationwide, even global, scale.

Not that Julia had been old enough to understand what was going on. Only that her mommy and daddy had gone away, this time never to return, and everything changed forever and forever. She'd been taken to the other house, the big dark heavy scary house, not allowed to bring more than a few of her toys, not allowed to wear what she wanted or eat what she liked, not allowed to laugh or run or make up stories.

"Screw that," she said now, cradling her baby-bulge in both hands. To the ever-popular ultrasound question, she and Bryce had chosen to wait and be surprised. "If you want a rocket ship bed when you're bigger, or a castle or racecar or treehouse, that's what you'll have."

Great-Aunt Linda showed up half an hour late, with lattes and donuts, and a carful of boxes. Although well into her seventies, she was spry as a gazelle, fond of bold colors and big clunky jewelry. She bounded up the porch steps more energetically than Julia would have been able to when *not* seven months preggers, smooched a fire-engine-red lipstick print on her cheek, and bustled her way into the kitchen without waiting to be invited.

"Your house is so cute I could just about barf," she declared. "You look good, too. Baby weight in all the right places. I bet Bryce *loves* what it's done for your boobies."

"Uh ... thank you, I think?"

"Just remind him, those are for the *baby*! Be too sore for anything else, more's the pity. Isn't it the way of things? Finally get a nice plump rack, and --"

"Are we one-hundred-percent sure you're related to the rest of them?"

"Sadly so, sweetie, sadly so. Black sheep, like your dad. Twigs off the rogue twisted branch of the ol' family tree. Drives them right up the wall, but they can't prune us all."

"I'm so glad I got away," Julia said. "It's horrible and ungrateful to say, but --"

"Ah-ah-ah, no you don't. It's not horrible, it's not ungrateful. I'm glad you did too. There were times when you were little I'd think about snatching you out of that dismal museum and keeping you for my own. Wish I had. Sorry I didn't. What matters is, you turned out okay."

"I guess I did."

"And that bun in your oven will, too. Wait 'til you see what I brought!"

"Granty-Lin, I told you you didn't have to --"

"Pssh. No, no, no. This is good stuff, sweetie. Found it in the attic, belonged to *my* great-aunt, Nana Ruth. Don't suppose you --?"

"Nana Ruth? I remember her, or I think I do, just barely. Or at least her being talked about. Didn't she end up in a ... um ... psychiatric hospital?"

Linda rolled her eyes and chomped a big bite of donut. "You mean looney bin, according to your ding-dong cousins? Who probably told you she was a witch and a murderess, didn't they?"

"Well ..."

"As far as most of the family was concerned, they might've preferred either of those to the truth. Now, yes, to be fair, she *did* end up in a looney bin, and not just because in those days people like her were considered mentally ill --"

"People like her?"

"Gays, sweetie. Nana Ruth wasn't a spinster or old maid or whatever they called unmarried women back then. She liked the ladies, if you know what I mean."

"I ... yeah ... wow ... really?"

"Not in any slutting around way; don't get me wrong. She and Elsbeth were devoted to each other. The kind who'd be described at their funerals as 'dearest friends and lifelong companions' though they slept in the same room for over sixty years."

Although still full from breakfast, Julia picked up a donut. Glazed buttermilk bar, her favorite. "I had no idea. It's ... uh ... cool though that, uh, you're so cool with it ... I mean ..."

Linda gave her a look. "Some day when you're old enough, I'll tell you how *I* spent the summer of 1967

--"

"*Old* enough?" She gestured at herself. "I'm --"

"Still a kid to me, sweetie. Still a kid to me. Anyway, never mind all that. It wasn't being a lesbian that got Nana Ruth sent to the funny farm, but she didn't snap and go murdering anybody either. It was a breakdown, simple as that. A stress breakdown. You see, she was a woman ahead of her time. Smart as any man, smarter than most, and not afraid to show it. But they wouldn't let her go to college, wouldn't let her study the sciences ... and by 'they,' I mean society in general, as well as the family. Back then, some things were Just Not Done."

"Even nowadays, there's too much of that hanging around," Julia said.

"Oh, don't get me started!" Linda hopped up from the dining nook. "Let me bring in those boxes, though. I found a bunch of Ruth's things, and one in particular she might want you to have."

"What is it?"

"Something she gave you when you were a baby."

On that tantalizing note, she commenced lugging boxes, refusing to let Julia help lift or carry. The boxes bore every sign of having been stored in an attic for decades, and the contents, as Linda rummaged, looked to consist primarily of books, with other oddball items mixed in. There was a light-up globe of the moon, another globe depicting the night sky with constellations, a polished brass sextant that could have come from an 18th century sailing ship, a set of handheld telescopes, a mounted telescope more complicated than Julia had ever seen, some sort of weird gadget all gears and revolving parts, and ...

"Aha!" said Linda with satisfaction, lifting out a case like a musical instrument might have been kept in.

She unlatched it and opened the lid, revealing a cluster of swirled-glass baubles on fine wires. Spherical, of differing sizes and colors, depending from a delicate metal mechanism on a hook.

"Oh my god," Julia whispered.

"You *do* remember?" Linda asked. "You know what it is?"

"It's the solar system. It's a mobile. It ... it used to hang over my crib when I was a baby. I'd watch it go around and around ..."

Hesitantly, as if it might shatter, she brushed a fingertip over the largest sphere, the brilliant grapefruit-sized blown glass Sun. Its surface felt cool and smooth against her skin, yet a warm tingle seemed to spread up her arm.

Not to scale, of course, obviously; in third grade or so, her class had done the thing where they took soccer balls and walnuts and marbles out onto the playground to try and grasp the vastness of size and distance and space. This mobile was far from astronomically accurate in that regard, but the intricacy and detail was nonetheless amazing. She marveled at it, the storminess of Jupiter with its myriad moons, Saturn's rings, the frosted blue-green jewel of Earth and its pale lunar companion *(the Moon like a pearl)*, even a garland of irregular glass beads meant to represent the span of the rocky asteroid belt.

"I cried," she said, tears welling at the memory. "Every night when they'd put me to bed in the other house, so dark and strange, and I'd lay there looking up seeing only shadows. They wouldn't let me bring it, even that one little thing. Oh, how I cried! I missed my parents, my home, everything, so much ... I'd never felt so small and alone."

"I really should have snatched you out of there --"

"It's all right; like you said, I still turned out okay."

208

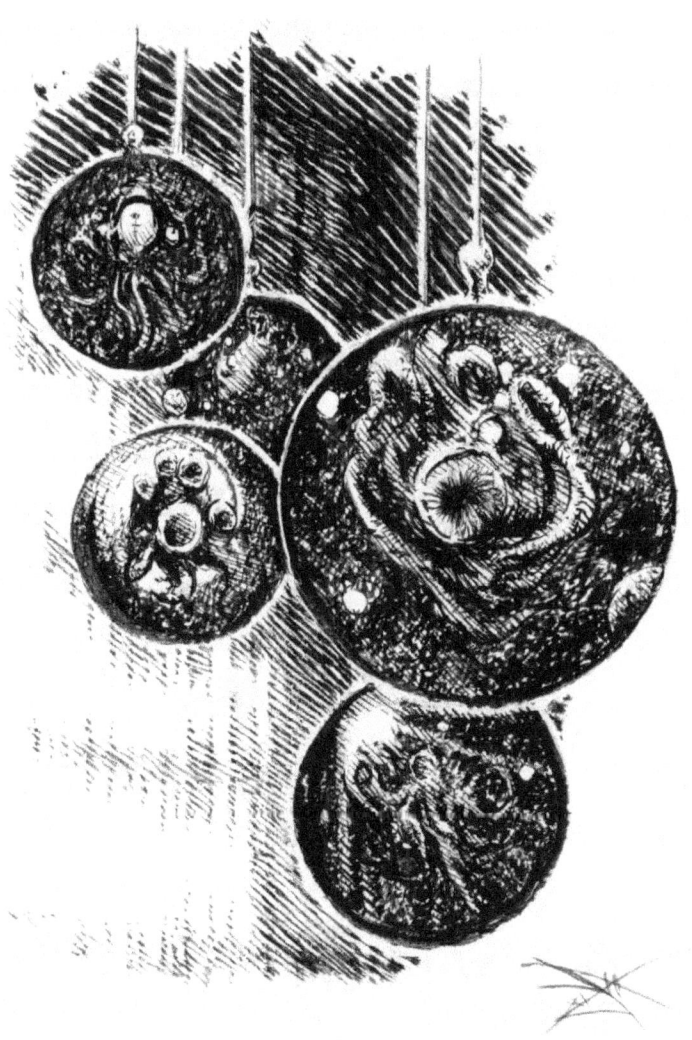

Linda gingerly raised the mobile from its case, which was fitted and lined with velvet, also very much like that of a musical instrument. "Elsbeth was a glass artist. This was her and Ruth's gift when you were born; your daddy always was one of Ruth's favorites. Oh, he'd spend hours as a boy playing with those telescopes and that star-globe, talking about becoming an astronaut someday."

As she held it aloft, the wires adjusted until each sphere was balanced at roughly the same level, with the smaller satellites suspended around their larger partners. The entire contraption hung, steady and even, until Linda flicked a tiny switch on the mechanism. Within its housing, a motor came alive with a faint hum. The wires began to move, each on its own rotation, carrying planets and moons and asteroids around the course of their orbits in a dance of beautiful simplicity and incredible complexity.

And, also from within the mechanism, a gentle music-box melody played. A melody Julia instantly recognized, one her mind put words to. As if someone, long ago, had sung those words to her, accompanying the tune.

The Moon, like a pearl

Went 'round the World;

The World, as it spun

Went 'round the Sun.

She let the tears flow, but they were happy tears as well as sad, bittersweet tears for all she'd lost, and for what was not so fully lost after all.

"When you told me your plans for decorating the nursery," Linda said, "I thought, if I could find it, you might want to hang it over the crib. Then I thought I might as well bring the rest of the boxes; no sense leaving them sit and gather more dust. If nothing else, some of those books and telescopes might be worth --"

Julia, careful not to jostle the mobile, hugged her tight. "I do, it'll be perfect! Thank you so much!"

The nursery had come together with almost ridiculous ease, from star-speckled blue curtains to a hammock of silvery netting filled with soft toys. Framed astronomy photos -- Earth from space, Horsehead Nebula, Andromeda Galaxy -- hung on the walls. The changing table was stocked with diapers, wipes, and powder. The drawers held plenty of onesies and blankies and cute little outfits. The constellation star-globe perched on a high shelf, beside the lambent Moon lamp and a mini home planetarium projection device with color-changing lenses.

Pride of place, though, of course, went to the crib, and the solar system mobile suspended above it. As the last few weeks of pregnancy wore on and the nesting frenzy faded into let's-get-this-over-with-already impatience, Julia had taken to spending most of her spare time in the rocker beside the crib, a lunar-phases fleece throw over her lap, watching the lovely glass baubles revolve in their intricate courses.

Some nights, she even slept there, feeling bad about disturbing Bryce with all her tossing and turning and heaving and wallowing as she tried to find a comfortable position in bed. Which, even if by some miracle she did, she'd then have to ruin within twenty minutes by getting up to pee. Or the baby would start in kicking, or doing somersaults or Olympic gymnastics tryouts in there, by the feel.

Bryce insisted he didn't mind, but she told him he should get what sleep he could now, and then she'd be more than glad to have him take over midnight feedings and changings for a while, giving her a chance to catch up.

Besides, the mobile helped with that too. The mobile and its soothing music-box melody, its lullaby of the spheres. Nothing at all like Holst's "The Planets;" awesome as those pieces were, they were far too stirring. The Mars one, especially. How could anyone drift off into dreamland with *that* going on? However active the baby was being, within moments of the first notes, the uterine acrobatics settled right down.

Things needed, after all, to be kept calm and quiescent. Mellow. At peace. At rest. As it was, as it had been, as it should be.

Quiescent.

The steady motion, constant, hypnotic. Orbits within orbits, synchronous, serene. As if the entirety of the cosmos, the very essence of nature and the universe and reality itself, depended upon it.

Strange thoughts to have, maybe, as she sat there rocking and humming along, but, given hormones wildly out of whack, she'd certainly had crazier ones. Some of which, she supposed, she could attribute to Nana Ruth's journals, detailing the difficulties and frustrations she'd faced throughout her long life.

Was it any wonder the stress eventually got to her, wore her down? Led her along more and more obscure paths, into esoteric theories and questionable controversies? Driven to the point of obsession, of conspiracy? Toward what could readily be deemed delusion, paranoia, and madness?

212

After all, even esteemed learned men like Galileo and Copernicus had been persecuted relentlessly for daring to challenge commonly-held 'truths.' Something as fundamental as the notion of the Earth going around the Sun, instead of the other way around ... of the Earth *not*, in fact, being the center and focus of all Creation ...

For crying out loud, here they were in the 21st century, and some still believed the Earth was flat. The Moon landing being faked or staged, or the Area 51, Bermuda Triangle, or Atlantis people had more credibility.

The melody trailed off into silence, the revolutions of the baubles stilled, and the baby stirred. As much as the baby *could* stir; this close to term, already in head-down position, there wasn't much room to maneuver. The sensation was ... disturbing, to say the least.

"All right, all right," Julia said, rubbing the solid rounded swell. She heaved herself up from the rocker, waddled to the bathroom, waddled back, reset the mobile, and sank into her seat again with a sigh.

Of course, toward the end, Nana Ruth *must* have been out of her mind. Perhaps senile, emotionally devastated by losing her 'lifelong companion' to cancer, ostracized by most of her remaining family, her name and legacy all but stricken from scientific or professional records, if it had ever been there to begin with.

Why not, under such circumstances, fall deeper into her theories? Why not go public with her findings, with what she'd witnessed through the electrospectum telescope she herself had modified? Humanity had the right -- the vital *need*! -- to know the truth, distressing though it might be, whether they wanted to believe it or not!

Damn it; she should have gotten something to drink while she was up, instead of now having to heave herself out of the rocker all over again and waddle all the way to the kitchen for iced tea. Which her compressed bladder would make her pay for in another twenty minutes anyway ...

Someone else, of course, was none too happy about getting up and moving either, shifting and pushing from within. Julia groaned at a dull, aching pulsation -- not onset of labor, she knew by now; just her lower back and pelvis protesting the strain of supporting the excess mass.

She got tea, contemplated a sandwich but decided against it, and returned to the nursery. To the rocker. To the mobile and the lullaby.

Calm. Content. Quiescent.

Just as she remembered, however vaguely, feeling in her own earliest childhood, watching the baubles revolve in their mystic patterns, listening to the melody, relaxing, resting.

Not seized by any sudden, petulant, tantrumy urge to disrupt, to destroy.

Julia paused mid-rock. Talk about strange thoughts ... where had *that* one come from? Had she let the ravings in Nana Ruth's journal get to her more than she realized?

Such a tragedy for someone so brilliant to succumb to insanity, postulating wild scenarios of unfathomably immense, indescribable, eternal entities existing beyond humble human comprehension. Or, to further speculate that, not only was their own Earth a speck so minuscule as to be all but subatomic by comparison, but their own solar system -- trillions of miles across! -- amounted to little more than a pretty trinket, a distraction to fascinate and lull the restlessness of some nascent Other, some Being, the rotation of moons and planets for billions of years mere moments in its infinite infancy ...

A cradle-mobile for an eldritch godling, nothing more. A godling who, just as a baby eventually learned to pull itself upright in its crib, might tire of merely watching the spheres go around and around to their celestial tune. Who might reach for them, jostle them from their orbital courses, set them swinging and swaying and crashing together in wild abandon and discordant arrhythmia. Or perhaps seize at them, seize the largest and brightest and shiniest of all, tug it loose from its moorings. A glorious golden ball of seething fires to play with, leaving the others anchorless, adrift, dark, cold, and lost ...

Drowsily, Julia rocked and rocked, hands folded protectively over her belly, gaze following the mobile's hypnotic motion, its gentle lullaby soothing her.

As it had done when she was a child. As it would for her own child.

As it did, perhaps, on a scale far beyond her capacity to imagine, for something newborn yet ageless, calmed and quiescent.

For now.

Smiling to herself, lulled by the sweet melody, she drifted off to sleep ...

o   nly to waken with a gasp and a start at Bryce's hands shaking her by the shoulders, Bryce's voice urgently calling her name.

The fractured remnants of a dream wheeled about in her head, a shattered kaleidoscope of monstrous images and vast distances, desolation, abandonment, loneliness. She jerked so violently she almost upset the rocker, triggering a spasm of pain in her lower back.

"Bryce?" she asked, groggily, pawing her hair from her eyes. "What are you doing home? What time is it? How long was I --"

He hugged her close, and she felt him shaking, clammy with cold sweat. Above them, the mobile had slowed its motions, the melody winding down into sluggish, plinking individual notes. The light through the window was weirdly *wrong,* somehow, a fuming wildfire-red that seemed to pulsate in the air.

Bryce rattled off spates of words almost too fast to understand: emergency alert, national crisis, massive solar flares, geomagnetic storms, electronics, the government, the military. "... phones out ...

radio ... the car on the fritz, its computer all zapped to shit or something ... close enough luckily to run the rest of the way ..."

"Wait," pleaded Julia. "I'm still out of it, give me a second --"

He kept right on going. Babbling, he was babbling, in a panic. "... what they thought Y2K would be, when we were kids ... shut everything down ... or a global EMP ... only bigger, only worse ..."

She'd never seen him like this and couldn't handle it, flinging her hands over her face and screaming, "Bryce! What the hell are you *talking* about?"

"Something ... Jules, something's wrong with the sun ... maybe even a supernova, and if it is --"

Her nightmare recurred full-force, swamping her in a bone-deep, helpless dread. The glorious golden bauble, the prize, so shiny, so enticing ... so close, almost within reach ... almost ... with determined effort, straining ... closer, and closer ...

There.

All in the same instant, the mobile went silent and still, a wrenching agony seized her entire midsection, and a rush of hot liquid soaked her thighs and her butt and the cushion beneath.

Labor ... her water had broken ... the baby was coming, coming *now*, with immediate undeniable urgency ...

As, in sudden and terrible total finality, absolute darkness fell.

PICTURES OF MY FORMER SELF

Terry Campbell

It's such an odd phenomenon, this concept of sanity. There seems to be a dividing line in the tedious balance of nature. The human mind appears to ride an invisible seesaw, teetering back and forth between the normal world and the unknown. One may live his entire life in the grip of insanity, and yet not know his true state of being.

For that matter, how does a person know he is the one with the wrongful mind? Why is he the insensate one, and not the rest of the world?

But enough dribble, I've babbled on long enough. I had never given much thought to the human mind and its limitations, that is until the passing of my uncle Myacin.

As a result of being raised in an orphanage, I was unaware that I had any family.

A lawyer representing my uncle's estate in Brazil contacted me at the Wittington Home for Boys.

There was no list of relatives when I entered the orphanage, but apparently my uncle had kept a family record.

The lawyer discussed the details of my uncle's death and the will within which he had left his fortune to me. His estate consisted of a small beachside house on the Brazilian coastline, some two hundred miles north of Rio de Janeiro. I reluctantly agreed, as busy as I had been, to take the next available flight and finalize all the legal matters.

On the flight, I mulled over thoughts of my late uncle. I wondered why I had never been told, especially as an adult, that I had a living relative. I peered out the plane window, studying the formidable statue of Christ the Redeemer atop Corcovado. What a spectacular sight it was.

I was amazed by how modernized the city appeared as I stepped from the plane. I suppose I assumed, in my ignorance, that the entire continent of South America was nothing but a rain forest.

The Lawyer greeted me at the gate. He was warm and friendly as he explained the will and all the formalities therein.

In the hotel lobby, we discussed my uncle's house over a few drinks. After a considerable amount of small talk, I was given directions. I thanked Mr. Laos for his graciousness, phoned a taxi, and waited patiently outside for its arrival.

As the taxicab weaved through a conglomerate of hilly roads, the Atlantic Ocean peeked through in intervals. I wiped sweat from my brow as a warm wind flowing from the open window bathed my face.

Coming from a Northeastern beach area, I had grown accustomed to cool damp weather and had not been looking forward to the sultry climate of Rio.

Mr. Laos had told me a British gentleman named Ebholtd, who had tended to my Uncle Myacin, had been minding the estate while he awaited my arrival. As the cab pulled up in front of my uncle's house, I was immediately stricken by the surprising number of iguanas that inhabited the shoreline. As I stepped out of the cab, I noticed that the reptiles lay there motionless, basking in the afternoon sun. As if this place was theirs as much as mine. I couldn't explain it, but the whole thing struck me as peculiar.

After the cab took its leave, I walked up the weathered steps, surmounted the shaky porch, and knocked on the door. Deadbolts pulled back and the door swung inward.

Ebholtd was as I had imagined. A smallish, elderly man garnered in a faded black tuxedo. The dress shoes adorning his feet were desperately in need of a shine. His tight and pallid face was pierced by small, dark eyes, tufts of white hair jutting behind the ears. He greeted me with a low, wheezy voice that matched the rest of his visage splendidly.

I introduced myself as Devin Inglemeyer, the long-lost nephew of my late uncle, Myacin Devonshire.

"Ah, yes."Master Inglemeyer. Do come in. I've been expecting you for several days now."

I stepped inside as Ebholtd took my bags. The virtual ease with which he lifted the heavy baggage impressed me. Even walking with a noticeable stoop, he seemed not to suffer as he wielded the luggage. Truly an interesting man.

The front room held all the charm of a cozy New England bed-and-breakfast. The low lighting, combined with the dark paneled walls, lent the room a homey atmosphere that delighted me almost immediately. The sofa, chairs and coffee table were obvious antiques. Probably brought from the Old World.

A sprawling rug of Asian origin spread out just in front of a huge brick fireplace. As I pondered the need for a fireplace in such a warm climate my eyes latched onto the portrait above the mantle.

It portrayed a dashing young man, early thirties I surmised, adorned in a splendid and colorful jacket. He was seated in a leather chair and drawing from a dark wooden pipe. I assumed the portrait was of my late uncle, but what really caught my eye was the boy standing next to him.

A young lad of about eight or nine, his features painted so exquisitely (minus brush strokes in a way I thought capable only of Michelangelo's touch) that it almost resembled a photograph. Something about the painting stirred a recognition deep in my bowels.

"Your uncle was a fine man, sir."

Ebholtd said.

"A fine man indeed."

"Who is the boy?"

"I know not, sir."

"A relative, perhaps?"

"Doubtful."

Ebholtd answered.

"Your uncle knew of no living relatives. It was only through the lawyers' diligent efforts that your whereabouts were discovered."

I nodded my head. It was strange that I had never known any of my relatives. Or that I even had any.

"Would you care for some tea, sir?"

Ebholtd asked, interrupting my thoughts.

"Yes, thank you."

"Why don't you retire to the parlor, and I'll bring the tea when it's ready."

"Lead on."

I followed Ebholtd into another small, poorly lit room that was furnished by still more antiques. A draped bay window looked out over the shoreline, and I could hear the faint crash of the waves. It was quite peaceful, apart from the room's decor. Scattered about, in an array of poses, were small stuffed animals.

"Your uncle was quite an avid taxidermist."

Ebholtd said.

It wasn't the presence of stuffed animals that baffled me, but rather the sequences that they had been immortalized in.

A rat poised over the dead body of another rat and chewing at its eyes. A vampire bat, its vicious teeth locked onto the throat of a small kitten. A large bird, perhaps a buzzard, pulling a long string of sinew from the flanks of a hare. An iguana, the legs of a small animal dangling from its gaping maw.

All were mounted in violent, albeit natural, poses.

Ebholtd, sensing my shock, spoke up.

"Master Devonshire enjoyed displaying his work in truly life-like poses, ones that mirrored nature and the everyday struggle for survival."

"I see."

I stated, attempting to buffer my shock.

"I shall return with the tea."

I retired that evening to the bedroom that had been my Uncle Myacin's. As I lay under the covers, marveling at how homey and familiar the old house was, I made up my mind that I would stay for a week or so before deciding what to do with my uncle's estate. I even considered keeping it and using it as a vacation home. It felt so welcoming. I was finding it hard to consider selling it.

As I lay in the darkness, I began to feel the urge for a late-night snack. Ebholtd had bedded down for the evening, so I slid out from underneath the covers stepped out into the hallway quietly, so as not to wake the kindly old gentleman.

Arming myself with a warm glass of milk and a toasted cheese sandwich, I made my way for the parlor.

I liked the atmosphere, despite the odd displays of animal life. As I sat down on the loveseat, the multitude of beady eyes glaring down caught my attention. I would not notice until later that one of the animal displays had been removed.

As I took a small sip of milk and was about to bite into my sandwich, I noticed the dead rat on the floor. I started as I rested the sandwich on the end table.

Slowly approaching the revolting creature, I noticed that its hair was wet and matted, a dark smear of blood staining its back. Cautiously, I kicked it to make sure it was dead. It didn't move. Hastening back to the kitchen, I retrieved a broom and dustpan. Just as I positioned the broom to scoop the rat into the pan, it squealed shrilly and leapt to its feet. Stumbling back, I watched as the rat streaked into a hole under the lamp table.

Once my nerves began to calm, I managed to convince myself that the rat had been either unconscious or playing dead.

Returning the broom and pan, I paused to wash my hands of any filth that might have adhered to them. I thought of my sandwich, which I wasn't certain that I wanted to finish, but decided to give it a try.

As I made my way down the hall, another rat scurried out from under the hat rack. Infuriated by the presence of vermin in my home,

I grabbed a small vase and lobbed it at the offending beast. I know I hit the thing square, but the vase bounced off it and shattered as it hit the floor. The rat disappeared into a hole that, curiously, I had not noticed earlier.

At first, I thought the vase had caused the hole, but upon closer inspection, I found that the force of the vase had merely opened a concealed entrance. Curious, I pushed on the door a little more. Groaning as it slid inward, I poked my head in, the fleeing rodent totally forgotten. Feeling along the wall for a light switch, I found none. Reaching above my head I felt a string. Jerking on it, a dim bulb lit up overhead.

A concrete staircase descended into a darkness that I felt an inquisitive need to explore. Reaching out to grip the handrail, I quickly withdrew when I noticed the iguana perched atop. My heart pounding, I stared into the reptile's red eyes. It sat nonchalantly, as if it had as much right to the banister as I. Composing myself, I shuffled down the stairs, giving the lizard a wide berth.

By the time I reached the bottom, I was in total darkness. Managing to find a light switch, I flicked it on.

This was apparently the room where my uncle practiced his hobby. The basement was quite small, considering the size of the house. In the center was a table bolstered by folding legs. On top were several knives, scalpels, various jars of paint, chunks of balsa wood, a bin of glass eyes, and other taxidermy equipment. The rest of the basement was apparently used for storage. Pieces of furniture with sheets thrown over them lined the back wall.

Approaching the table to inspect my uncle's tools, I picked up a stuffed raven, minus its glass eyes. My uncle must have been working on this at the time of his passing. Setting the bird back down I reached for the tray of knives. As I looked upon the implements, that same odd sensation of recognition from when I had seen the portrait swept over me. I felt familiar with taxidermy, even though I had never studied the hobby before.

Pushing the tray back to its original spot I yawned. The evening's events had seemed to tire me more than I realized. Turning off the basement light, I ascended the steps, once again hugging the innermost rail to avoid the iguana. Which still stared at me menacingly with its beady blood-red eyes.

The more I explored my uncle's home, the more disturbing facts I discovered. Ebholtd directed me that morning to my uncle's private library.

It was aesthetically pleasing, the entirety of the wall constructed of oak and stained in a dark, mahogany finish. Next to the room's single window, was a large roll-top desk, stained in that same mahogany color. The deep plush carpet made me feel that I was floating as I crossed the room. Sitting atop the shelves, amidst the hundreds of books, were more disturbing mountings of small animals.

Perhaps the most unsettling of all was another painting of my Uncle Myacin and that strange boy.

The boy was so familiar to me that I began to assume that he was my uncle's son, a cousin that I didn't know I had. Perhaps he had died, thus allowing me to be Myacin's last relative.

I dismissed the thought, sliding down into a recliner in the corner of the library with a few books I had pulled from the shelf. The first one had the odd title Aiyk-Shamir. Flipping open the pages I began to read.

Many of the passages were scribed in a language which I could not decipher. Some passages were in English, speaking of an ancient evil being, apparently the product of some age-old local superstition. Aiyk-Shamir was a great lizard-man who held power over all reptiles. According to the beliefs of the local religion, Aiyk-Shamir and others of his kind had existed since the dawn of time. They had eventually been captured, where upon they reverted to the egg from which they had come. Now the horrid gods lay hidden, awaiting their hatching, the day when their horrors would again return and claim the world. Large cults worshipped these loathsome gods. Many of the believers had been given the ability to reanimate dead tissue, both that of animals and humans alike. I flipped a few more pages, and came upon a startling, repulsive artist's rendition of Aiyk-Shamir. The drawing depicted it as tall and scaly, yet moist, as if its scales oozed some bodily secretion. It had long, thin appendages that resembled human arms and legs, with long, black claws sprouting from the fingertips. But what was most distressing, was the being's head. It seemed disproportionately larger than the body. Scaly like the rest of the creature, but somehow it did not seem reptilian. Scales hung loosely over its face. Huge folds draped over the cheekbones. The mouth was barely visible over the dangling skin, but a long black tongue protruded from under a nose which consisted of only two small slits. Its eyes seemed to glow blood-red and the head was adorned by no ears. Although this was merely a pen and ink illustration, it had a feeling of life.

I slammed the book shut in disgust. It disturbed me that my uncle would be involved with such foolishness, but I decided not to judge him.

The other books I had chosen also contained verses pertaining to Aiyk-Shamir and his evil followers. I had never realized that such strange cults abounded in South America but, considering the virtual melting-pot of inhabitants, mysterious religions probably were more common than I initially thought.

Closing the cover of my last book I rubbed my eyes. The sky had darkened, and as I glanced through the curtains, I could see black storm clouds blowing off the ocean. I closed the drapes and turned to my uncle's desk. As I sat at the rolling chair I probed through the paperwork scattered across the top.

There was nothing of any major interest- bills, returned checks, receipts, and the like. I opened the side drawer and pulled out a battered old loose-leaf notebook stuffed with dry, yellowed pages.

Opening the pages revealed a journal entry. This was my Uncle Myacin's diary. Interested, I turned to the middle of the notebook and began to read.

Journal Entry—March 20, 1960

Oh, but if I could only know the exact date and the exact time. The incubation is surely reaching its final stages. All the signs are there. But alas, I must wait. I shall continue my work as planned, for all is going well. The things I've learned, the sights I've seen.

What did all this mean? What was my uncle speaking of? I turned a few more pages and read on.

Journal Entry—November 3, 1960

The boy is doing well. The tragedy that he experienced seems to have had no permanent hold on his mind. Sometimes, I curse myself. If there had been any other way, I would surely have done it. But my choice was a simple one. There could only be one way.

The boy! Could the boy mentioned in this passage be the same boy in the portraits?

Journal Entry—January 2, 1961

It is a new year, and with it comes renewed hope. I am getting much closer now, closer than I ever dared dream. I can only guess that with each degree of strength I gain it is a sign that the time of the hatchings draws nearer. Then, the day of Aiyk-Shamir and the Ancient Ones will arrive.

I slammed the diary shut. Aiyk-Shamir. The Ancient Ones. Hints of hatchlings.

Could it be that my uncle believed in the nonsensical ravings I had read earlier? Could it be that my uncle had been directly involved with this cult? And what of the boy? Where did this poor child fit into all of this? Had my uncle been engaged in something horrible, such as kidnapping? Had the mysterious boy been a hapless child who had been abducted and forced to commit serious crimes?

I shuddered at the thought. I had to find out the truth, and I suspected Ebholtd knew more about this boy than he was telling me.

Just then, I noticed movement from one of the bookshelves. The iguana that I had earlier believed to be stuffed was animated. As I stared into its unblinking eyes, watched its black tongue slither in and out, my heart began to pound. Continuing to hold its gaze, I could not look away.

For the third time since entering this home, I sensed that tinge of familiarity. It frightened me yet filled me with a feeling of great content.

There was much more to my uncle than I had imagined, and I wondered how deeply involved with the Aiyk-Shamir cult he had been. Most of all, I wondered who the boy was.

"I believe I have some explaining to do, Master Inglemeyer."
Ebholtd said when I questioned him.

"Yes, that would be nice."

I answered quaintly.

"There is much about Myacin Devonshire that you do not know."

"I have become aware of that recently. Could you let me in on it, starting with the boy in the paintings? You said earlier that you did not know who he was, but I think that may not be the case."

Ebholtd nodded and reclined onto the parlor sofa. Sighing deeply, he loosened his bowtie and leaned back.

"Yes. Yes, I know who he was. He was a nephew of your Uncle Myacin."

I had been right. The boy was an unknown cousin of mine.

"The boy's parents were brutally murdered before his eyes by members of an evil cult."

I sat straight up, wide-eyed.

"Aiyk-Shamir?"

"Yes. You've heard of them."

"I read about them in the library."

"After his parents' death, the boy moved here and lived with Master Devonshire. I remember him well. He was a quiet lad, rarely ever spoke. I always assumed that his shyness was due to the tragedy he had experienced. He took right up with your uncle and they became the closest of companions."

I felt somewhat relieved. Just knowing that my uncle had not been involved in kidnapping or the like set my mind at ease.

"There's more."

Ebholtd said.

"Your uncle didn't die in this house, as you may have been led to believe."

I nodded. No one had told me differently, yet I had assumed he had died here. Leaning forward, I struggled to better hear his low, soft voice.

"Your uncle passed away in the confines of a mental hospital"

"What?"

I exclaimed.

"A mental hospital?"

Ebholtd nodded.

"I am afraid so."

"But why? Was it the cult? Was my uncle deeply involved?"

Ebholtd paused, staring straight ahead.

"That is all,"

He muttered.

"I'll tell you more some other time, Master Inglemeyer."

I decided not to press the issue. I was sure Ebholtd knew more, but I would find out in time.

"Ebholtd, where is my uncle buried?"

Ebholtd pointed towards the rear of the house.

"There is a small necropolis atop a hill not far from the house. He is buried there alongside his dear wife, Lily Devonshire."

"I think I would like to see his grave."

I said as I rose from the chair.

"I shall return shortly."

Exiting through the back door I headed across the sand toward the grassy hills beyond the beach house, absorbing the beaming warming rays of the sun as I walked. My skin had started to dry and flake in the days since my arrival, but I was beginning to enjoy the warm, humid atmosphere.

It did not take me long to reach the little cemetery.

The area was very small, with only about a dozen markers. I wondered if any of the other occupants were relatives of mine, in addition of course to my aunt and uncle. Perhaps I would ask Ebholtd later.

Pushing open the rusted front gate of the cemetery I made my way towards what appeared to be a fresh grave. Reaching the marker, I stopped and read its façade.

"Myacin Devonshire. Born April 12, 1915. Died June 2, 1992".

I glanced at the headstone of my Aunt Lily, more worn and cracked than my uncle's. Lily had died in 1963. I sighed as I shook my head. Myacin had lived a long time without her. It was a good thing that the boy had come along. Perhaps his presence had filled a void in my uncle's empty life.

I thought of searching for the grave of the boy when I realized that Ebholtd had never mentioned his name. Deciding to explore the other tombstones, I saw the first iguana.

It was perched atop Uncle Myacin's stone, although it had not been there a moment ago. As I stepped back instinctively two more iguanas slithered from the foot of his marker, their black claws sending tiny pebbles of dirt scooting down the mound of the grave. Hearing the crinkling of leaves and grass, I became aware that there were dozens of green lizards crawling through the cemetery and towards me. They were in the trees as well. I could make out their hisses overhead. Backing against the gate I watched in awe as the multitude slowly moved to face me. They stopped advancing, merely traveling in circles as they crawled over each other. I began to think there was no purpose, when my mind grew dimly aware that they were linking together. Tails touched heads, curving about, each lizard positioning itself in a premeditated fashion. They were spelling out a word. As I moved farther away, my mind raced, and my heart pounded when I noticed what they had spelled out.

Aiyk-Shamir, 1992. Emitting a defenseless yelp, I fled the cemetery.

Sleep did not come easy for me that night. Aside from the dreadful itching of my skin, sapped of its moisture by the insidious climate, the events of the last few days had put me on a razor's edge. All the strange facts I discovered in my uncle's library had set me wondering. But the unnatural display by the loathsome lizards had convinced me that this was something not a part of our safe, brightly lit world of normalcy. It reeked of the dark side and screamed of evil doings.

No, sleep did not come at all that night.

I returned to my uncle's library at morning's first light. Though I had been unable to sleep, I could not bear to face the books in the dark of the night.

I needed to find out more about this ancient being named Aiyk-Shamir.

I had previously read of the creature being a lizard-man, which sort of explained the strange behavior of the iguanas. But I still had no idea how the boy fit into all of this. I thought I might find a clue in my uncle's books.

Just as I prepared to sit down, I heard a fluttering overhead. Followed by the cry of an animal. As I looked up, something flashed by my face and thudded at my feet. It was the remains of a kitten whose throat had been slashed. But the kitten was not dead. It mewed pitifully and stood on weak legs as its bloodied head swiveled grotesquely on its broken neck. Staggering and swaying, I watched in horror as it disappeared among the back row of shelves. When I moved to investigate, something struck the back of my head. I wheeled about and saw a bat flitting across the room. Shrieking in anger I reached for an umbrella that was propped against the wall. Swinging at the bat, I missed and lost my balance. The bat swooped in, and I swung quickly, hitting it squarely. To my surprise, the bat did not fall, but instead flew from the room. Even more shocking, the umbrella had bent nearly in two. It was only when my shock faded that I remembered the diorama in the parlor. Running from the library to the parlor, my heart pounding, the stuffed bat and rats, were missing. Suddenly feeling extremely weak-kneed, I stumbled over to the sofa and collapsed from shock and exhaustion.

As I slept on the sofa, I dreamed. Dreams that must have spawned images of Hell in prehistoric man.

Uncle Myacin, armed with picks and shovels was there with the boy. They were in a graveyard, the likes of which I could never imagine in a conscious state. The tombstones were massive, as large as any modern skyscraper.

My uncle and the boy approached one of the gigantic graves and began to dig. After a short period of time, too short it seemed for the task at hand, they had cleared the dirt from the grave. Inside was a giant egg.

U nable to drive the vivid memories from my head, I decided to investigate the basement once again. As I made my way down the damp staircase, I turned on the light. The room was just as I had left it-the table, the equipment, the incomplete bird, and the covered furniture.

I approached the stuffed bird. Upon picking it up and turning it over, I began to wish that I knew the entire story of my uncle's past. And any connections he may have had with cults. I heard movement from a corner of the basement and peered into the darkness, my heart pounding.

"Do these surroundings seem familiar to you, Master Ingelmeyer?"

It was Ebholtd.

"Yes."

I said, my heart slowly returning to normal.

"The boy in the portraits."

He said.

"He is you."

"M-m-m-e?"

I stammered.

"But . . . how?"

"Your parents were murdered by the cult to which your uncle belonged. Your uncle needed you, lad. He needed to teach someone his craft. Needed to transfer his secrets to another. Oh yes, it seemed innocent at first. A loving uncle teaching his young nephew a new hobby. But that all changed after your parents learned of the cult."

"Did my uncle have my parents executed?"

I should have been more shocked at the news of my parents' murder. But I didn't remember my parents. Their deaths were no more painful to me than deaths on a television show.

"Yes."

Ebholtd answered.

"Of course, it was made to look like a random slaying. That's the way the police explained it. Myacin was awarded custody of you, and that's how you came to be in the portraits."

Some of this insane charade was coming together. Missing pieces were slowly being linked as the picture became clearer.

"Why was my uncle locked away? Did the authorities finally connect him to the cult?"

"Yes, they linked him to the cult, but not the murders. You see, Master Ingelmeyer, there was a terrible problem of grave-robbing in the early sixties. After your Aunt Lily died and her grave was subsequently desecrated, the authorities' efforts began to intensify."

"My uncle was a grave-robber?"

I asked, trying to conceal my disgust.

Ebholtd nodded.

"That was when you were taken away and placed in that orphanage in the States."

"Why can't I remember any of this?"

"The orphanage brain-washed you. They stripped you of all childhood memories."

" Are you saying I was a grave-robber as well?"

Again, Ebholtd nodded.

"Why didn't you tell me these things when I first arrived?"

"And what would you have said, Master Ingelmeyer? You'd think me daft."

"Whatever happened to Aunt Lily? Was she laid to rest again?"

Ebholtd shook his head and shuffled slowly over to the rows of covered furniture.

"The authorities never found Lily Devonshire's remains. Nor did they find any of the others."

Ebholtd seized the bed sheets. Looking back at me, he smiled and tugged.

I felt an overwhelming, almost intoxicating burst of remembrance. As the sheets dropped, seemingly in slow motion, they revealed the nude, mounted display of my dead Aunt Lily. I now remembered helping my uncle disinter her remains. The tedious hours spent as we mounted Aunt Lily in a facsimile of the same form which she had when alive.

"You remember now."

Ebholdt said.

"Yes."

I answered, as I approached the fleshy statue.

"The authorities never found this basement, never found the majority of your uncle's works. We concealed this room well. They were only able to judge him unfit to be a part of society."

"It's all foggy,"

"It will come back to you, lad. It will all come back."

I should have been shocked. Sickened and repulsed. But somehow, I was not. I could only marvel at the craftmanship. At the sudden realization that I was home.

Ebholtd took my arm and led me over to the table. The iguana was once again balanced on the banister. At the top of the stairs, the kitten and the rats from the parlor watched. I looked down at the prone bird on the table.

"Your uncle was very close,"

"Close to what?"

"Close to learning the secrets of the Ancient Ones. Closer than any who came before him."

Ebholtd said, suddenly sounding older and wiser.

"The time wasn't right. Now, perhaps it is."

"How do you know so much?"

Ebholtd approached me slowly. His eyes had become dark and deeply set. His breathing shallow and raspy.

I looked back across the room at my Aunt Lily. Her eyes shown like the glass they were, but somewhere deep inside there was a faint sparkle. An almost undetectable glow of awareness.

"Finish the bird, lad."

Ebholtd said softly.

"Finish the bird."

"But . . . I don't . . . remember."

"Trust your feelings. You'll remember."

I picked up the raven, and my hand instinctively reached for the small box of sawdust. As I spread apart the bird's chest, it all began to come back to me. As if watching a previously viewed, almost forgotten, film.

I sewed up the bird's chest cavity and reached for a set of glass eyes. Dabbing a bit of glue into the empty sockets, I gently pressed the orbs into place. The black raven began to squirm in my grip. It squawked once, and as I released it, the bird stumbled about on the table, screeching and flapping its wings.

"Do not be alarmed."

Ebholt said.

"It has been dead for quite some time."

Finally, the bird stood straight, flapped its wings, and began to flit about.

It flew up the staircase, past the iguana and the other revived animals. I turned back to Ebholtd. He had moved back behind Aunt Lily and was removing sheets from all the others. They were all there, the mounted corpses that my uncle and I had exhumed. I marveled at how close my uncle had been, and for that matter, how close I was now.

It is truly an odd phenomenon, this thing called sanity. How it stays in the darkest recesses of our minds, covered over by mounds of normalcy. But always there, awaiting the time when it can bring itself back to the forefront. As it had once altered the mind of a frightened, lonely boy, it now altered the mind of a sane, rational adult.

If insanity can be so incredibly mind-altering, might it not lead one to believe in feats imperceptible to the normal mind? Is that not how the Roman Empire began its conquest of the ancient world? Or how

Hitler viewed himself. Savior of the world, the annihilator of the undeserving?

I cannot yet fully appreciate my uncle's doings. I do not even know how fully involved he was with the cult of Aiyk-Shamir or if if the cult still exists. But I do know that the belief in Aiyk-Shamir must be true. How else could animals be reanimated? The time for the return of Aiyk-Shamir must be drawing near. I must pursue my uncle's dream. As I've come to learn, it was always my dream as well. I was there from the onset. I helped rob the graves. I helped mount the corpses. I have sent Ebholtd up to the little cemetery to fetch Uncle Myacin's earthly remains. So that, in the event I discover human restoration, I can bring him back. I feel the need to keep a journal, some sort of record, of my findings. I must study my uncle's entire library, I need to know all I can about the cult of Aiyk-Shamir. I must find out if there are any more followers left in Brazil, and if so, revive the cult to its past glory.

Now I sit in the parlor. Staring up at the portrait of my Uncle Myacin and the lad I know now to be me. Aunt Lilly rises beside me. I hear the back door open, and Ebholtd shuffles down the hallway, dragging something in his wake.

"Do not worry, my beautiful Aunt Lily. You will soon be reunited with Uncle Myacin."

The crow flies into the room and alights on Aunt Lily's shoulder. It squawks and flaps, then settles quietly.

In the corner of Lily's mouth, the glue cracks and the smallest of smiles forms.

PLAYGROUND

Nathan Robinson

They said it was the war to end all wars.

Though, they said that about every war.

Wiser men had said that WW4 would be fought with sticks and stones.

But what about WW5? Six and beyond?

Every bomb had left its womb (or detonated there within), rendering vast swathes of the planet inhospitable. Little tracks of land ran between the red zones. You'd think these would be peaceable, but oh no. These had become corridors of hate, funnelling death to and fro on all sides.

As he awoke, Narren often pondered and mused in his cot about the futility and necessity of mankind's obsession with warfare. Man versus man, man versus machine, machine versus man. Now back to man versus man with sticks and stones.

For what?

For oil?

For land?

For nothing? Killing for the sake of killing because we disagree on politics?

He had forgotten. Maybe it was his memory, or maybe everyone else had forgotten as well. He wanted to wake from happy dreams. Instead, he came into life after each sleep immediately thinking about war or the prospect of. He thought about fighting or the moments before a fight. How to kill an enemy. How to avoid being killed. He thought about how he would die a lot. He thought about as he awoke, and it was the last thought on his mind as exhaustion finally took him to sleep. He thought about all those he had killed and had yet to kill. The dead were the only faces in his dreams. In his memories, remembering his wife conjured the face of someone he didn't recognise. She had been replaced with a stranger, the image of her taken by his own faux memories. Her body, by the war. He hadn't been there when she died. He supposed that was a saving grace. What memories he did have wouldn't be polluted by the sight of her death.

Narren sat up from his cot and wiped his face, moving mud and old sweat around.

The rust-stained mirror in the bunk room displayed a skeletal figure that the youth in him no longer recognised. His clothes looked too big despite the six feet of him. With his deep-set eyes in dark sockets, he resembled a ghoul. He felt like he had left himself behind in another life. He looked hungry, but he had no appetite. He only ate when hunger truly gnawed at him. He didn't enjoy eating, as the food was barely palatable in the boggy front where rats and rot got into nearly everything. When he did eat, he ate fast. He took no enjoyment in partaking in such meagre cuisines.

He put on his battered helmet and left the warmth of the bunker and headed outside, his bones creaking, joints popping as he headed up the concrete stairway. There was no door. Old curtains had been screwed into the wooden lintel to keep some of the heat from escaping. The door had been blown off in a previous explosion, killing everyone inside. It could happen again, but a roof was a roof, and he was just as likely to die inside as he was out.

Outside was swathed in mist and darkness. They had no exterior lights and were told to rely on the moon, which seldom made an appearance from behind the near permanent fog that clung to the surface of the earth like grey grease. A good day brought sight of the sun.

He peered into the gloom. He could make out the spectral shape of the dead tree maybe twenty feet away. Apart from the mud, that was it.

He waited a moment. Listening to the death stillness of night. Sometimes you could hear bombs falling in a distant city. Or sirens. Or sirens then bombs.

Tonight, and for the past few weeks, the nights had been silent as a tomb. The radio had been the same. Their last orders of any sense had been weeks ago.

Narren and his troop had been asked to maintain position. So, they had done so. They couldn't leave anyway as they had no vehicles, and they were miles from the nearest semblance of a base. All their meagre food and supplies were here, so they saw no reason to risk the wilderness. They had voted and their best chance had been to stay. Apart from Pryce. Rickety old Pryce had volunteered to head out into the dim beyond. No one had contested as it meant more resources for those staying behind. He had taken one week's worth of food, filled his revolver with six shells. and ventured forth. They watched as he became one with the smog, stick in hand, like a set of haunted bagpipes shuffling away, never to be seen again.

Darius, the radio operator, had quietly approached Narren an hour after Pryce's departure and dropped six shells into his hand.

"By the time he'll need them, it'll be too late. We need them more."

Pryce was older than us both.

"He isn't coming back; we both know that. So, I took them from him before he left."

Narren didn't say anything. He understood. He pocketed the shells and never mentioned it.

Thinking about Pryce made him think about everyone else that he had lost. Narren removed a tobacco pouch, the leather as old as his own skin, and rolled a cigarette as he mused.

Tomas froze to death on duty one night, rifle still pointed out into the snowy wastes, pipe still in his mouth.

Brigit had a suspected heart attack during a bombardment, adding to the chaos, but still the only casualty of the attack.

Yeal caught his leg on barbed wire and contracted sepsis and died in agony a month later, as they had no medical supplies in which to treat him. No one had the heart to put him down as they all held the hope that help would come. Yeal screamed himself to death one night.

Now, everyone was very careful around the bunker, careful not to snag themselves on anything. A bullet was instant, so was a bomb. But a cut opened you up to a world of disease and infection that could lead to prolonged agony.

There were countless others, but Narren was starting to forget their names as time moved on. They were just faces. Faces in the mud.

Something moved in the night, shifting the gloom. A half second spark shone from within the fog.

Narren froze, though it didn't take much effort. He hadn't finished rolling his cigarette, though it seemed someone had started theirs.

They had a small concrete wall at the entrance to the bunker, a wood wormed chair with a missing leg leant against it. He ducked down behind the wall, put his unrolled cigarette back into the pouch, then paused.

The exterior lighting had failed long ago, so Narren had to wait until his night vision adjusted.

He saw two more dim glows slow blinking on the tree line. He could make out the spectres of smoke rising, then more shapes of hot breath imitating the smoke.

They weren't theirs. They would have whistled by now.

Narren had no radio on him, so he gathered a few loose stones and tossed them down into the bunker. A moment passed, so he threw a few more. There was a shuffling, then Vrack and Darius emerged from behind the curtain, both still chewing their grey evening meal.

He held up a hand to silence their approach. They ducked and moved along the wall toward Narren.

Narren pointed to beyond the dead trees. He held up his fingers to indicate ten. Then pointed up to indicate that there may be more.

Darius wiped his mouth and nodded, then headed back into the bunker to alert the others.

Vrack removed his pistol and remained with Narren. He checked the weapon, then focused on the new arrivals that skulked in the dark. They were beginning to encircle the bunker. Vrack lifted the eyepatch that adorned what used to be his right eye and scratched the ghost eye underneath. His left eye blinked a few times to adjust to the dark.

Including Narren, there were seventeen soldiers stationed at the bunker. He watched as the ghostly breaths spread out further around their camp, doubling in number. Now there were at least forty. He began to see actual movement as shadows began to move in the fog as they got closer, angled limbs machining into position. Vrack trained his weapon on the lead figure as he moved around the horizon.

'I'm going to load up. Guard the door.' Narren ordered Vrack. Vrack nodded and Narren headed inside, down the and straight to gun racks and cupboards that served as their armoury. Others rushed about with weapons, heading to their assigned stations. He grabbed a rifle and slung it over his shoulder. As his hands were sourcing some magazines, Narren noticed that they were shaking.

It wasn't just the cold.

This might be it. This might be his last battle.

He felt an ache in his chest, an immense pressure that seemed to radiate outward to his left side and brought tears to his eyes. Narren took a deep breath and felt one of his ribs pop. He held the breath, and the ache subsided somewhat. He took a few more breaths, holding them as the pressure abated.

Somewhere above him, the sound of a gunshot rattled around the concrete walls.

They had three above ground nests. The turret had been demolished in an airstrike before they arrived. The other two were observation posts that could be sealed off from the rest of bunker, namely Ob-1 and Ob-2. Narren headed to Ob-2 as it was closer. Another gunshot ran out as he reached the stairs and headed back up to ground level. He opened the metal door and barged in, closing it behind him. Darius was crouched beside the concrete opening, his face a grimace.

'I can't see a dammed thing.'

Peggie and Farls were by the opposite wall adopting similar positions.

'Who fired?' Narren asked.

'Me,' said Darius. 'I think I got one.' Darius stood up, brought his rifle to his shoulder, and moved to the opening. As he did, he jerked and stood straight. A guttural rasp came from his mouth. There were no lights in this part of the bunker, and for good reason. Floor space was kept clear to avoid tripping. People became shapes and smells that you identified in the near dark. But even with the lack of light, Narren knew that glinting black liquid coming from Darius' neck was blood. He could see that an arrow had come from behind, from Farls' window, the head now emerging from under Darius' chin.

Darius' last words were lost in a wet gurgle. He crumpled to his knees, then fell face down on the bunker floor.

Machine gun fire let rip from Ob-1. Narren looked out and saw small shapes illuminated by the blast of bullets. He raised his rifle, took aim, and fired. Taking one down by the treeline. He had a feeling that his fight would use up the last of their ammunition.

'I need a flare.'

Farls reached down into box beside them.

'Where?'

'Treeline. Northwest. Light them up from behind.'

Farls did as he was told, leaned out and with a pop, fired the flare.

As he pulled back, a hand reached down from above and grabbed his wrist. Another, with knife in hand, ran the blade across his forearm, drawing a thick well of blood.

Farls screamed and dropped the flare gun. He grabbed the knifed hand and pulled it down, pulling the small body in through the window. Peggie pulled out her pistol and aimed shakily at the intruding shape. She fired. The room illuminated for a second, followed by a yelp.

'They're on the roof!' Narren rushed over to the other window whilst Farls used the attacker's own knife on them. Across the way at Ob-1, Narren could see three figures above. He watched helplessly as one threw a canister down in. More machine gun fire spewed forth from Ob-1, chopping down the already dead trees as bodies ducked and fell. Narren shouldered his rifle and fired through the opening, picking off the three distant assailants in quick succession. Despite his age, at least he had his eyes. The bodies fell as plumes of thick yellow gas began to billow from the neighbouring pillbox and into the night air, grim fingers reaching for the pink of the flare.

Screams came from across the way.

Narren leapt across the room and thumbed the intercom that connected them to Ob-1.

"Get out of there and close the damned door. You've been gassed. Do you hear me?'

There was a crackle as he depressed the button. The only reply was distant screams.

He returned to one of the windows and looked out. Shapes coming from every direction. They were surrounded. No gun fire came from the enemy. It was either hand to hand or gas bombs. Some held bows, others cross bows. They were silent. Aside from the ones on the roof, he couldn't see where they were coming from.

As he realised this, an arrow punctured Peggie's temple, spraying dark blood into her white hair. She dropped to the floor and onto of Farls.

Narren returned to the intercom and flicked a switch so he could speak to the entire bunker.

'Cobalt. Repeat Cobalt,' he ordered. 'Anyone acknowledge?'

He waited. The code fell on deaf ears. The gunfire had stopped. He heard bodies shuffling outside the bunker, soft voices scheming in the night.

Again. No reply. It would be up to him.

Narren abandoned his post, slamming and locking the metal door behind him. He rushed down the stairs so blindly he tripped, righted himself but overcorrected and missed the next step, falling down the next four on a twisted left foot. He landed hard, with his ankle snapping, head smashing into the dusty concrete. His helmet took the brunt of it, but he still scraped his cheek. He landed and righted himself, immediately tensing at voices. They were banging on one of the interior doors. They were nearly in.

More gunfire from inside. More screams took over the echo of bullets ricocheting off bones

He loped deeper into the bunker, meeting no one else, friend or foe.

In the deepest room, he found the solitary switch on a back wall, cables snaking out of the top and bottom. He jammed the loose wires into their ports and hand tightened the screws the best he could, hoping it would be enough to connect. Below this was a hand crank, which he wound for ten seconds to build a charge. He pulled down the switch and waited three seconds. A whirring came from within as power surged in the ground above him. A light blinked alive green. Narren thumbed the button beneath it, then held his hands to his ears as he dropped to the floor.

The lights went out and destruction rang in his ears.

The room shook, threatened to collapse, but held following the boom.

The room filled with darkness.

Narren waited, crouched on the floor, then emerged and felt his way up the stairs, coughing and blinking through the dust and made his way to the main corridor. Through the ringing in his ears, he could hear screams from Ob-1. screams that descended into gurgles as gas melted throats into lungs as his unit literally drowned in their own homemade soup. They couldn't be helped.

The curtain had been blown off and a body wearing Vrack's boots lay across the doorway. As Narren got closer, he saw countless arrows in Vrack's body from every direction. He still held his pistol in his hand.

Once outside he took a lungful of clean night air and coughed again. It was still dusty, and he was sure he could taste metal.

He smelled cooked meat and felt a pang of guilt as his appetite momentarily returned. It quickly dissipated.

The eruption of dust added to the night mist and reduced visibility to a few feet. Narren stepped carefully over the upturned soil, rocks and bodies, feeling with his feet before committing to a step in case he fell into a self-induced crater. He pulled the pack of matches from his pocket. It was a pack that he had liberated from a body a few weeks ago. They had been half-soaked with blood that was now the colour of mud. He lit two. He didn't know where he was going, but he still had a sudden urge to see.

The match struck and a second later a broken face lurched toward him. The jaw was missing, the skin was patchy at best, but mostly blood. A dark tongue flapped loosely, dripping black blood on Narren's uniform. The thing had no eyelids, just staring eyes flaked with soil. Somehow the skull with a pulse managed to scream. It reached out to

Narren with skinless, bony hands caked in mud and blood. Tendons hung loose. The walking corpse was essentially naked as uniform and skin had been blown off indiscriminately. Flesh and cloth hung as rags.

The scream turned into a bloody hiss. Narren dropped the lit matches, pushed the thing to the ground, and leapt on its skinless head. His boot hit the wet flesh, and he slipped on the slick gore. He fell beside it and scurried back from the abject thing, raised his foot again and brought back of his heel down upon its head until the screaming stopped.

It didn't stop. Narren carried it on until the once a head became a puddle of broken human soaking into the dark chaotic soil.

He scurried back, away from the tomb of his dead comrades and away from the thing that may have also been a comrade, though he suspected not.

His back hit something solid and he screamed. Feeling around he expected another faceless monstrosity, but his searching fingers found something hard and rough.

Bark.

It was real and it grounded him. He leant again the twisted trunk and relaxed some.

He looked left and saw that some of the dead trees had been uprooted and were burning, giving some illumination to the cratered scene. Absence of life had become carnage. He could see a half a body in the upper limbs of a tree. Bits and pieces of human and torn roots were everywhere.

A hand raised up from the turned soil in front of him and grabbed hold of his jacket. Narren pulled back, pulling the entombed body with him. He felt its other hand searching past his neck and towards his face. Soily fingers invaded his mouth. Narren pulled off his helmet and pushed the emerging body away. He put his knee into its chest, held his helmet in two hands and brought it down again and again. He felt something punch his chest, but Narren kept pounding his helmet into the grave emergers skull until it parted, and it was digging soil.

Something clicked and his eyes became alerted to light. He turned towards the spark.

A first he thought it was an old man because of his size, but as his eyes adjusted to the lighters flame, Narren realised it was a boy. A boy that looked so old he looked ancient. He was laid on his side, propped up on a body that was torn asunder.

'Okay,' Narren said. Not sure if it was a realisation or an acceptance when he saw the gun. He dropped the helmet and his limbs became locked.

The old boy placed the lighter on the soil in front of him, settling it carefully into the disturbed dirt until it sat upright. The flame flickered, then settled as the boy let go. He had a pistol in his hand, and it was pointed at Narren. The boy's eyes glinted yellow from the glow of the lighter. His uniform was caked with mud and gore. His legs were maroon ribbons.

'I'm not afraid,' the old boy spoke. But it wasn't a boy's voice, or an old man's voices. It was a little girl's voice. Sweet, musical, but burred with sadness and a life lived too young.

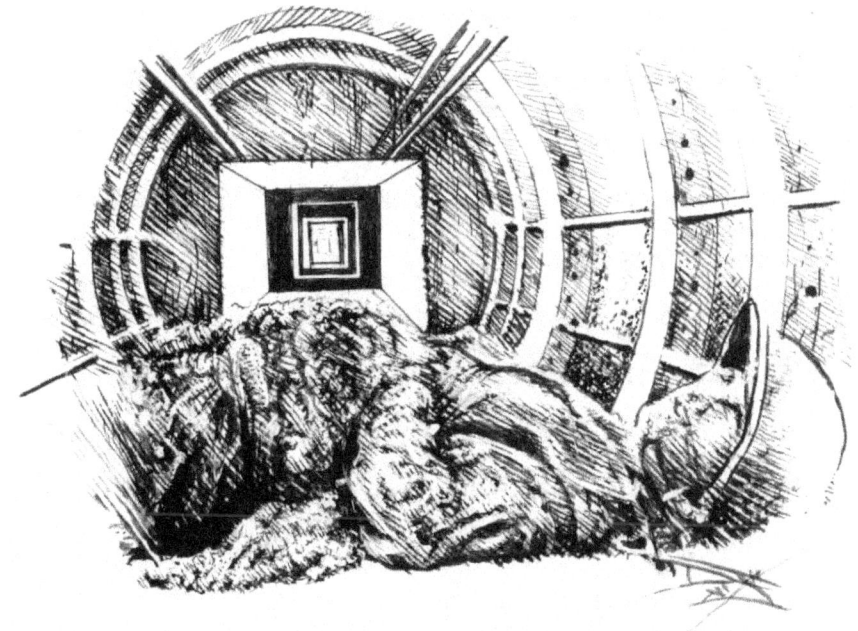

'They said I would be afraid. They said that we would all be afraid and that it was okay to be afraid. But we shouldn't be scared, and we should keep fighting no matter what because it was for the good of our country. They said we should fight for our parents. A boy asked why. Why should he fight for his parents. He said his parents were dead. He wanted to fight for his children, that he would never have.

They shot him and sent out us out into the night to kill the enemy. The last of the enemy. You are the enemy.'

The girl looked down at the flame. She winced from the pain and moved to ease herself into some form of comfort. She looked back at Narren. The glint in her eyes had gone.

'Before this flame dies, I'm going to kill you.'

'Why?' Narren asked. He said it involuntarily. The sound just came out without a thought.

'Because someone must win. And it can't be you. Not after all you have done to our people.'

'Your people have done just as much to me. My son, my daughters. My grandchild still in the womb. My wife.'

'I have no one. I've not lived.'

'It's nothing personal. I didn't have a choice. I had to fight or risk losing my homeland.'

'Do you still have a homeland?'

Narren didn't answer. He hadn't had anywhere to call home for years. Various impersonal bunkers along the front. He supposed his current digs had been his longest home for a while now.

Wherever I lay my helmet, he mused. Narren felt a sting of something. He looked down. A knife handle, buried to the hilt, stuck out of his right breast. Internally he shrugged. He left the knife in. He could feel the blade pressed into his lung. He couldn't tell if it had pierced it. He didn't want to know.

'I never had a home,' the girl continued. 'My childhood was robbed. I don't know what it is. I read about it books before we burnt them.

The flame flickered and they both looked at it. Just the wind passing through.

'I wasn't in charge,' Narren offered. 'I was just a grunt. Millions died before me. All the young men. Then the women. They came for the old people last.'

'Not on our side they did. There's no one left. They emptied the schools. They emptied the orphanages. I remember sizing a child up for his uniform. He thought it was a game. He thought he was playing war.'

'Take it up with your generals. We never used kids. There were none. Your bombs made sure of that. It's just old folk. We're already doomed. What were we fighting for? Nothing. There's nothing left. All the art has gone. No one creates anything anymore. Just more bombs. More bullets. The battlefield is their canvas. So are our bodies. The battle is lost, but we kept fighting because we have nothing else to do. We didn't know anything else. We were afraid to turn back because we were afraid of losing the nothing we fought hard for. We were fighting for existence. There's nothing back home. I'm tired. I don't want to win because there's nothing to win. This is how they end all wars. You kill everybody. I don't want to win this world. Shoot me if you want. You're not winning. No one is.'

'Okay.' That all the hesitation she had. The girl pulled the trigger. She shot low and Narren felt a punch in his gut, then a hotness on his skin as his warm insides spilled out.

'If I had my gun I'd shoot you.'

'I'd let you,' she replied.

They looked at each other for a long time as they both bled and breathed their last. One couldn't tell if the other had died they were both still. Narren was sure he could still see his breath long after hers had stopped, but he couldn't be sure.

His thoughts turned to his wife as he tried to remember her name. Her face came back to him. She was smiling. She was happy. A version of her that existed somewhere. Not here. Not now.

Annie, he thought, and smiled.

THE LIMINAL DEAD

Lucas Mangum

1

I awoke on a spit-covered floor for the second morning in a row. Everyone else was still asleep—on beds, sofas, chairs, and beside me on the laminate—so I tried to be quiet as I went to leave. Coming down the steep path from the house in the woods, I took it slow because I was still a little drunk and didn't want to bust my dumb face.

I reached my car, slumped into the driver's seat, and fired up the engine. Cradle of Filth screeched at me through the car's speakers, and I twisted the volume knob down until it clicked to silence. I checked my phone for messages and felt something heavy in my chest when I saw none. I flexed my hands on the steering wheel and took a breath I hoped would revive me.

Before putting the car into gear, I tried to replay the events of the night before. It was a series of blurs and shadows. Gray, black, and forest green, broken by occasional flickers of white fluorescence.

Nothing good could have happened, but I didn't recall anything with consequences beyond taking a few more years off my life. I reversed out of the gravel driveway and headed home on winding, wooded roads.

She was already clawing at the closet door by the time I got to my room.

"I'm not up for it right now," I said to the mirrored door at the foot of my mattress. "Can't it wait?"

Her fingernails scraped the material behind the glass—a clear response if I ever heard one. I'd come to know what she meant, though I'd never heard her utter a word in English. She only ever scratched at the door like a dog or grunted like a cavewoman. Her insistent scratching now told me she wouldn't be taking 'no' for an answer.

And truthfully, if I wanted what she offered, I had no power to refuse.

"I'm hungover," I said. "What if I can't get it up? Huh? What then?"

She continued clawing at the mirrored door. My gaze flicked to my laptop, inside which lay an abundance of pornography. Just thinking of it got things moving down in my pants.

"Yeah, who am I kidding?"

I got naked and opened the computer as her fingernails quickened their scraping. I clicked on a POV video with a blonde who I'd seen once or twice and took myself in my hands. The woman in the wall began to grunt and snort. I once found it distracting, but now I couldn't imagine getting myself off without those guttural noises of hers.

When the climax arrived, I came into a wad of tissues, and she squealed with girlish excitement. Once I cleaned up, I twisted the tissues into a neat package and left the soiled materials in front of the closet door.

She was wheezing now, could hardly contain her glee.

I hugged my knees and looked at the door over my forearms. The mirrored door inched open, and she stuck her blue-gray hand through the gap. Her fungus-crusted fingernails closed over the tissue before dragging it across the floor into the darkness.

I hoped it wouldn't be much longer now.

2

After my honorable discharge from the U.S. Air Force, I came home to find the declining neighborhood I'd enlisted to escape had changed into an idyllic suburb. Porches and gutters no longer sagged. Roofs no longer wore the scars of hailstorms from decades past, and the chipped siding on my house and the neighbors' homes had been replaced. Every window looked modern and energy efficient; every door was freshly painted. The homes themselves stood up straighter, as if the ground beneath the foundations had leveled in the time I'd been gone. Even the sidewalks were no longer cracked from bulging roots, and all the potholes I remembered pocking the streets were filled.

I'd enlisted straight out of high school. My parents had hoped for community college, but I needed to get away. The last recession had hit the neighborhood hard. Every week, it seemed another one of my friends' parents was getting laid off. Those who kept their houses let them fall into disrepair. Yards went to weeds. Old cars sat in driveways getting rusty and blanketed in pollen. Foundations split and sunk into the earth, and vines crawled up the walls and chimneys like parasitic tendrils feeding off the human-made structures. The houses that were abandoned stayed that way, For Sale signs growing a layer of grime or falling apart altogether.

During that time, Dad's moods went from nervous and uncertain to full-fledged panic. He worked on the assembly line in a manufacturing plant, not the most recession-proof job in the era of outsourcing and automation.

As an elementary school teacher, Mom had tenure to keep her job secure, but she was drinking a lot, especially on weekends and over the summer. The alcohol was making her mean. To my father. And to me, for looking like him.

I needed to get away—and get away I had. I was gone for eight long years. It felt even longer now as I rode through the neighborhood in the back seat of a Lyft, taking in how different everything was. I never came back to visit—I never even returned to the same state during those eight years. Now, I wasn't sure I'd come to the right place, although I had given the driver the right address.

The front yard, once a patchy lawn that was more clover than grass, had been replaced by a gorgeous rock garden, complete with a fountain in the middle. Pygmy palms and other tropical plants provided nice pops of green and shade in spots.

One of the garage's bay doors was open, and what I saw next was almost enough to convince me that I'd slipped into an alternate reality. A classic car with faded red paint, the body raised on jacks. Someone was underneath, wearing faded jeans and tan work boots. From the bottom of the driveway, I recognized the figure, but I couldn't believe it. I thanked my driver and got out of the car to get a better look, just to be sure. I approached, draping an arm across my forehead to shield my eyes from the sun, which hadn't quite yet slipped behind the roof. The closer I got, the more the figure's identity became unmistakable.

"Dad?" I said.

Boots first, the mechanic shimmied out from under the car—a Ford Fairlane, by the looks of it. As he looked down the driveway at me, his face scrunched, then softened. He stood and wiped his hands on his shirt.

"Sully," he said and for a second, I thought he might open his arms and move in for a hug. Instead, he kept wiping his hands. "I almost didn't believe it when your mom told me."

He closed the distance, still sizing me up. His eyes held the green vibrancy I remembered from before things got bad.

"It's good to see you," I said.

He opened his arms then, and we embraced.

"Yes," he said.

He held me at arm's length and looked me in the eyes as if checking to see if I wasn't a mirage brought on by the heat. Then he laughed and clapped me on the shoulder.

"Yes. It's good to have you home."

He sounded different too. No longer did his voice waver with the simmering anxiety I'd come to know so well. He sounded even-toned—placid and content were the words that felt the most apt.

I looked past him. "So what's going on in there?"

He followed my gaze and smirked. "Oh, that old hunk of metal?"

He headed back to the garage and motioned for me to follow.

Back when I was still living at home, the garage had been only a place for storage, where seasonal items collected dust until their designated holidays and shared their space the rest of the year with no-longer-needed things that were too sentimental to throw away but too ugly to be considered heirlooms or keepsakes. It was a disorganized haven where tools went missing just when the occasion arose that they were needed, and where old furniture went to die.

Now the garage was still a little messy, but in that charming, gearhead shop kind of way. Some stray tools, some splatters of oil and droplets of paint. But otherwise, the room was organized. There was a large, brand-name tool chest up against one wall and underneath a hot rod calendar for the current year. On the opposite wall, several framed photos of classic cars and sports heroes sat on shelves. A stainless-steel meat freezer stood beside the door leading into the house.

"So, what do you think?" he asked.

My father stood beside the car. He looked old—his hair was mostly white, and his face was starting to have the texture of an old shoe—but there was something youthful about him now, standing in this completely redone space beside the car he was restoring.

"It's … different."

"Different good, though, right?"

I looked around again just to take in the new vibe of what should've been a familiar place.

"Yeah, just …" I gestured at our surroundings. "When did you get all this done?"

"I'm sure you have lots of questions, and I've got a few for you, but let's not keep your mom waiting. She's missed you."

The mention of my mother took my mind off unanswered questions about the garage. At the times I allowed myself to think about the neighborhood I'd left behind, I felt most guilty about how me leaving might have affected her. The fact that I didn't even visit must've hurt—only she hadn't sounded hurt when we spoke on the phone the previous day.

When I stepped into the kitchen, I had a good idea why.

The garage wasn't the only room that had changed in the house. The kitchen, too, was not the one I recognized. All the cabinets and appliances were new and modern. There was a marble island in the center of the space, illuminated by dangling pendant lights and housing a stainless-steel sink. Everything in the room had brightened, as if imbued with new life. It was a far cry from what had come before. The room smelled like roast chicken and potatoes, which couldn't be right—Mom was never much of a cook.

The kitchen could've been in a different house entirely from the one I'd grown up in; again, I reminded myself that I'd used the correct address. And the house was the same shape I remembered. Only the guts had changed.

A flush emitted from the powder room, followed by the sound of washing hands. The faucet shut off, and the powder room door opened.

"Is that you, Bo?"

"Not just me," Dad said.

My mother turned, spotted me, and her eyes went wide. "Sully!?"

Facing my mother head-on, I could already tell she wasn't drinking anymore. Her skin, though wrinkled with age, had more color to it. She didn't have bags under her eyes. She'd lost some weight but not too much to cause any worry.

She reached for me and pulled me in tight. When she released me, I stepped back and looked at each of my parents.

"You look good," I said. "You both do. And the house looks completely different."

"Different good, though, right?" Dad said again.

I cocked my head at his repeated turn of phrase. Mom clamped a hand on my bicep.

"I bet you're hungry," she said.

Again, I noted the smell that filled the room. She took her hand off me, leaving the ghost of a throb from gripping me so tightly. I watched her go to the oven, put on some mitts, and pull out a pan with a whole seasoned chicken partially submerged in a ring of potatoes. My stomach responded with a growl.

Dad put his hand between my shoulders and guided me toward the dining room. "Come on, let's eat."

As I shuffled forward, it dawned on me just what was the biggest difference about this house: it finally felt like a home.

Someone knocked on the door not thirty seconds after the three of us were seated at the dining room's new glass table. I looked up from a forkful of buttery potatoes. Dad and Mom exchanged glances. Mom got up from her spot and went to the door, while Dad looked at me, eyes gleaming. Something was up, but when I tried to come up with some possibilities for what that could be, I drew a blank.

I cocked my head to the side for further explanation, but Dad turned his attention back to his plate. I watched as Mom opened the door and stood aside. When I saw who was standing on the opposite side of the storm door, a not-entirely-unpleasant pang jabbed at the inside of my chest. I pushed back my chair and stood.

"Audrey," I said—I practically gasped it.

The girl I'd loved with a nearly obsessive fervor back in high school had blossomed into a sleek-figured brunet. She smiled when she saw me, and I thought I'd melt back into my chair. Though I'd had a couple of flings while in the Air Force, none of them amounted to much beyond a few intense liaisons and a whole lotta heartbreak. Seeing Audrey again, I wondered if maybe it was because I'd been waiting for her this whole time.

She gave me a visual once-over, still smiling as if she knew what the vibrance of it was doing to me.

"As I live and breathe," she said. "I had to see it for myself, but here you are."

"In the flesh," I said and laughed nervously.

"I wasn't sure you were stopping by," Mom said to Audrey. "Let me fix you a plate."

"Are you kidding? I wouldn't miss this for the world."

I crossed the room and met her on her way to the table. We embraced; she was warm and smelled like fresh-cut lilies. We pulled apart and our gazes met. Her sunflower eyes seemed full of light, devoid of the shadows I remembered from when we were young and always feeling like the ground would give way.

Mom set Audrey's plate in front of the chair next to my seat and we all sat down for dinner. Conversation centered around my time overseas where I inspected and repaired reconnaissance aircraft at Al Dhafra, but it occasionally shifted to Audrey moving back into the neighborhood after college and how my parents were enjoying their retirement.

At times, I attempted to steer the conversation to how the neighborhood had changed, but I could never get a straight answer. Mom simply said that I was gone a long time, while Dad reiterated how nice it was, and Audrey said it had occurred when she was away. Eventually, I took the hint and stopped asking.

The food Mom cooked was delicious, which I still could hardly believe. I didn't want to bring it up out of fear of insulting her, so I just quietly assumed that she'd taken the time to hone her craft now that she and Dad weren't working all the time. That could be the only explanation and as Dad kept saying it was a nice change, so there was no point in harping on it.

After the main course, Mom brought out coffee and key lime pie. As a kid, I only ever ate key lime pie on those rare occasions when the family went to a restaurant. It was always by far my favorite dessert. The first bite of pie I took seemed to melt in my mouth—a phrase I'd never quite understood, not until that moment. I even closed my eyes to savor the taste. Key lime pie was supposed to be a relatively simple recipe, but, like everything else she served, it delivered an extra complexity, a homemade flair that I grew up never thinking was possible.

"How did you get it to taste so good?" I asked, looking at Mom with newfound wonder.

She shrugged as if to say it was nothing. It was most certainly not nothing, but I decided to let her have her secrets. What I feared would be a night full of awkward conversations and misplaced emotions was shaping up to be something I hadn't expected. Everything was nice, the way coming home should feel. I didn't want to ruin that sentiment by asking too many questions.

Mom and Dad held hands and watched me eat, their eyes gleaming with what could only be parental pride. I looked at Audrey and found her staring too. She blushed and looked to the side. Something was up; a big part of me wanted to know what, but a more powerful part of me didn't care.

When dinner was over, a warm contentedness settled over me. I felt so relaxed, I thought that I might fall asleep in my chair. I offered to clean up, but Mom said absolutely not on my first night home. Dad said he would help instead, so I walked Audrey to the door.

The sun was still out but was on its way down, turning the sky a hazy orange. Audrey and I stood in the concrete walkway outside the front door. In the dusky light, she looked even more enigmatic. A well of emotions rose within me. I couldn't believe I was back and that she was here too. Surely, she would've found someone in college, got married, and never have come back to the neighborhood of Hyacinth Hills. Back in the day, she wanted to get out every bit as much as I did. That was true for all our friends.

And yet, she and I had both returned.

"It feels almost like a dream," I said.

"I know what you mean," she said. "It's a good dream, though, isn't it?"

"I haven't decided yet," I said, and that was true.

As nice as it felt to sit down like a proper family with my parents, as great as it was to see Audrey again, something felt off about all this. Even eight years didn't seem like enough time for the entire neighborhood to make such a dramatic change. To go from a declining pit to the picture of prosperity. My parents seemed so happy—Dad was finally living his dream of restoring cars. Mom finally had a home she could be proud of. And then there was Audrey—

She brushed the side of my face with her fingers.

"You'll get used to it. You'll be happy here, if you're planning to stay, that is."

The truth was I hadn't decided yet. Not wanting to confess this to her, I changed the subject and asked if she was married now.

"No," she said, with a coy smile before sashaying down the driveway toward the darkening sidewalk. When she reached the edge of my property, she stopped and turned back toward me. "Oh, Sully? Don't go walking around outside after dark."

"What?" I asked, but she was already walking away.

I looked at the sky. It was turning purple, streaked with gray and orange, the sun giving its last fiery stand before retreating over the horizon.

I awoke sometime around midnight. The disorientation of waking in a strange place made my senses swim. I was in my old room, but it wasn't how I remembered it. For one thing, it was clean and tidy; learning how to do both of those things had been one of basic training's biggest challenges. All my books and some of my old toys were there but organized on new wooden shelves. The stained carpet had been replaced with a dark wood floor, and the window was covered by a strong-looking shade. Even in the dark, I could tell all the walls had been repainted.

I remembered where I was, and my disorientation retreated. I knew I was lying in bed in my old room at my parents' house, but like everything else in the house, and the entire neighborhood, it had undergone a dramatic transformation.

I put my head back on the pillow to try falling back asleep but gave up after a few minutes and got out of bed. Slipping my feet into my shoes, I went to the restroom to relieve myself, and headed downstairs. When I reached the front door, Audrey's word of warning echoed between my ears.

Don't go walking around outside after dark.

I again wondered why she'd say such a thing. Did the neighborhood have a curfew? That was silly. Most likely, Audrey had been joking with me. It wasn't out of character for her. She'd always had a peculiar sense of humor, usually centered around the macabre—serial killers, monsters, and the like—so I assumed that's what her warning was: a strange joke with not enough context for me to immediately get. Some things never changed, I thought, and opened the door.

The outside air was cooler now but tinged with humidity. I walked down the driveway, giving the moon a passing glance before turning onto the sidewalk. The street was empty save for some parked cars, and the air was silent in that way that it can only be at a late hour. No, it was even quieter than that. I should have at least heard some crickets pulsing dissonantly in the nearby greenbelt. Though I thought it strange, I continued walking and told myself to just enjoy the fact that my shuffling feet were the only sound.

277

In the nighttime shadows, the houses looked almost like their old selves. As I walked on, this seemed less a trick of the light and more like the daytime illusion had slipped, revealing the true nature of things. This of course couldn't be right. My imagination was wandering, the way it sometimes did at a late hour.

I reached the end of my street and stepped onto the main drive. The shadows in front of the house across the way were moving. It could've been that the tree was casting them as it swayed in the wind, but there was no breeze.

I watched as the shadows moved across the door. The longer I looked at them, the more I realized they were one shadow, one shape: a human shape. The figure looked to be scratching something onto the house's door, something indecipherable. It repeated the motion, thickening the lines, further darkening the image. As I passed directly behind the shadowy figure, it stopped and so did I. Slowly it turned, and a half-greeting/half-explanation began taking shape on my tongue.

I never got it out. The sight of the figure's eyes froze me in place. Even in the dark and across the street, I could see the whites; they seemed to both glow and be much larger than normal. The dark irises seemed as if they were all pupil.

The figure began to walk from the house's front door, its eyes zeroed in on me. When it reached the sidewalk across the street, I turned and headed toward home. I couldn't hear its footsteps, but I knew it was following.

I turned back onto my street and quickened my pace. To my horror, other shadow people stepped out from in front of some of the other homes. All of them were headed toward me. As some stepped out of yards on my side of the street, I broke into a run.

I reached my house and nearly collided with one of the figures striding across my lawn, on legs that seemed too long and too thin. I wove around it, sprinting for my front door.

Once inside, I slammed the door behind me and engaged the deadbolt. Instinctively, I went to the window to make sure none of the shadow people were attempting to get inside. Around a dozen of them were out there, standing on the sidewalk and watching the house as if to ensure I didn't reemerge.

I backpedaled from the window and turned to head upstairs. I knew full well I wouldn't be falling asleep anytime soon. But looking at those figures another second was bound to cause my mind to snap.

I got into bed and lay in the dark, Audrey's warning swirling through my head like a record locked in a groove.

3

I remembered now: our little ritual. How I'd built the life I'd wanted, the life that had been stolen from me the day Mom pushed Dad in front of that train. We were downtown, having just gotten out of a baseball game. By the time we reached the platform at the station, they were fighting again. Red-in-the-face screaming, sticking fingers in each other's face, calling each other awful names as spittle flew from their lips. People were staring, and I put my head down, pretending I was somewhere else—perhaps in my room, staring out my window and hoping for a good dream.

I didn't even see her shove him, but I heard the train and the screams. By the time I screamed, Dad was gone.

Mom tried to stop me from looking over the side, but I jerked out of her hold on my bicep and glanced down. Only a lumpy puddle of meat remained. Raw, red, and glistening, nothing among the mess resembled a human being. Someone could have just as easily dumped a slop bucket of offal onto the tracks, and it would've been no different than the sight below.

All around us, the people clamored. Cries of "she pushed him" and "call the police" echoed through the station. I looked at my mother, and my lips quivered as questions and condemnations filled my head. I could speak to none of them because if I opened my mouth I would only scream again. And I knew right down to my marrow that if I screamed again, I'd never stop.

From the platform at the station, life became a blur: hospitals, jails, courtrooms, shelter after shelter swam by like cinematic images on a liquid screen. I became convinced that I, too, had died that day at the train station, and that death meant living forever in a transitory, pre-ritual state.

All that ended when I met her—the woman in the walls. She introduced ritual, a cycle, purpose to my aimless life. With every offering of bodily fluids wrapped in tissue, she grew stronger. I grew weaker, but that was okay because I was moving toward something, some as-yet-intangible goal that would reset everything and give me back what was stolen from me when Mom pushed Dad into the train's path.

Once the woman in the walls had enough power from gathering enough of my seed over the years we spent together, she gave me what I wanted. She didn't ask what I wanted because she already knew.

On her instructions, I hailed a Lyft and told the driver to take me home—my real home of Hyacinth Hills. As the ride progressed, unwanted memories faded and new ones took their place, filling the holes like Tetris pieces.

I had the life I wanted, complete with false memories and programmed emotions. I was surrounded by people who cared for me and always acted how I hoped they would. And I could keep all of this, too, but only if I stayed inside after dark.

THE END

A

AUTHORS

Jeff Strand is the Bram Stoker Award-winning author of over sixty books, most of them horror/comedy. He lives in Duluth, Minnesota with fellow Splatterpunk Award-winner Bridgett Nelson. You can visit his Gleefully Macabre website at www.JeffStrand.com.

Christine Morgan, after several traumatic life-upheavals, is now enjoying the peace and quiet of the remote high desert, with her dad and the cats for company. Author of the Splatterpunk Award winning LAKEHOUSE INFERNAL and many other works, she writes, reviews, edits, does weird crafts, and has way more sharks and dinosaurs than someone of her age probably should. She can be found online at: ChristineMarieMorgan.wordpress.com, on various social media platforms, or by email at ChristineMarieMorgan@gmail.com

Patrick Lacey was born and raised in a haunted house. He spends his time writing about things that make the general public shiver. He lives in a hopefully un-haunted house in Massachusetts with two hyperactive cats, his daughter, his son, and his wife.

Robert Essig is the author of fifteen books including *Baby Fights, Secret Basements* and *Broth House*. He has published over 150 short stories and edited three small press anthologies such as *Chew on This!*, which was nominated for a Splatterpunk Award. Robert lives with his family in east Tennessee. For updates, subscribe to his free newsletter at **robertessig.substack.com**. You can grab signed copies of his books at **essighorror.bigcartel.com**.

CODY GOODFELLOW has written nine novels and five collections of short stories. His writing has been favored with three Wonderland Book Awards for excellence in Bizarro fiction. His comics work has appeared in *Mystery Meat*, Dark Horse's *Creepy, Skin Crawl* and *Slow Death Zero*. As an actor, he has appeared in numerous TV shows, videos by Anthrax and Beck, and a Days Inn commercial. He also wrote, co-produced and scored the Lovecraftian hygiene films *Baby Got Bass* and *Stay At Home Dad*, which can be viewed on YouTube. He "lives" in San Diego, California.

Dan Henk was born on a small army base in the deep south.

He's been homeless, made it through brain cancer, got stabbed by a crackhead, totaled three cars, three bikes, and plunged backwards through a windshield. After four hours in a coma, he sprung back and resumed his normal life. There is a running theory that he is a cyborg. Despite all that, he has three novels, two anthologies, two chapbooks out, and has done a slew of artwork for books and magazines. You can see his latest travails and triumphs on his website, **danhenk.com**

Ryan C. Thomas is an award-winning journalist and editor in San Diego, California. He is the author of 14 novels (including the cult classic, *The Summer I Died*), numerous novellas and short stories and can often be found in the bars around Southern California playing guitar. When he is not writing or rocking out, he is at home with his wife, son, daughter and pets watching really bad B-movies. Visit him online at **RyanCThomas. Com**

Lucas Mangum is the Splatterpunk Award-winning author of Snow Angels, Barn Door to Hell, Saint Sadist, Haunted Hearts, and Gods of the Dark Web.
With Ryan Harding he wrote Pandemonium, which was nominated for a Splatterpunk Award. It pays tribute to the Italian Demons films, and showcases his love of professional wrestling. With

Wesley Southard, he wrote The Final Gate, which takes its cue from the films of Lucio Fulci and went on to inspire a death metal EP of the same name by UK artist Seven Doors. He lives in Austin with his family. For more information, go to LMHorror.com.

Terry Campbell is a 60-year-old author living in McKinney, TX. Graveside Press will publish his novella The Seething Below as a Tiny Terrors in August, and his werewolf novel Shun the Moon will be released later this year by Water Dragon Publishing. He can be found on Threads @aintelmo11

Thomas R Clark is a two-time Splatterpunk Award Nominee (Best Novella, 2021 for BELLA'S BOYS and Best Short Story, 2022 for FIREFLIES & APPLE PIES). His most recent release, WE ARE 13, is available through his personal imprint, Nightswan Press. He is the blog manager and senior columnist for Memento Mori Ink magazine. Tom's journalism and entertainment critiques have appeared in Rue Morgue, Stranger With Friction, House of Stitched Magazine, This Is Infamous, and miscellaneous internet outlets. He lives in Central New York with his wife and their canine companions.

Nathan Robinson is the author of Starters, Ketchup On Everything, Midway, and Devil Let Me Go. He lives in a haunted house in the north of England. By day, he works as a high school librarian, by night, he sleeps. Follow him @natthewriter

www.facebook.com/NathanRobinsonWrites

Authors

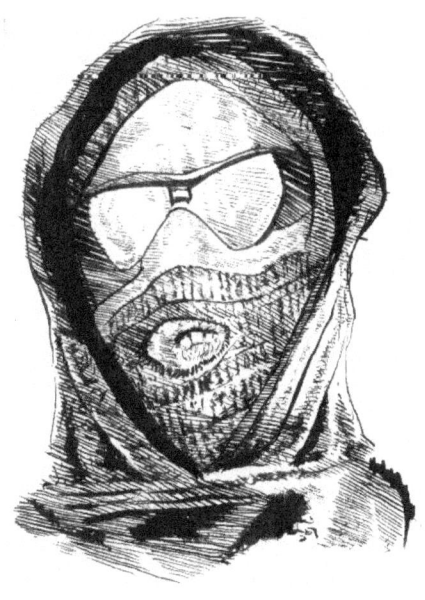

Merrill David is a brain tumor survivor who now resides in East Texas with his wife and their Chiweenie dog Vinny. Merrill's list of works includes his Wicked Awake zombie novel series, a splatterpunk sci-fi novel named Fester, the paranormal amusement park novel Season Pass, the horror/mafia crime novel Lasagna, and a short disgusting story on the Godless platform entitled Bloodcum.

Dicey Grenor, also known as Spicy Dicey, is an attorney, author, podcaster, and screenwriter. As author of The Narcoleptic Vampire Series and other dark erotic romance, sci-fi, fantasy, horror books (15 in total), short stories (30+), and scripts (4), Dicey enjoys crossing genres while writing inclusive, character-driven stories about sexy creatures that don't stay dead.

diceygrenorbooks.com

289